DEATH MAIL

'But if the sack with the telltale letter in it has already been dropped behind the German lines...?'

'They reckon, under present conditions, what with Allied raids and priority for munitions trains, that the stuff salvaged from the wreck won't be in Berlin for another four days.'

'OK,' Kane said. 'Even so, I don't see how – ?'

'How we can stop the letter being delivered?' Colbert cut in. 'That's easy, old chap. That's why you're here. You're going into the Reich to find that letter and bring it back here.'

'You must be joking!' Kane said.

Also by Peter Leslie and published by Star

ANVIL

DEATH MAIL

Peter Leslie

A STAR BOOK

published by
the Paperback Division of
W. H. ALLEN & Co. PLC

A Star Book
Published in 1985
by the Paperback Division of
W. H. Allen & Co. PLC
44 Hill Street, London W1X 8LB

First published in Great Britain by W. H. Allen & Co. PLC, 1984

Printed in Great Britain by
Hunt Barnard Printing Ltd, Aylesbury, Bucks.

ISBN 0 352 31668 3

Author's Note

This is a work of fiction. All of the characters, and a few of the places, are invented, and are not intended to bear any resemblance to actual places or persons, living or dead. But – although the real factory was not in Perugia – Operation Cornflakes did in fact exist as described. By the end of the war in Europe, the Allied Psychological Warfare Department claimed that almost two million letters had been delivered in this way.

The man of intelligence applies himself to the study of letters and wisdom, but not to military matters.

Lao Tsze (*c.*570–490 B.C.)
The Tao Teh King

There is no stratagem so extreme, no ruse so absurd, that men will not in time of war recourse to its use in the hope of securing an illusory advantage.

Hugh Miller (1802–56)
The Witness

Intelligence is the motor that drives all nations, the conductor of all armies, the artillery of all wars. Without intelligence idiocy itself would be meaningless.

Giovanni Papini (1881–1956)
Hymn to Intelligence

PROLOGUE

Wednesday, 16 August, 1944

The locomotive and seven of the twelve freight cars were blown off the rails when the first wave of fighter-bombers flashed into sight over a wooded ridge and strafed the train. They were P.38 Lightnings of the American 15th Air Force's 46th Bombardment Group – silver, twin-boom planes that howled down on the tracks in groups of three, pulverising the wagons with cannon fire, rockets and small high-explosive bombs.

The road, the railway and the Tagliamento River ran together there in a narrow valley that twisted through the eastern foothills of the Dolomites on the way to the Austrian frontier. Udine and the plain lay twenty miles downstream.

By the time the second wave swooped over the hilltop, a pillar of black smoke veined with crimson was leaning away from the wrecked permanent way and the flaming freight cars. The Lightnings in the second wave flew very low, streaking through the smoke to hose cannon shells among a detail of German soldiers who had fanned out from an undamaged coach at the rear of the train to fire automatic weapons at the attackers. Planes in the third wave dropped incendiaries and 250-pounders.

The train was on its way from Bologna to Berlin, loaded with fruit and vegetables and light engineering components from the commandeered Fiat factory in Turin. Three wagons immediately behind the locomotive carried sacks of mail from an army post-office in the rear of the Gothic Line, where seasoned Wehrmacht men pinned down the

Anglo-American advance on the far side of the Arno. Routed through Klagenfurt, in Austria, and then Linz, Prague and Dresden, the train was not expected to complete the 650-mile journey in less than four or five days.

The war, and the air raids and battles that would be responsible for the delay, had seemed very far away until the Lightnings appeared over the valley. It lay between Venzone and Carnia, at the foot of the long grade that rose past Malborghetto to the border, and although it was more than two thousand feet above sea level, thin skeletons of vines still clung to the stony terraces on either side of the line. Across the river, the red roofs of a village showed among the trees on the edge of a chestnut forest.

For some time after the roar of the last fighter-bomber had dwindled to a drone and then faded away, the silence was broken only by the crackle of flames and the cries of a man whose legs had been blown off by a 40mm cannon shell. Then gradually the natural sounds of the upland valley reasserted themselves: a tremble of sheep bells, the shallow river babbling over stones, wind hissing through the grasses before it teased out the smoke rising from the martyred train.

At the same time movement was visible beyond the splintered wagons. Soldiers ran toward the locomotive, which was lying on its side with steam still seething from the ruptured boiler. Others rose cautiously from a ditch or emerged from the shade of alders bordering the line. On the far side of the water, villagers had assembled to stare across at the aftermath of the raid.

The railway lines, twisted and bent, were strewn with broken crates which had been packed with apples. Cabbages, onions, peaches, littered the bomb craters between sacks of mail thrown from the forward freight cars. Several of the cars, split open by shells and then fired by incendiaries, still blazed.

'God in Heaven!' the NCO in charge of the guard detail said. 'The salvage boys are going to have a ball clearing up this lot!'

'Peaches!' the corporal with him said savagely. 'Apples! I haven't tasted fresh fruit since I left the hospital after Stalingrad.'

'You should join the lads defending the Gothic Line,' the NCO told him, 'Orchards, vineyards all around.'

'Oh, sure,' the corporal said. He nodded toward a confetti of army postcards scattered around a ripped sack at their feet. 'We wish you were here in beautiful Tuscany. The weather's fine. An X marks our foxhole.'

'Better see what we can do,' the NCO said.

The two men moved towards the smashed loco. They had sheltered beneath the river bank during the raid; their uniforms were soaked to the waist.

The engineer was dead in his cab. The fireman crouched among the coal spilled from the tender with his hands clasped over his head. He was shuddering uncontrollably. Further back, half a dozen men carried wounded comrades beneath the alder trees, where a *Stabsgefreiter* from the last coach was already laying out the contents of a first-aid box in the shade. The soldier whose legs had been blown off was no longer screaming.

One of the survivors who had been the first to reach the engine was staring from the flame-licked freight cars to the empty sky. 'What the hell do the bastards think they're doing?' he cried. 'This is the fifth mail train attacked this month! I mean what's the point? There's no damned sense in it: we're not carrying munitions, for God's sake . . . and in any case all the trains strafed have been heading north, away from the front.'

'I'll tell you one thing,' his companion said angrily. 'If they want to keep any of their precious rolling stock intact, they'd better damned well couple on a flatbed truck armed with 75s each time they run a train.' He threw his Schmeisser machine pistol to the ground. 'How the hell are we supposed to guard against air attack with these?'

'All right, all right,' the NCO said. 'Put it in writing and mail it to the *Herr General*. I'm sure he'd be happy to oblige.'

'What's the use of that?' the soldier said sourly. 'The train carrying the letter would be blitzed!'

'You'd better get across to that village, Bergmann, and find a phone,' the senior man said to the corporal. 'Report the raid and ask for salvage crews and an ambulance.'

Glad to escape the stench of blood and excrement and cordite, the corporal walked away towards the river. It was a hot day; his wet trousers were already steaming in the sun. At the head of the valley, the mountains stood bare and brown against the blue sky.

The river here was shallow, flowing fast between banks of shingle. He had no trouble wading across.

It was curious, just the same (Corporal Bergmann reflected, climbing the bank on the far side), the way the enemy aviators had concentrated recently on mail trains. Stranger still was the column of smoke that had risen at once from the strafed train: as the soldier had said, there were no munitions aboard, and no merchandise among the freight could have produced a cloud so dark and so dense. Or so quickly. If the idea had not been so ridiculous, he could almost have imagined that it was some kind of smokescreen laid by the raiders.

He put the thought from his mind. Why would they bother? What good would it do them? Right now there were more pressing problems to solve.

The villagers fell back, leaving him a free passage as he squelched across the mountain grass towards the first houses. Nobody said anything and no one volunteered to help: the Wehrmacht were not popular in northern Italy.

There was a post office at the far end of the single dusty street. While he waited for the call to be put through, Bergmann tried to marshal his recollections of the hell that followed the first appearance of the Lightnings. He was not one hundred percent sure – who could be under such conditions? – but he could have sworn that one of the planes, at least one, in the second wave had dropped some kind of missile that had failed to explode on impact . . . and had still not exploded.

11

The planes had been very low, but in the brief glimpse he'd had, Bergmann had thought the missiles were not shaped like normal bombs. What could they be? Landmines with delayed-action fuses? Some deadly secret weapon? Cannisters of gas? Germ warfare?

Whatever they were, he was happy enough to be several hundred yards away from them. It would not surprise him if there was still some unpleasant development to come on the far side of the river.

The corporal was surprised all right. But his astonishment was due to a development nearer than the train wreck and the mysterious missiles.

Turning away from the antique phone after he had made his report, he discovered that he was surrounded by a ring of grim-faced Italian partisans armed with shotguns and World War I revolvers.

He was more surprised still when, later the following day, he was taken to a clearing in the forest and put aboard a Lysander reconnaissance aircraft with British markings and flown to a temporary airstrip near Perugia, behind the Allied lines.

PART ONE

Very Special Delivery

Chapter 1

'This feller Kane,' the red-tabbed brigadier said suspiciously. 'Seems a bit of a bolshie, what? I mean to say, no sense of discipline; won't toe the line; makes tactical decisions off his own bat. Mad as a hatter, if you ask me.'

The colonel from the Intelligence Corps who was sitting on the far side of the desk pushed back his chair and rose to his feet. He walked across to the window and stood staring out at the rain. Below, in the courtyard of the *palazzo*, Italian soldiers were loading sacks of mail into a Bedford three-tonner which carried no divisional markings superimposed on the camouflage. 'It was because of his . . . individuality, his enterprise, if you like, that Kane was chosen for this particular assignment,' the colonel said carefully. 'One is obliged to take certain risks – as I am sure you know very well, sir – one has, as it were, to cast one's bread upon the waters in the hope of getting a positive return in jobs of this kind.'

'Yes, Colbert, that's all very well,' the brigadier said, 'but surely we should be able to expect, well, a modicum of respect, a certain amount of deference to the powers that be, even in this kind of job? Otherwise, where will it all end?'

'Satisfactorily, sir, one hopes,' the colonel said.

On the desk in front of the brigadier there was a buff folder ornamented with a red Top Secret seal. He opened it and took out the single sheet of typescript it contained, settling a pair of gold-rimmed spectacles on his nose – a short, pink-faced man with an angry moustache. 'Says here that he organised a couple of cloak-and-dagger raids on the French and Belgian coasts,' he observed. 'Testing the strength of the Atlantic Wall an' that sort of thing.'

'Yes, sir.'

'It appears they were successful enough.' The brigadier cleared his throat. 'But what's all this Eagle Squadron nonsense?'

'Kane's mother is English, but his father was an American,' Colonel Colbert explained. 'He joined the other US citizens who volunteered to fly with the RAF before America entered the war.'

'Ah, yes,' the brigadier said. 'The Yanks.'

'He was shot down over France, bribed the skipper of a Breton trawler to offload him in a rubber dinghy five miles from the English coast, and wangled a commission with an American armoured division after Pearl Harbour. As I say, sir,' Colbert murmured, 'one does rather favour the individualist, the chap with enterprise, in one's particular job.'

'Before the balloon went up' – the brigadier flipped over the page and scowled at a filing card that had been stapled to the back of it – 'he was apparently a . . . a stuntman – whatever that is – in Hollywood.' The dry voice was scandalised. 'That's the film place, ain't it? Greta Garbo, Mary Pickford, an' all that?'

'More like Douglas Fairbanks, actually,' said Colbert. 'Kane, I mean. One can't swear that he's been over Niagara Falls in a barrel, but he's certainly pretty nifty when it comes to diving through a window or leaping off trains at 50 mph. Quite a dab at cat burglary too. That's one of the reasons why the firm wanted to row him in on this show.'

'Yes. Well.' Brigadier Terence Honeywell gestured helplessly at the folder, stayed his hand in mid flight, and then shrugged. 'I must suppose you people know what you're doing – all you want from me is a signature, what?' He stared with disfavour at the intelligence colonel. Like many Sandhurst-trained regulars, he disliked this new breed of wartime officers: either they were pipsqueak temporary gentlemen, or else they were brainy types owing their rank and position less to soldierly qualities than to their social or mental equipment. Dilettantes, he called them. Their uniforms were tailored in Savile Row, their hair was too long, they removed the wire stiffeners from their dress service hats . . . dammit, they lounged about the place instead of standing up straight and setting an example to the men!

Honeywell fervently wished that he himself was back in a position where he could set examples. This beastly Staff job, acting as liaison between the American Office of Strategic Services and the most hush-hush of Britain's military intelligence units, was certainly not of his own choosing. Nor were the armchair warriors with whom he had to deal. He looked at Colbert again.

The man's face was long and sallow, with a straight nose and heavy-lidded eyes. Of all the Allied officers billeted in the requisitioned *palazzo* he seemed the least out of place. With that face and his straight, dark, lustreless hair, he could have been one of the conspiratorial *quattrocento* nobles whose portraits hung in the picture gallery downstairs. And certainly (Honeywell reflected) this damnfool operation he himself was being asked to underwrite now was Machiavellian enough.

'I know the whole idea sounds hopelessly batty,' Colbert said, as though reading his thoughts. 'Frankly, I doubt if we'd have touched it with a bargepole if some PWD bods with an in at SHAEF headquarters in London hadn't twisted Ike's arm. But the word has come down: like the jolly old tennis pro, we do but stand and serve.'

'Quite.' The brigadier removed his spectacles, folded the earpieces, slid them into a morocco case which he buttoned beneath the three rows of medal ribbons into the breast pocket of his tunic. He replaced the sheet of typescript and closed the folder.

Colbert said: 'One should add, sir, crazy though it is, this show does call for a chap with a plus ration of guts and savvy.'

'With a what?'

'With more courage, determination and enterprise than your average Nobby Clarke. Kane has those qualities. He's tough.'

'I don't doubt it.'

'Would you like to see him for yourself? Should one roll him in for inspection, cast the official eye, so to speak?'

'Who, me? No, no. Good Lord, no. Absolutely not. I leave all that kind of thing to you and your opposite . . . this OSS feller, Whatsisname.'

'Lieutenant-Colonel Georgopoulous.'

'Yes, him. You two carry on. Come back to me when you've buttoned it all up, and I'll sign the movement orders, request for seconding, pay transfer chit an' all that.' Abruptly Honeywell stood up. 'That's all I'm good for in this damned job,' he growled. 'Pen-pushing and coping with the other feller's bumph!'

'Yes, sir.' Colbert flicked a speck of dust from the green Intelligence Corps tab at his left shoulder. 'There's a bit of a panic on this one: Kane has to be briefed and then fired off PDQ. We shall be in touch soonest.'

'I shall be here all day.'

'Very good, sir.' The peaked cap settled at a rakish angle on the head, a languid hand raised in salute, and Colbert strolled from the room.

His opposite number in the OSS was also his opposite in appearance. Colbert was tall and lean; Irwin Georgopoulous was short and chunky with curling iron-grey hair. Colbert's face was long and solemn; the American's was round, red and animated. The I Corps colonel spoke in a lazy drawl; Georgopoulous's delivery was staccato and rapid. About the only thing they had in common, Brigadier Honeywell saw, passing them in the picture

17

gallery on his way to lunch at the improvised mess, was the fact that each had transformed the stiff crown of his headgear into the floppy shape Honeywell detested.

Martin Kane wore the bars of a captain in the United States army on the shoulder straps of his olive-drab uniform jacket. He had worn other insignia on other uniforms in the course of his undercover work, but these were the ones to which he was officially entitled. There would have been crowns or stars on the straps if Kane's devil-may-care attitude and disreputable, rake-hell activities had not antagonised a series of commanding officers and almost all the uniformed bureaucrats with whom he came into contact when he was not actually on active service.

'That bloody man Kane,' they used to say when he flew with the Eagle Squadron, 'what the hell is he up to now?' And the American brass was no more tolerant when he enlisted under the Stars and Stripes at the end of 1941. 'Thank Christ the sonofabitch is off my back,' his colonel enthused eighteen months later when Kane was finally ingested within the secret ranks of the OSS. 'Face it, the moment that guy shows up, law and order goes out the window!'

Something of this showed in Kane's appearance. He was a compact man, not too tall, but muscular. His hands were large and immensely strong. Beneath the short, crisp blond hair, his face was raffish and hawklike, with a prominent nose and a ruthless mouth. It was nevertheless the cleft chin and the wide grey eyes that made him irresistible to so many women.

At 14 hours 50 on the afternoon of Thursday, 17 August, 1944, he rapped on the panels of a third-floor door in the *palazzo* that was labelled MILINTEL 7. *All passes must be shown.*

Kane had no pass. He gave his name to the British corporal clerk who opened the door, and strode across the anteroom.

'Yes, sir. If you would just come this way . . .' the clerk began – but Kane was already ahead of him, opening a door that led to an inner office whose windows looked out onto terraced vines.

Georgopoulous was tilting back a swivel chair behind a large, empty desk. His ankles were crossed; his feet, shod with rubber-soled combat boots, rested on the polished wood of the desk. Colbert stood in the window with a well-filled brandy balloon in his hand. Nearby, bottles and glasses showed in the open drawer of a green steel filing cabinet. It was still raining outside.

'Kane?' Georgopoulous said. 'You're early.'

'I'd eaten,' Kane said. 'No point hanging about.' The voice was mid-atlantic, the American inflexions scarcely noticeable.

'More to the point,' Colbert drawled, 'have you drunk? I can offer you scotch, gin or brandy – Italian stuff. Stock 84. It's not bad'.

'Brandy would be fine. Thank you, sir.' Kane was always prepared to show respect to a senior offier when the man had earned it. With the glass in his hand, he visibly relaxed. It was clear that these two characters were not the rank-pulling type.

'We'll come straight to the point,' Colbert said. 'Time's short on this one. Very short. But you have to be filled in on the background first.' He glanced at Georgopoulous. 'Your witness.'

'The mission,' the OSS man said, 'is ass-about-face. What I mean, we're not asking you to launch an operation; what you have to do is recuperate one that already fucked up'.

Kane waited patiently, sipping his brandy.

'A smart idea dreamed up by the boys of the Psychological Warfare Department,' Georgopoulous said. 'We threw the Krauts out of North Africa, right? Stalin's beating the shit outa them in Russia, we have bridgeheads in Normandy, we're attacking here in Italy, OK? Now, only two days ago, Patch's 7th Army pulls off successful landings all along the French Rivera coast.'

19

'Don't tell me,' Kane said drily. 'I just came from there.'

'OK. The Reich, you could say, is under pressure, right? Has been for quite a while now. So back in the Spring the PWD eggheads figure the time is ripe for an attack on the enemy's morale.'

'His morale?'

'Sure. We're gonna win this damned war: that's obvious now. So how can we speed up the end, minimise the losses, and like that? Put the German soldier in a rebellious mood, they figured. At least that would help, if the guy really wanted out.'

Georgopoulous lifted his feet from the desk and leaned forward in his chair. He fished a crumpled sheet of paper from the breast pocket of his jacket and smoothed it out. 'I'll read you the relevant para from the original PWD report to SHAEF,' he said. 'Quote. It is considered that weary frontline troops, especially in the east, would be particularly susceptible to three approaches: number one, doubts about the fidelity of their womenfolk at home; number two, the idea that there was already, within the German army, a widespread peace movement desirous of ending the war; number three, news of an organised anti-Hitler underground working within the Reich. Unquote.' The OSS man grinned. 'You know this man's army. Generous to a fault. The PWD chiefs decided to feed the Krauts all three!'

'Yeah, but . . .' Kane shifted in his chair. 'For Christ's sake! Have any of these smartasses faced a Kraut with a Schmeisser recently? Or been the wrong side of a Tiger tank? Jesus, I don't see any sign of the German soldier letting up, not from where I stand.'

'No,' Colbert agreed. 'Not yet. There is of course no peace movement and no underground – and the Fräuleins sleep around no more and no less than other war wives. But you have to remember this is a long-term plan, no immediate effects expected. The water wearing away the stone, and all that.'

'In any case,' Georgopoulous said, 'that ain't the heart of the problem. The $64,000-question was: how the hell to get the guys to believe these cooked-up stories. The Master Race has been too well brainwashed, and for far too long, to fall for anything so crude as leaflets dropped by airplanes.' He paused for effect, and then said slowly: 'But if details of these so-called "movements", if evidence showing that the chicks did put it about, came genuinely from inside the Fatherland . . . well, the story might be different.'

'OK,' Kane said dubiously, 'but how the hell – ?'

'However crackbrained the original scheme,' Colbert interrupted, 'one has to hand it to the boffins for the way they worked that one out. Get the ideas across, they said? Simple: we use the Nazis' own internal mail system. After all, it can hardly be enemy propaganda if the mailman brings it with the morning post.'

Kane stared at him.

'It's true.' The OSS man was smiling again. 'They invented a mythical "Union of German Partisans" with messages sent in counterfeit military envelopes. They faked up a supposedly underground newspaper called *Das Neue Deutschland* – and printed it badly, deliberately, on god-awful paper, to suggest that it came from some clandestine cellar press in the Reich. Smartest of all, they formed the "National League of Lonely Women" – headed notepaper and all – with personal letters to individual Wehrmacht men, telling them that this was a nationwide network of part-time whores, hungry for horny men, who could be contacted like this and like that, any time the guy was on furlough.'

'The sting in the tail,' Colbert added, 'being the line: Don't feel guilty about contacting us; your own wife and/or girlfriend has been a member of the club for some time.'

Kane shook his head. 'Jesus!' he said. 'Yeah, but – shit! Use the internal mail system, you tell me. Great. But how the hell do you guys get this stuff into the system?

Parachute agents into Germany with orders to buy stamps at the local post office and then drop the envelopes into the bloody box?'

'Not quite,' Colbert said. He passed between them with the bottle, replenishing glasses. 'But the way this falsified material is inserted unsuspected into the Nazi postal system is pretty smooth, just the same. You tell him, Irwin: your people dreamed it up.'

Georgopoulous said: 'It's smart, I agree. Pursuit planes based here in Italy attack northbound German mail trains on the far side of the mountains, derailing and strafing the rolling stock. But one ship in each wave is loaded not with small bombs but with sacks of fake mail, franked as though it came from wherever the train started. Dropped among the wreckage, these sacks are recuperated by salvage teams along with the genuine stuff – and assumed by the guys clearing up the mess to be part of the original freight consignment. After which, of course, they get shoved in with the real McCoy and distributed along with the normal post.'

'Crazy,' Kane said. 'So what's gone wrong?'

'We'll explain on the way to the factory,' Colbert told him. 'No time to lose on this one.'

'What factory?'

'Where all this merchandise is printed up,' Georgopoulous said. 'You don't think the stuff is tapped out between lunch and dinner by a couple of girls with a typewriter apiece, do you? Shit, there's going on for a million of these letters gone out already!'

'A million!' Kane echoed. 'How do you know where to send that number of letters?'

Georgopoulous chuckled. 'Telephone directories smuggled out of the Reich. All mail to serving soldiers is automatically forwarded to the nearest Army Post Office.' He jumped to his feet. 'C'mon, guys, let's go. The carriage is waiting!'

The *palazzo* that served as intelligence headquarters was in San Gimignano, a mediaeval hilltop town near

Siena whose fourteen tall, square, stone towers presided over the Umbrian countryside. The 'factory' had been installed in – or, more precisely, beneath – Perugia, seventy miles to the east. 'An Etruscan duke, or somesuch,' Colbert said to Kane, 'became cheesed off sometime in the Dark Ages when the town was sacked for the umpteenth time and razed yet again to the ground. OK, says His Grace, this time we'll rebuild the place *under*ground – and the bloody Saracens, or the Florentines, or whoever, can sit up top and whistle: we'll just pull down the trapdoors and sit it out until they've gone. If the buggers are looking for rape, let them go find some Sabine women.'

'You mean they dug out an underground city?' Kane asked.

'Sort of. Perugia's built on a boss of solid rock. They hollowed out a bloody great warren beneath the main square, with streets, houses, storerooms, an assembly hall, little kiosks that were obviously some kind of shop or boutique. The streets are cobbled and they even have names – Via This and Via That. The whole shoot looks exactly like Pompeii or one of those other Roman towns, except that instead of the sky there's a rock ceiling.'

'And this is where they fake your German mail?'

Colbert nodded. 'It seemed safer. If they'd moved the stuff into some commercial site outside the old town, sure as eggs there'd have been a leak. Don't forget, we've only just chucked the Krauts out of this part of Italy: there'll still be fascist sympathisers around. Bound to be. And if someone can see, someone else can talk. But down below in those caves they can control who comes in and who goes out . . . and nobody can see a thing.'

'Can't the workers faking the material talk?'

'Ain't nobody for them to talk to,' Georgopoulous said. 'We moved them in from outside. Poles, Frogs, North Africans. Pioneer Corps characters. They live in a military hostel, and very few of them speak Italian.'

The Humber Staff car taking the three men to Perugia

turned out of the *palazzo* courtyard, clattered across the Piazza Cisterna, and passed through an arched gateway in the ancient walls. The rain had stopped but there were few people to be seen among the dun-coloured jeeps and army trucks parked around the square. Looping down into the valley below, the road dissolved beneath scarves of mist that wrapped around cypress trees and veiled the terraced vines.

'We've filled you in on the Clever Dick part,' Colbert said as they joined the main Rome-Siena highway. 'Now we'll give you the gen on the disaster . . . and that's really where we come into it. Members of the Island Race, I mean. Because Operation Cornflakes was originally an American show: they thought it up, and they worked it . . .'

'Operation what?'

'Cornflakes, old boy. So called because the product, so to speak, is delivered by your friendly army postman at breakfast time.'

'I don't believe it!' said Kane.

'True. Honest Injun. As I was saying, it was originally Irwin's baby – but it was the Special Branch and the lads from MI5 in London who stumbled on the fact that something was wrong.' Colbert lit a cigarette, shook out the match, and flipped it out of the open window. 'So now it's a combined op,' he said.

'I guess you'll tell me what did go wrong sometime before they invalid me out?'

'Not to put too fine a point on it' – the Intelligence Corps colonel signed – 'someone did talk. We don't know where, when or even why, but the whole damned plan, every smallest detail of the scheme, was communicated to a big time Nazi agent in London. Shortly afterwards, this cove was nabbed. It was while the interrogators were bargaining with him – you know: everything about the German spy ring in Britain against your miserable life – it was while they were tooling around with that one that the chap let slip that he'd been fed the Cornflakes, as you might say.'

24

'But of course he'd already passed the information on to his masters in Berlin?'

'In a manner of speaking, yes. But you can't just breeze into a phone box in wartime London and dial Tiergarten 1234, please can I speak to Herr Ribbentrop.'

'He'd sent it by radio?'

Colbert shook his head. 'Too risky. We think he suspected the SB were on to him; he wanted a less obvious, more certain channel. No – he popped the information into an envelope and sent it by mail.'

Kane stared from Colbert to Georgopoulous and then back again. The Humber turned off the main road and sped along between groves of olives. After the fall of Rome in June, the Allied advance through Italy had been rapid: Umbria and southern Tuscany had been relatively untouched by the war. 'Are you telling me. . . ?' Kane began.

'BIC and DI, they call it in LA,' the OSS man said. 'Built-in conflict and dramatic irony. Yeah, you guessed it: Herr Kraut used the system he was going to blow wide open as a means of getting his report to Berlin! You have to admit it's a nice touch. I figure we should be flattered he thought the service was reliable enough for such an important message!'

'But . . . how come he managed it? To get his own letter in?'

'Clearly,' Colbert said, 'the leak must have come from some bod working actually in the factory. An agent posing as a refugee Pole infiltrated into the Pioneer Corps. Something like that. All the London spy had to do was encode his report, bung it into an envelope, and then post it back to this sleeper via an APO, with orders to slip the letter in among our beautiful fakes when the next delivery was made.'

'Was the sleeper fingered when this guy was interrogated?'

'No. He stopped short of that. Wouldn't budge on it.'

'But the letter did go in? The delivery has been made?'

'Sure has.' Georgopoulous said. 'It was in one of the sacks dropped on a mail train that was blitzed near the Austrian frontier yesterday. We got the signal from London just too late to stop the delivery: the P.38s were already over the target.'

The Staff car raced through a village of lakeside houses. Kane saw a sign, *Castiglio del Lago*, and the gleam of water between red brick walls. Away to the north, sunshine filtered through the hurrying clouds to silver the wet roofs of a small town perched on a ridge. 'Cortona,' Colbert said. 'There's a two-room museum there with rather a fine ceiling.'

Light flashed suddenly from the hillside below Cortona – a car windscreen? an opening window? – and now the road ahead was steaming in the August heat. Kane said: 'So what happens? Your telltale letter drops into a mailbox in Berlin? The German intelligence services are wise to the set-up? You mean you'll have to scrap the whole fucking plan, factory and all?'

'That's about the size of it. Once they're on to the wheeze, the Jerries will expose the whole thing as a dastardly enemy plot to besmirch the purity of German womanhood, question the loyalty of the German fighting man, and so forth. Naturally. And of course they'll keep an extra close watch on strafed trains, with some tricky way of telling their own mail from ours.' Colbert shook his head. 'No point in going on.'

Georgopoulous said: 'The tear-jerking scenario you just heard is predicted on a conditional.'

Kane frowned. 'Come again?'

'That's what would happen' – pause for dramatic effect – 'that's what would happen *if* the telltale letter was delivered in Berlin.'

'If?'

'The top brass are very concerned that it shouldn't be. For some reason – you tell me why – the guys up there pin a lot of faith on this zany operation.'

'But if the sack with the letter in it has already been

26

dropped behind the German lines. . . ?'

'They reckon, under present conditions, what with Allied raids and priority for munition trains, that the stuff salvaged from the wreck won't be in Berlin for another four days.'

'OK,' Kane said. 'Even so, I don't see how – ?'

'How we can stop the letter being delivered?' Colbert cut in. 'That's easy, old chap. That's why you're here. You're going into the Reich to find that letter and bring it back here.'

'You must be joking!' Kane said.

Chapter 2

Approached from Assisi, Arezzo and the east, Perugia presents the classic aspect of a fortified town dominating the olives and vines and orchards spread over the flat land below, its only entry a massive Etruscan gateway in the form of a triumphal arch. To the traveller approaching from the direction of Siena, the view is less impressive: the ancient city is reduced to walls, roofs and spires surmounting a sprawl of railway yards and apartment blocks. The Humber Staff car carrying Colbert, Georgopoulous and Martin Kane clattered over a level crossing, passed warehouses and shuttered gas stations, and then climbed the zigzag route that led to the Governor's palace and the Piazza Italia.

Military traffic along the steep streets was heavy.

British, American and Polish soldiers stood at every corner. The Gothic Line, straddling the country from Pescaro to Viareggio, was only twenty-five miles away, and the Allied advance had halted there once troops had been withdrawn to mount the invasion of southern France. The heavy grumble of artillery was clearly audible over the manoeuvring of trucks and transports in the crowded square.

Colbert's driver parked in a compound controlled by white-helmeted MPs. The three officers hurried past Renaissance façades and plunged down flights of steps leading to the slope where the entrance to the catacombs pierced the old city wall.

There were more snowdrops here, armed with M.1 Garand carbines, and a technical top-sergeant inside, who compared the special passes he was shown with a printed list in a cellophane cover.

Despite the information he had already been given, Kane was amazed at the complexity of the operation and the pressure under which the personnel worked. The underground 'streets' stretched away in every direction, some slanting quite steeply up or down. In line with the usual heavy-handed army waggishness, they had been renamed to suit the code-name of the project: Kane saw a Frosties Avenue, an All-Bran Lane, a Kellogg Square.

A subdued electrical hum and the clatter of machinery overlaid the sounds of voices echoing off the rock walls. The miniature 'shops' and 'dwellings' hollowed out along each paved thoroughfare – they reminded Kane of the souks in an Arab kasbah – were staffed by men and women busy about a multiplicity of jobs. He saw shirtsleeved journalists pondering the copy that would become the text of the next batch of deliveries, designers with drawing boards, secretaries cutting the stencils for a German Gestetner copier. One kiosk was stacked from floor to ceiling with bales of yellowish paper; another housed a small team guillotining each bale into standard sizes. 'No expense spared,' Georgopoulous said at Kane's ear. 'We had German wartime paper laboratory-analysed: every ream you see here was specially milled in Pittsburgh and flown across secretly by the guys delivering Fortress replacements to the USAAF.'

In one larger space, overalled technicians rolled ink onto an old-fashioned hand press turning out smudged copies of a one-page news sheet headed with the legend *Das Neue Deutschland* in Gothic type. Behind the press, compositors picked individual characters from a case with tweezers and arranged them in columns on a forme.

At the far end of one corridor, stone steps led to a suite of rooms that must have been reserved for the seigneur and his family. Of all the openings Kane had seen, this was the only one with a delicate wrought-iron grille barring the entrance. Inside, a line of girls working German Adler typewriters composed the letters informing Nazi soldiers of the supposed infidelities of their women.

'The underground peace movement stuff can be roneoed,' Colbert explained, 'but the League of Lonely Women material has to be typed out separately, letter by letter. In case the guys compare notes, you see.'

They passed through sectors where men stencilled mailbags, gummed wrappers and envelopes, laboriously transferred long lists of names from telephone directories to information sheets. In an ante-room near the assembly hall, an electrical machine was spewing out sheet after perforated sheet of perfectly forged twelve-Pfennig stamps. The hall itself – which was the nearest part of the labyrinth to the exit tunnel – was used as a final assembly and dispatch section.

Clerks sitting at long trestle tables folded paper, filled envelopes, gummed flaps, added addresses, stuck on stamps, and then passed the envelopes on to a moving belt that fed them through an automatic franking machine. After that they were stuffed into the prepared sacks and slid down a chute into a waiting truck at the foot of the ramparts. A few letters from each batch were put aside and manually franked by a girl with a wooden-handled rubber stamp and an ink pad.

'Variety, you see – they say it's the spice of life. But not a word in here,' Colbert warned. 'We still haven't identified the sleeper. It could be any of these girls, any of these blokes. Better to pretend that you're part of a normal inspection team, someone who knows all the secrets already.'

'Incredible!' Kane exclaimed when finally they led him through the tunnel and out into late afternoon sunshine at the foot of the city wall. 'It's the detail that fazes me. How the hell do you know that those mail sacks will pass as the genuine article in the Reich? How come you don't fuck up on the cancellation of stamps, the stencilling technique, and the like?'

'Material from refugees, agents in Germany, but mostly from very intensive interrogation and cross-examination of Jerry POWs,' Colbert said. 'Any Kraut with postal or railway connections in the compound, and there's a team of experts ferreting out the tiniest crumb of info on packaging, franking routines, and so on.'

'It's the individual slant that bugs us,' Georgopoulous said. 'It would be another story if it was simple leaflets – but playing it this way, except for the phoney news sheet, we're really blocked from any mass-production approach.' He shook his head. 'With the set-up we have here, the most we can produce is twenty-five thousand letters a week.'

'How sad for the Panzers on the eastern front,' said Kane.

On the far side of the palace, behind the *carabinieri* headquarters in the Corso Vannucci, British and American military intelligence chiefs had commandeered the top floor of the Albergo Posta and made a combined mess, intelligence library and operations complex from the tall rooms with their classical murals. 'It seemed the right choice – *l'Hôtel de la Poste*,' Georgopoulous smiled (his French accent was good). 'Better still, according to a publicity throwaway they still have under the counter at Reception, the place was already famous in the eighteenth

30

century . . . and guess who stayed here: not Queen Elizabeth, not Napoleon, but Goethe, Heine, Humboldt – and Hans Christian Andersen, the best faker of all!'

'OK,' Kane said. 'I'm wised up on how the operation works. I'm duly impressed with the routine. I know how it got fouled up. Suppose we quit horsing around, and you tell me what you want me to do?' He looked at the OSS man and smiled. 'Sir.'

They were sitting in a room with a domed ceiling that sported *trompe l'œil* balconies with ladies in crinolines eavesdropping on the conversations below. Plaster panels on the walls contained classical landscapes portraying ruins and waterfalls.

'We drop you into Germany early tomorrow,' Georgopoulous said. 'We can give you the co-ordinates that will identify the particular sack containing the letter with the spy's report: the numbers are stencilled on the outside. You'll have a small, hand-picked team with you, each one an expert on some aspect of skullduggery. They'll help you ease your way into whatever sorting office you choose to bust.'

'If I find the sack,' Kane asked, 'how do I identify which of the hundred letters inside is the one we want? Or do you want I should trudge back like Santa Claus with the whole fucking sack over my shoulder?'

'*When* you find the sack,' Colbert corrected, 'it won't be hard to locate the right letter. There are only a limited number of ways in which the addresses on the letters are laid out here: we'll show you examples. The one you're looking for will be different from all of them – and the envelope will be English, not made from German-style paper like the rest.'

'How do you know?'

'The spy they caught in London wouldn't finger the sleeper here,' Georgopoulous said, 'but he did say that his instructions had been for the letter to remain unopened when it arrived from Britain, that it was to go straight into the sack the way it was.'

'Will the stamp be cancelled? Will it be franked?'

'You tell me. Depends where the sleeper works. It's got to be near the end of the production line: a sealed envelope that appeared before would alert an overseer. If the bastard's located on the inner side of the belt feeding the franking machine, the stamp will be cancelled; if he's in Dispatch, it won't be. That's all we can say.'

Kane smiled crookedly. 'I don't suppose he told you the address?'

'Where he was sending the letter? Uh-uh. He spilled just enough to have gotten himself off the hook, no more. The guys in MI5 told us he was kind of an intelligent character: he was even amused at the thought of the odds; with what he'd told us, would we be able to identify the sleeper? Would we be able to stop the letter? Or would it still get through to Berlin and kill our project?'

'You do know it was going to Berlin?'

'Yes,' Colbert said. 'All the post in that particular sack was. Jerry organises kind of a preliminary sorting at the APO nearest to the mail train's starting point: in this case, Bologna. You know – just which general area the stuff's for: Westphalia, Palatinate, Reinhesse, Berlin, Württemburg – the way it might be divided into States in the US.'

Georgopoulous said, 'The report will be in code or cypher, you bet your life. But the envelope could be addressed to a ministry, a safe house, a cover office, the spy's dear old Momma, you name it. It could be typed or in longhand; we just don't know.'

'If I locate the envelope,' Kane queried, 'I guess I can open it, and like check out the contents? Just to prove that it *is* the right one? If it's in cypher groups or an obvious code, that would be the clincher.'

'It should be clear enough,' Colbert agreed. 'The information is sufficiently complex to show up even in an apparently innocent letter to a girlfriend – to show that it isn't innocent, if you see what I mean; that even if the subject's hidden, the text is some kind of code.'

'And when I've got the letter, I chew it up and swallow it, and then put everything back the way it was?'

'Good God, yes. The sack must show no sign that it's been tampered with. If you have to open several envelopes before you find the right one, the others must either be resealed or destroyed. Otherwise Jerry's attention could be drawn to that particular consignment, that particular train, and thus that particular raid. It could blow the whole thing wide open, if he started asking questions.'

There was a knock on the door. An American military policeman stood outside, his white webbing equipment and helmet bright in the dimly lit corridor. He sprang to attention and saluted. 'Colonel, sir,' he said to Georgopoulous, 'the prisoner and escort have arrived. Captain Ceccaldi says to tell you he's ready for interrogation any time you want.'

The OSS man nodded. 'Tell the captain we'll be right over,' he said. And then, to Kane and the Englishman: 'OK, guys – let's go.'

In answer to Kane's raised eyebrows, Colbert said, 'We're off to meet a member of the Master Race, the chap who's going to work out your route for you and turn the job into a piece of cake!'

Corporal Willi Bergmann neither looked nor felt like a member of the Master Race. He was dog-tired, he was unshaven, he was frightened – and above all he was totally bewildered.

Nothing that had happened to him in the past twenty hours made sense.

After the horror of the attack on the train, there had come the sickening fear of imminent execution when he was captured by the Italian partisans. This had increased to the point where he could hardly stay upright when he was marched with chattering teeth into the chestnut forest. Then, suddenly, stupefaction . . . the spidery monoplane in the clearing, the long flight, the exploding anti-aircraft shells as they flew over the front line. Temporarily, Bergmann lost his fear in curiosity: he had never been in an aircraft before, and the birds-eye view of the terrain through the Plexiglass windows of the Lysander intrigued him. At the height chosen by the pilot – it was less than five thousand feet – the casemates and redoubts of the Gothic Line were as clear as the symbols on a map, and behind a great swell of high ground a long line of enemy tanks and artillery was advancing across country through which he himself had retreated only a few weeks before. Apart from the AA fire as they crossed the line, there was no sign of activity, nor (Bergmann's major worry) did any Messerschmitts or Heinkels of the invincible Luftwaffe appear to challenge the reconnaissance plane's right of way.

Landing on the strip near Perugia, he was astonished to recognise the landscape: he even knew the town; he had been several times to an army brothel there when his unit had been based on Spoleto and the trains they guarded started in Rome. There had been a smart hotel near the whorehouse, out of bounds to all but the most senior officers.

Bergmann's confusion when he was taken in a jeep to this same hotel was total. Had he not been a simple man, he might have imagined himself the victim of some kind of time-warp, or simply that the whole crazy scenario was an unlikely dream. He had not been maltreated, he had not been beaten, he had been fed – rather better than he was accustomed to, as it happened – but he had been told nothing. The Lysander pilot and the officer who had covered him with a service revolver throughout the flight had said no more than that he was to consider himself a prisoner of war; the armed escort in the jeep had refused to talk at all. Now here he was in this plush hotel room with the same Italian-looking man who had been on the plane.

The man produced a shiny white packet with a picture of a camel on the front and offered him a cigarette. 'You have no need to be afraid,' he said. 'The men coming here to talk to you only want information.'

Bergmann's face blanched. Lurid visions of torture flashed through his mind. We have ways of making you talk. But what could he possibly know that would interest an enemy? They must have mistaken him for someone else: a spy? a senior officer in disguise?

The door of the room opened. He saw two soldiers with machine pistols standing guard outside. Three officers he had never seen before walked in and stood staring at him. The man who had given him the cigarette stood up. Hesitantly, Bergmann did so too.

Two of the newcomers wore American uniforms. The third was a tall, thin man with a grave expression. The battledress that he wore, with its green shoulder tab, was unfamiliar to the German.

The chunky American with the round face was speaking. 'As soon as they tipped us off that Mata Hari had spilled the beans,' he said, 'and that his report was already on the way to Berlin via our special delivery service, we sent off Ceccaldi here with a Lysander – and orders to snatch one of the crew of the strafed train and bring him back here. Luckily the jolly old brigadier was able to radio a partisan group in the area and ask them to organise the snatch and hold the guy until we arrived.' He gestured at Bergmann. 'This is the guy.'

Bergmann stared uncomprehendingly. He spoke no English.

'Sit down,' the tall, thin officer said in German. And then again: 'Do not be afraid. All we want is a little information.'

'The conventions of war', Bergmann said in a trembling voice, 'require only that I should communicate my name, rank, and number.'

'Yes, yes. We are familiar with the conventions. However, you find yourself in the hands of – shall we say? – a somewhat unconventional unit. With unlimited time and unlimited means at its disposal.' The officer paused, to allow the implications of his words to sink in.

Bergmann swallowed.

'In any case,' the officer pursued, 'the information we want is strictly non-military. It will not imperil the life of a single one of your comrades. It is really . . . how shall I put it? . . . no more than a matter of verifying a routine.' He turned towards the second American, the stocky one with the cruel face. 'You ask the questions,' he said. 'After all, you're the one who'll be making use of the gen.'

Kane stepped forward. His German was accentless and perfect – he had spent two years at Heidelberg in the early thirties. 'What we wish to know,' he said, 'is simply a confirmation of the route your train would have taken if it hadn't been . . . if it had not been attacked.'

Bergmann shifted uneasily in his chair. He had heard about the tricks of interrogators: the soft voice followed by the threat, the cigarette before the whip. What sinister purpose could underlie so simple a question? 'I do not know that I should . . .' he began doubtfully, aware that he had already had the cigarette.

'It would have crossed the Austrian frontier beyond Malborghetto, would it not?' Kane had been well briefed. 'And then perhaps passed through Klagenfurt in southern Austria?'

'That is so,' the German admitted cautiously.

'And then? Salzburg? Linz? Vienna? The freight – the merchandise and the mail – was destined for Berlin, was it not?'

'Some of it. The machine tools, certain cases of fruit, one of the mail cars were for Munich.' Questioned about his own particular work, his scarcely military work, Bergmann answered almost automatically. What had railway timetables got to do with the war? 'That train would have halted at Linz,' he went on. 'The wagons bound for Munich would have been uncoupled and shunted into a siding. They would have left the following day . . . today, that is. The remainder would have been added to another train, routed through Prague and Dresden to Berlin.'

36

Ceccaldi and the other three officers exchanged glances. 'When would the Berlin train have left?' Kane asked.

'That would depend on many things. If there were terror attacks – that is to say, air raids. How many munitions trains were scheduled. If there were to be troop movements. The train had a low priority.'

'When would you expect it to leave? If you were to stay with that train, I mean? Unless of course you were to go to Munich or return here to Italy?'

'No, no,' Bergmann said, almost conversationally; he was rapidly gaining confidence. 'The *first* train would return to Bologna, but my detail stayed with the Berlin portion all the way. Because of the mail, you see.'

'Does all of the mail go right through to Berlin,' Colbert asked casually, 'or is some of it dropped off along the way?'

'Again, it depends on the amount. If there is a big provincial delivery, a whole van might be loaded, and then uncoupled at Dresden, say, or even Linz. Otherwise, sacks are off-loaded at the big towns for local sorting: no point wasting valuable space sending the stuff all the way to Berlin and then having to bring it back again.'

'Quite. You still didn't say when you would have expected the Berlin train to leave Linz. If it hadn't been attacked.'

'Not before this evening. Then it would normally be scheduled for an overnight run as far as Prague, when the traffic was light.'

'Since your train *was* attacked and wrecked' – this was Kane once more – 'how would you expect any mail salvaged from it to be treated? Would it take the same route, perhaps a day later?'

'Well, of course. They will have sent breakdown crews from Udine. Once the line was cleared, a relief train would have been organised, from Klagenfurt maybe – they have more rolling stock available there. After that,' Bergmann shrugged, 'yes, it would continue as originally planned.'

'So your comrades should still be at Linz tonight – and possibly until tomorrow evening? If the Berlin stuff leaves then, is it on a through train, or is there another switch?'

'There's always a change at Prague. They switch locos and make up a fresh train when the lines are clear enough to let one through. Some of the freight is stored overnight in the goods sheds, but the mail is transferred to the central sorting office there: it's across the road from the station and it gives us a chance to get some sleep.'

'How long does it stay there before the new train is made up?'

'I told you: until they get a clearance. It may stay in Prague twelve hours . . . or two days. Tomorrow is Friday. If the stuff doesn't leave Linz until the evening, it could remain in Prague until Monday morning.'

'Thank you,' said Kane, 'that's just what I wanted to know.'

Bergmann was suddenly alarmed. What had he done? Why would they have brought him all this way, sent a special aircraft to kidnap him, just to ask a lot of tomfool questions about routine railway working? There must be some trick somewhere. 'Why do you want to know all this?' he asked suspiciously. 'Why should I – ?'

'Just checking,' Colbert told him. 'Thank you, Captain Ceccaldi. You can take the prisoner away now.'

'Will they shoot me?' Bergmann asked in a tremulous voice as the two MPs came into the room.

'Not unless your table manners are *very* bad,' Colbert said solemnly. 'Not this side of the Gothic Line anyway.'

He turned to Kane when the German and his escort had left. 'So far, so bloody good,' he said. 'All we have to do now is organise you a plan of the central sorting office in Prague, and introduce you to the villains who'll help you get in there.'

Chapter 3

The three NCOs locked into the Nissen hut near the Perugia airstrip regarded each other with mutual suspicion.

The reaction was hardly surprising. If it had been possible to comb the entire listed personnel of all the Allied armies in Europe, it is unlikely that a more disparate trio could have been found. Two of the men were English, one was a naturalised American of Polish descent; one was a regular with twenty years' service, one was a wartime volunteer, and one was a conscript. Of the latter two, the conscript was an ex-jailbird and the volunteer a small businessman from the Jewish quarter of New York. The regular soldier, although he was an archetypal British NCO, nevertheless spoke perfect German: his father had married a nurse from Kiel after the First World War.

Victor Hawkins had been a colour sergeant with the Green Howards before his language qualification, plus an extraordinary strength and toughness, had qualified him for Special Operations. He was a monolithic man, long-armed, barrel-chested, shaven of head – a fighter of few words, and those few largely unprintable. He possessed a third qualification that could not be evaluated in terms of words on paper: unswerving loyalty towards authority and 'the officer'.

The conscript's name was Daventry. A thin, balding, taciturn man of forty-five, he wore heavy horn-rimmed spectacles and looked as though he might be a librarian or the manager of a rather superior gentleman's outfitters. He was in fact a locksmith by trade and a safe-breaker by choice, and he had arrived in Special Operations via HM Prison in Wandsworth and the Pioneer Corps. His Christian name, which he preferred not to reveal, was Vernon.

In contrast to the Britishers' reserve, Vladislaw Zygmund, the Polish-American late of the United States Marine Corps, presented the world a façade of unremitting vivacity and cheerfulness. He was a short, round, bouncy little man with an inexhaustible fund of energy, the owner and operator of a small-time print shop in the Bronx that specialised in letterheads, invitations, business cards and other minutiae in the private sector. More privately still, although the Federal authorities had never been able to prove anything, Zygmund was an expert forger of documents.

The Nissen hut was bare except for a trestle table and half a dozen canteen chairs. After twenty minutes of silence, Zygmund said: 'So what the hell are we doing here? You guys figure we been singled out for special leave already, on account of our exemplary behaviour?'

'Some fuckin' 'opes,' Sergeant Hawkins said mournfully.

'Don't ask me,' said Daventry. 'Pulled out of the line this side of the Arno. Not a bleeding word of explanation. Never is. Some dirty job they want us to do, if you ask me.'

'You been on special soddin' ops before, mate?' Hawkins asked.

Daventry nodded.

Hawkins looked at Zygmund. The Pole spread his arms and shrugged. 'Me too,' he said. 'If you call it special, sitting in a back room making out ID documents for German officers they have names like Quinn and O'Hara and Meredith in their Uncle Sam pay books. You two guys never met before, is that right?'

'Never set eyes on the bleeder,' Hawkins confirmed cheerfully. Daventry nodded again. There was no point wasting a word.

'I like a man he should be frank,' Zygmund continued, 'so tell me frankly: why are we here? Locked in like rented waiters after the silver is gone? What do you think?'

'They'll tell you just before the fucking parachute opens', Hawkins said, 'an' that'll be a bloody lie.'

'If I had me twirls, we'd be out of here quicker'n you could say Wormwood Scrubs,' Daventry said. 'But what'd be the use?'

'I see light already,' said Zygmund. 'By me, they get in, as you might say, officially. Like with passes. By you, the entry is unofficial, like when the cat should be away.' He turned to Hawkins. 'Aside from being big, what is your speciality?'

Before the sergeant could answer, a key turned in the lock, the door opened, and Colonel Colbert came in with Martin Kane. 'Sorry, chaps, for the melodrama,' the intelligence officer said easily. 'It's just that we think it's important that nobody puts two and two together to make you three . . . and we couldn't get here any earlier to fill you in.'

Hawkins and Daventry regarded him with that sullen impassivity that characterises Other Ranks waiting for an officer to prove himself. Zygmund raised his eyebrows. The British were an alien race to him and his knowledge of the officer class was restricted to celluloid images of Ronald Colman and David Niven.

'This is Captain Kane,' Colbert said. 'He'll be in charge of your show. Captain Kane is an Anglo-American – so none of you need feel that you're being bossed by someone from the other side of the fence. I should tell you too that he is an officer of immense experience, working behind enemy lines, so I expect one hundred percent loyalty and co-operation from all of you, at all times. Is that clear?'

Colbert's cool gaze rested on each of the three men's faces in turn, and then he continued: 'In any case, this is a combined operation in every sense of the word. Each of you has been picked because of some special – er – skill without which this little jaunt would be unlikely to succeed. I'll stress that each of you is as important as any of the others . . . but the orders come at all times from

Captain Kane. Now pay attention while I tell you what this is all about.'

Briefly, he sketched in the outline of Operation Cornflakes and then explained about the spy's letter and why it was so important to retrieve it.

'Cor,' Sergeant Hawkins burst out when Colbert had told them about the mythical League of Lonely Women, 'I know what I'd bloody do if I got a letter like that! AWOL and the first train home, that's what!'

'Sort out the old lady, you mean?' Daventry asked.

'Not on your bleedin' life, mate! Do in the fucker what wrote the letter, more like. Blimey, the idea!'

Kane repressed a smile. The blind trust implicit in the man's indignation was a good sign. He thought he was going to like Sergeant Hawkins.

Colbert said, 'Now, we have to accept in this kind of undercover operation that reliability – the fact that any one of you can count absolutely on the special skills of the other four – is more than half the battle.'

'Strewth!' Hawkins murmured *sotto voce* to Daventry. 'First it was two and two makes three; now he's upped us to soddin' five!'

Colbert heard. He grinned. 'There *is* a fifth chap in the team,' he said. 'Name of Fischer. He's a Swiss-American, based on Schaffhausen, near the German frontier. Fischer's OSS liaison for the whole of southern Germany. He breezes in and out of the Reich as regularly as a commuter, running escape lines, serving agents, and that kind of thing. He'll be waiting for you when you land, and he'll be your guide. Now, any questions?'

'Yes, Cap,' Zygmund said, unsure of the Englishman's rank. 'Where do we land? And how? A drop already? Also, where exactly are we heading, so we pick up this Nazi spy's letter?'

'Where and how? We won't know until later tonight, just before you leave. We're waiting to hear from Fischer – whether it's a better bet to drop you, land you in a Lysander, or smuggle you across the border from Austria.

We leave it to him to decide.'

'And the target?'

Kane spoke for the first time. 'We're too late to catch the mail sack in Linz,' he said. 'We're gambling on their leaving it over the weekend in Prague. So the central sorting office there is the nut we have to crack. Which means, of course, whichever way we get there, we shall home in on the southern part of Czechoslovakia.'

'I can't wait,' Zygmund said. 'They tell me the glassware in the shops is sensational.'

So far, Daventry had shown little interest. Now he asked, 'When do we leave?'

Colbert looked at his watch. 'In about three hours – providing Fischer has contacted us, of course. We want to give you as many hours of darkness as possible, let you steal up as near as you can to the target.'

'What about gear?'

'We'll do the best we can. Paper, inks, stamps, stencils and whatnot in a specially fitted attaché case for you, Zygmund. Skeleton keys, probes, and a neat little magnetic toy for listening to the tumblers, all in a handy body-belt, for Daventry.'

'Ah,' said Daventry, 'now you're blooming talking.'

'I have to point out,' said Colbert sombrely, 'that this is a damned dangerous job. When you've nabbed the letter – which I'm sure you will – your chances of making it back home are . . . slim.'

'Now he tells us!' said Zygmund.

'You know the rules in Special Operations: you don't have to accept the job. We've all heard the funny joke – I want three volunteers: you, you, and you. But this really is, in a way, a volunteer show. I can't make it an order. So if anyone wants to back out, now's the time to speak up.'

Colbert looked around. Nobody moved. Then Hawkins asked, 'Sir? Supposin' someone did chicken out? What then?'

'He gets posted back to his unit, that's all.'

43

'Czechoslovakia,' said Hawkins, 'here I bloody come.'

'There's one other thing.' Colbert looked this time at Kane as well as at the three NCOs. 'When you do meet Vincent Fischer, don't be deceived by his appearance. He looks like a meek little post office clerk, but he's tough as nails. And he's very, very strong.' Once more the intelligence officer glanced at Kane. He smiled. 'Your four chaps!' he said. 'About the only thing they have in common is that their Christian names, all four of them, begin with a V!'

'Let's hope it's also a V for Victory,' Kane said.

Chapter 4

Finally, it was a 15th Air Force DC-3 Dakota that was assigned to transport Kane and his men to Czechoslovakia. The radio message from Fischer had said that contacts south of Prague were not sufficiently stable to risk the temporary use of an improvised landing strip, even one small enough for a Lysander. Added to which was the problem that the full 840-mile round trip was far outside the Lysander's range, whereas the Dakota could make it with one hundred miles to spare. The intruders were therefore to jump from fifteen hundred feet, relying on electrical beacons for the rendezvous with Fischer.

The Dakota was identified by the letter R for Rosie, but she was known to her crew – according to a lurid picture and lettering below the greenhouse – as *The Whore of*

Babylon. Two days before, the plane had delivered parachutists of the 1st Provisional Airborne Division to their dropping zone near Le Muy, inland from the 7th Army's invasion beaches on the coast of Provence.

'This is going to be just another bloody milk-run,' the pilot complained to his navigator as Kane's team climbed aboard. 'Might as well be skippering the Staten Island ferry.' The navigator made no reply. They were nearing the end of their third tour, and he could not remember a single mission on which the pilot had not made some similar remark. He felt for the rabbit's foot in his pocket, and turned his attention to the cellophaned clipboard strapped to his knee.

Behind and below him, livid in the greenish light from the console in the radio operator's cubbyhole, Kane surveyed the Dakota's cabin. Strips of the soundproofing material that jacketed the stressed metal fuselage had worked loose and hung down between electrical junction boxes. The curved walls, veined with a complex of cables and control conduits, were scarred with patches where flak had penetrated the skin on the plane's more hazardous flights. Daventry, Zygmund and Hawkins were buckling themselves into the canvas seats behind the hatch.

A voice crackled incomprehensibly from the radio set. The operator leaned forward and tapped the pilot on the shoulder. The pilot slid back a panel of Plexiglass and thrust an arm out into the night, pointing at his port starter motor and then turning a gloved thumb up. Twelve feet below on the artificial runway, an RAF flight sergeant jerked his head at the engine cowling and revolved his index finger. The pilot pressed a switch labelled '*Energise*'.

The light in the cabin dimmed further. Over the stutter of the booster pump, a faint whine in the starter motor increased as the flywheel built up speed. The pilot thumbed the switch to '*Mesh*'.

The port airscrew wheezed, coughed, began to spin.

Then, when the pilot had stabbed the prime button and thrust the throttle forward, the 1,600 horsepower Wright Cyclone engine caught with a racketing rumble that shook the whole aircraft and made conversation impossible. As soon as the starboard motor fired, the plane began to trundle towards the far end of the runway. They were to maintain radio silence for the whole of the flight; in any case there was no control tower on the airstrip, and the green Aldiss lamp that was their only link with Colbert's operations room was already glowing.

The pilot swung R for Rosie into the wind, pushed the throttles up to 30in. of boost against the brakes, and took a last look at his instruments. Throttle and pitch locks off . . . booster pumps to '*Emergency*' . . . supercharger to low gear . . . mixture control OK . . . engine and oil temperatures collecting a tan with the needles flickering into the red sector . . . harness and hatches secure . . . flaps . . .

He flipped off the brakes. The Dakota surged forward, gathering speed as the dry clatter of the engines rose to a roar. Fifty . . . sixty . . . seventy miles per hour showed on the dial as the wheel stiffened in his hands. The pedals grew hard. At eighty, he dabbed the brakes and feathered in a touch of right rudder to counteract the leftward pull of the engines. At eight-five, the nose lifted . . . and then smoothly, with the indicator into three figures, they were airborne, the white runway marker lights streaming beneath the wings like tracer, the Nissen huts, a line of trees, and finally the spired bulk of the town sliding away into the dark as he heaved the column back against his stomach, banked, and settled the plane into a long climb to operational height.

In the cabin, Kane strapped himself into an isolated seat by the hatch and plugged in his headset. He heard the pilot call 'Gear up!' into his microphone. The navigator jerked a lever. There was a sudden roar while the undercart flaps opened and the oleos folded inward to tuck the wheels into the aircraft's belly . . . then they were

46

alone in the night with only the blue-white flames from the Dakota's exhaust stubs to keep them company.

Trying to accustom himself to the vibration of the airframe and the appalling clamour of the piston engines, Victor Hawkins studied his team leader's silhouette against the glow from the radio compartment. He knew nothing about Kane yet: the man had done nothing, said scarcely a word, given no hint of character. He was an unknown quantity. According to canteen gossip, he was something of a hell-raiser, a bloke who stuck up two fingers at the top brass. That could be good or it could be bad; it depended on the way he behaved under fire. In profile, the hawklike face was certainly strong, almost predatory. But they would have to wait until they were down there where the action was before they knew what stuff the bleeder was made of.

Daventry stared glumly ahead without seeing. He was a man who dealt in precisions: the smallest sound, the tiniest shift of a tumbler, one hundredth of an inch more or less on the width of a steel tongue, made the difference between success and failure for him. It was natural for him to be a counter, to have facts and figures at his fingertips. According to his calculations, they should be over the Gothic Line, flying into German-controlled air space, in less than thirty seconds. Radar-activated searchlights perfected by Hitler's technicians, Daventry knew, could probe almost seven miles into a clear sky once they had locked onto a plane that showed on their screens. The deadly 88mm flak was accurate up to 18,000 feet. If coastal defence radar could direct a night-fighter to within two miles of an intruder, at approximately the same height, the enemy would appear as a vulnerable blip on the Nazi crew's own radar screen. Daventry tensed, waiting for the blinding light that would flood the cabin through the ports, the orange flash of bursting shells.

Beside him, Zygmund was thinking of a Jewish girl from the Bronx: a pliant body, a taste for T.S. Eliot, and legs that were best kept hidden. She was a great lay, but she preferred Sardi's and the Stork Room to Shraft's. A pity.

They were flying at 10,000 feet. In the distance, the outline of a cloudbank was silvered by a moon not yet risen above the horizon, but the dark wastes of sky around them were clear. Hitler's new searchlights were concentrated near the channel coast and in the Ruhr. Most of the 88mm guns below were trained on the British and American tanks on the far side of the Arno, and the few Focke-Wulff 190s left in the Mediterranean theatre had been switched to the invasion sector in southern France.

The featureless, milky streak of the coast near Rimini slid rearward to disappear beneath the Dakota's wings. They droned on northward across the sea towards Venice and the Austrian Alps.

Kane could feel his heart beating over the uneven pulse of the two Wright Cyclones. Now that action at last was in sight, he sensed his whole system tuning up, taut as the strings on a violin, as the adrenalin sped through his veins. This was his life – the adventure, the danger, pitting his own skills and determination and judgement against the throw of the dice that might give fate the advantage. This was the throat-tightening, breathtaking thrill that he craved: a rough sea, a river in spate, an unmanageable horse, a sniper in a tree, an unattainable woman or an autocrat in power – they were all challenges that Martin Kane had to meet. And it was the step into the unknown that mattered, not the result. It was this almost Taoist approach – the Way more significant than the End – that lent Kane in his wartime roles his peculiar and personal strength.

Tense as a coiled spring, he knew – as he had known all day, husbanding his energy against the time when it would be needed – that he risked squandering this inner force if he permitted his mind to race ahead. The future was conditional; it could be seized only when it relapsed into the present. In this transitional stage it was better to concentrate on the past. As an exercise, he directed that mind to recap the events of the past twelve hours.

The summons to San Gimignano had come via the

advance headquarters of the American 3rd Division near St Tropez. Kane had been parachuted into France a month before as leader of one of the three-man 'Jedburgh Groups' whose task was to co-ordinate Resistance fighters and put them in contact later with the invading forces. It was while he was making his report to General O'Daniel amid the ruin of Pampelonne Beach that the top-priority signal had come from Headquarters, MELF: a helicopter would pick him up from the beach-head and take him to one of the carriers moored offshore – and from there a plane would fly him to his destination. It was a night flight and the destination was Fallonica military airfield, near Rome. The driver who raced him along the damaged roads through the remaining hours of darkness made the towers of San Gimignano as the sun was rising; by seven o'clock they were eating bacon and eggs in the dining-room of a small *albergo* that had been requisitioned as an informal mess for OSS personnel.

After all the talk with Georgopoulous, Colbert, Ceccaldi and the German POW, Kane had met the pilot of the P.38 which had carried the mail sacks on the last disastrous Cornflakes raid. He remembered the relevant phrases from a transcript of the young man's debriefing.

'She was kind of capricious today . . . I mean, you know, like veering . . . I wondered, when they repaired that former in the starboard boom, had they maybe warped her some? . . . Shit, I had to keep on feeding the crate a touch of left rudder . . . O for Orange had laid the smokescreen good: in any case, the Krauts were running from the wreck like ants from a nest. A few were firing, but mostly they hit the dirt. Some of them legged it for a belt of trees between the tracks and the river. Alders, I guess . . . (laughs) goddamn, I almost zapped those guys with my first stick. She was still pulling to the right and I guess I over-corrected, concentrating on the train. But the next run was a lulu: smack on the nose! . . . The first

*three cars were ripped open: I could see the genuine
sacks lying around. My second stick should have
dropped right in there . . . We didn't see a single
sonofabitch bandit, in or out.'*

The Dakota, most reliable of the Old Faithfuls, was anything but capricious. She thundered on across the sea as
the cloudbank built up in the east and eclipsed the light of
the rising moon, ploughing her way through the sky
towards the lagoons at the head of the Venetian gulf and
the mountains beyond.

Venice was blacked out, but now there were searchlights in the sky and pinpoints of fire twinkled through the
dark far away beyond the plane's starboard wingtip.
Allied bombers must be raiding the docks in Trieste.

They crossed the coast. 'Steer zero-eight-two,' the navigator's voice ordered suddenly over the intercom. The
clumps of light tilted and then swung away as the DC-3
changed direction. Seconds later, flak hosed up at them
from the invisible land below. White streaks of tracer rose
lazily upward from the flickers of gunfire pricking the
blackness and then suddenly accelerated with astonishing
speed to flash past the greenhouse or curve away harm-
lessly beneath it. The sky ahead was punctuated with spark-
les of orange as anti-aircraft shells burst. The plane lurched
and a wisp of smoke whipped past the light penetrating the
Plexiglass screen: they had flown through a near-miss.

Daventry nodded his head. It was exactly as he had
expected. Kane could hear the pilot cursing while he
wrestled with the controls to haul the Dakota back on
course. Owing to their low power-weight ratio, most of
the twin-engined World War II planes pitched, yawed,
dropped or rose like a lift at the mercy of any turbulence
in the air, and demanded all of a pilot's strength to keep
the non-power-assisted control surfaces in the airstream,
even in supposedly level flight. Evasive maneouvres, as
Kane knew, were something else.

A red glow pulsed on the underside of the cloudbank,

and now the brighter flashes of exploding bombs stabbed the dark in the distance. The central beam in the nearest group of searchlights moved abruptly towards them. Inexorably, the thin cone of brilliance traced a path through the night, drawing the subsidiary shafts after it. The pilot muttered something inaudible and the navigator's suddenly indrawn breath hissed sibilantly in Kane's earphone. But the beams steadied a quarter of a mile away, and the men in R for Rosie could see the shape of an aircraft trapped in them.

It was a four-engined bomber flying on a course crossing their own about fifteen hundred feet below. A B.17? No, the ship carried a twin tail-group: it must be a Liberator.

The skipper tried the time-honoured ruse of side-slipping down the main beam, but the others clung relentlessly to the plane, pinning it against the dark like an insect on a board. The machine twisted, turned, banked, dived, vainly trying to escape the blinding lights. But flak was already peppering the sky around it with flashes of red. Kane could see the silver streaks of bombs falling away as the Liberator jettisoned its load . . . and then the crucified silhouette seemed suddenly to stagger in mid-air. A flame-coloured ball of fire blossomed from the centre section, spreading rapidly into a maelstrom of crimson that whirled white hot and then livid green before it vanished to leave only a stain of smoke in the searchlight beams.

'Jesus!' The pilot's voice was shocked. 'You'd think they could have – Christ! There goes another!' Further away to the east, a flaming torch burned suddenly in the sky, blazing furiously downward until it erupted in an explosion that illuminated a jigsaw of wharves and jetties in a momentary glare.

The searchlights were advancing again, probing the dark. The pinpoints of fire dropped from sight as the pilot hurled the Dakota into a vertical turn, kicking hard on left rudder. He dived, and they swung back into view and then slid slowly across the greenhouse roof. Tracer sprayed upward once more, falling away when the pilot banked steeply to regain his former course . . . and then *The Whore of Babylon* had flown into the comparative safety of the clouds that been massing ever since they left the Italian coast.

The radio operator left his cubbyhole and handed out oxygen masks. 'We have to fight our way up to fifteen thousand,' he yelled at Daventry's ear. 'At the height we're flying now we risk, you know, to run into an Alp.'

Daventry nodded. He knew.

Thirty-five minutes and a great deal of turbulence later, the cloudbank thinned, dissolved, and left them suspended above a glittering wonderland of white.

Behind them, the moon rode in a clear sky, sculpturing with pale brilliance the crests of ridge upon ridge of snow-capped mountains below. To the left, the Hochgolling and the 10,000-foot summit of Dachstein stood above the peaks separating Salzburg from Kitzbühl. Here and there, a vertical rock face or an isolated crag showed blackly through the snow, but for the most part the carpet of white lay unblemished as far as the eye could see in every direction.

The Dakota's shadow raced across the undulating snowfields and then out over the Danube plain beyond. They passed unscathed through a storm of flak above Linz, and then it was the Czech frontier and the final 75 miles to the rendezvous.

Fischer had specified a dropping zone near the town of Zivohost, east of Lake Slapy, the northernmost of the three reservoirs that dammed the Vltava River on its way to Prague. It was an agricultural region, not over-populated, and it was only a dozen miles from the outskirts of the capital. Weighing up the safety and accuracy of the drop against the risk of discovery and the difficulty of arriving undetected in the city centre – Fischer's message had explained – it seemed the best bet for a successful start to the operation.

The pilot had eased them down to 3,000-feet and the

glint of water in sinuous drowned valleys ahead was clearly visible when the radio operator told Kane that he was receiving regular bleeps on the frequency allotted to Fischer's directional beacons.

The bleeps were at maximum volume as they droned over the curves of the first long, narrow lake. The navigator prepared to home in on the beam. 'We'll try to make it on the first run,' he told Kane. 'No point arousing their suspicions, tooling around as though we were doing circuits and bumps.'

Kane nodded. The radio operator opened the hatch and let in the roar of the wind. Kane signalled his men to hook up and stand in position by the hatch. 'We're looking for a sandpit, three fields west of a village with a church tower,' the navigator said. 'Your target's a stretch of heath beyond that.'

Kane nodded again. The navigator studied the large-scale map on his clipboard, glancing from it to the patchwork of country visible between the edge of the cockpit and the cowling of the starboard motor. The pilot dropped the plane lower, shifting the control column slightly to keep the machine centred on the beam. The thunder of the engines sank to an alto whine.

'Got it!' the navigator exclaimed triumphantly. 'There, Hal . . . over there! Below that crescent of woods. Visual fix: steer any goddam course you like!' The pilot's eyes crinkled above his mask. He held up a thumb and put the plane into a shallow dive. On the bulkhead aft of the radio compartment, a red light glowed.

Kane motioned Hawkins to take his place at the hatch. He could see fields and hedges and trees, like cardboard cut-outs in the moonlight, streak past the opening. The red light changed to green. Kane slapped Hawkins on the shoulder, and the big sergeant stepped out into the night. He was followed instantly by Daventry and then Zygmund.

Kane's pulses were racing. His mouth was dry. At last, this was it! He heard the pilot's 'Good luck, guys!' before he ripped off the headset and hooked up himself. Then he was ready to go, shouting his thanks to the radio operator, who was standing ready to close the hatch.

Kane jumped.

Before the pilot chute opened, the cold air hit him like a fist. He gasped as the tears sprang to his eyes. For an instant, feeling the wrench of the harness at his shoulders and groin, he saw another canopy behind and below. *The Whore of Babylon* hurtled away like a leaf in a gale. Then a dark cloud slid across the face of the moon, and the landscape spinning up towards him dimmed.

Kane could think of nothing but the last line of a comic monologue by the English actor Stanley Holloway. The monologue was in Yorkshire dialect. It was called 'Sam, Sam, Pick up tha' Musket'. The last line was: *Right-o, boys; let t'battle commence*!

PART TWO

Bad King Wenceslas

Chapter 5

Vincent Fischer parked the car in the disused sandpit and took up his position on the edge of the wood soon after midnight. But he waited until fifteen minutes before the Dakota's ETA before he actuated the shortwave transmitter that would send out the VHF signals directing the plane to the rendezvous. The batteries had a limited life, the aircraft could have been delayed – and there were too many Gestapo radio detection vans, in an area where partisans were numerous, to warrant the risk of any long-term, static emission.

He heard the faint but unmistakable drone of the Wright Cyclones when the Dakota was still many miles away: it was a very different sound from the synchronised beat of Dorniers and Heinkels, or the rasp of the twin Klimov motors powering the Czech-designed Tupolev bombers used by the Russians.

Tupolev Archangelski dive-bombers had raided an important railway junction northwest of Prague earlier that night – which must make it tough for the Nazi radar and gunnery spotters, Fischer thought, since the same planes were also used by the Luftwaffe and the air forces of Bulgaria and Finland. Maybe after a while they just gave up, fearful of making a mistake; maybe that was why they had not opened fire on the Dakota – they could simply be waiting until the fix was visual, until they could be certain of its identity.

Fischer hoped that the pilot wouldn't mess around, would locate the heath and unload his passengers on his first run-in, and not circle the area interminably. The less attention they attracted, the better chance they would have themselves for a trouble-free run-in to the city.

He could see the machine now, a shadowy cruciform shape against the sky – between 1,500 and 2,000 feet, perhaps? Maybe a mile and a half away?

Switching on the continuously blinking red lamp that was to act as confirmation of the radio beacon, Fischer stepped out into the moonlight. He was, as Colonel Colbert had said, an unremarkable man, although 'meek little bank clerk' was, as a description, perhaps a trifle unfair. He was a middle-aged, middlebrow middleweight of medium height – a sandy-haired nobody whose very anonymity was his strongest point as an agent: the unremarkable man goes unremarked.

Fischer checked that the lamp was flashing the agreed signal – three short, one long, a pause, then two short again – and focused his binoculars. The Dakota was very close now, planing down with airscrews feathered and the wind whining over the aerofoil surfaces.

As he watched, four shadows streaked beneath it, bloomed into circular canopies, and then drifted down towards the heathland on the far side of the wood. Fischer gave an exclamation of satisfaction. He turned and began to hurry through the trees. The moon vanished behind a mass of alto-cumulus that was moving across the sky. The plane banked and flew away toward the south.

Five miles away, outside a guardhouse protecting the barrage that dammed the waters of the Vltava to form the Slapy Reservoir, a young Wehrmacht officer had also been watching the plane through binoculars. He stood on a narrow catwalk above the lip of the concrete dam, cursing the cloudbank that had dimmed the light from the moon. The aircraft was no more than a blur now, dwindling fast as the pilot used full boost and began to climb.

Oberleutnant Rudi Halder was a Sudeten German. He had been born in 1919, in the western, German-speaking part of Bohemia that had been ceded by the Treaty of Versailles to the newly formed country of Czechoslovakia. Throughout his childhood he had been subjected to the rantings of Henlein and his followers among the German minority who craved reintegration with the parent country. He had been in the forefront of the cheering crowds when Hitler, after the Munich débâcle in 1938, had marched in and annexed the Sudetenland. Now, at the age of twenty-five he was eager to prove himself as good a German as anyone born in the Reich itself.

Halder was an infantry officer. He had served on the Eastern Front and lost a leg at Stalingrad. Here, he was restricted to light duties that were purely defensive. His job was to protect the dam against possible sabotage by Czech partisans. No more than that. It was not his business to interfere with Air Defence or to question the decisions of Anti-Aircraft Command, nor was it in any way his concern that the artillery had not fired on the aircraft. Doubtless they had their reasons. And yet . . .

And yet Rudi Halder's hobby was aircraft identification. He had received the highest marks of any cadet during officer training, and he had fashioned more than one hundred balsa-wood models during his convalescence and while he was undergoing re-education with his artificial leg. He lowered the field glasses now and bit his lip. He shook his head. 'It wasn't a Tupolev or an Ilyushin,' he said to the *Feldwebel* standing beside him. 'It was no Luftwaffe machine. It wasn't a Dewoitine or a Caproni 135, and it certainly wasn't a Savoia-Marchetti from Italy. It has to be British or American.'

'Sir?'

'Twin-engine,' Halder mused. 'Low-wing dihedral . . . no nose blister . . . tailplane with single fin . . . It must be an Avro Anson or a Douglas DC-3. They call them Dakotas.'

'A Dakota, *Herr Oberleutnant*? Isn't that the machine

they use for towing gliders?' the NCO asked.

'No, that is a C-42. But they do use them for transporting airborne troops . . . and for parachuting agents into occupied territories,' Halder said, his voice quickening. He stared out across the surface of the water. The drone of aero engines faded beyond the steep walls of the valley. He decided. He would risk the mind-your-own-business snub, the chance that those in authority already knew all about the intruder. After all, if there were enemy agents, they might be saboteurs, and then it would be his business. 'You will call Army Group headquarters and ask for the Duty Officer in the intelligence division,' he told the NCO.

The man saluted and went into the guardhouse. Halder remained for a short while on the catwalk. The moon sailed out from behind the cloudbank and burnished the ripples of water lapping the rim of the barrage. The plane was no longer audible: it was clear that it was not returning. Hearing the thin screech as the *Feldwebel* cranked the handle of the field telephone, Halder too limped inside.

'Sector D-3, Slapy, reporting, sir,' he said when the sleepy, irritable colonel on duty was at last on the line. 'I beg to report that the unidentified aircraft briefly entering the sector and then retreating four minutes ago was of British or American origin.' He paused, then decided to back his hunch. 'It is suspected that enemy saboteurs parachuted into the area between the dam and the town of Zivohost,' he said firmly.

The nebulous blur of land below Martin Kane abruptly gained outline and dimensions as the moon reappeared. In the wan light he could distinguish woods and fields, the sandpit, a ribbon of road, the onion dome of a church rising from a huddle of roofs. The few lights that had been visible on the outskirts of the city had swung out of sight in the inexplicable way things do, seen from the air.

Kane tugged at the shrouds rayed out on either side of

his shoulders, trying to coax the parachute more to the east. But a breeze from that quarter was carrying him obliquely away from the heath, toward the gleam of distant water that marked the Vltava and the reservoirs.

Trees and hedges were speeding up to meet him now. He was going to land in a large sloping field some three hundred yards on the wrong side of the sandpit. He sailed over the outbuildings of a farm, across a shadowed lane, and just avoided a line of telephone cables slung between posts along the edge of the field. When he hit the ground, the impact knocked the breath from his body and he was dragged twenty yards before he could twist around, seize the shrouds and spill the air from his parachute. Panting, he hauled in the nylon cords, rolled up the canopy and unclipped his harness.

He looked cautiously around. No torchlight beam to supplement the moonlight, no tramp of jackboots, no guttural shouts from a Nazi patrol. Just wet grass, the smell of cool, damp earth, a creak of branches as the wind stirred trees in the wood. Carrying the bundled-up chute, Kane tramped down the slope.

The sandpit was on the far side of the wood, and the heath was beyond that. It had been agreed that the parachutes, together with the radio beacon and the signal lamp, should be buried in the pit. Since he had to pass the place to reach the rendezvous, Kane decided to rid himself of the bundle on the way. He scooped a hole beneath overhanging brambles that masked one side of the depression and stuffed the incriminating canopy and harness inside.

It was as well that he did so. He had barely scraped sand and stone back over the hole and scrambled up the bank when a figure materialised from among the trees behind him, and a rough voice demanded. 'Hey, you! What the devil are you doing here?'

Kane swung round. Like the other members of his team, he was wearing German-made working clothes – corduroy trousers, a coarse wool windbreaker, a shiny peaked cap of the kind favoured by Czech labourers and minor functionaries. If they were going to spend their time in and around railway yards and postal depots, it seemed a better protective cover than bourgeois clothing or spurious Nazi uniforms. He couldn't see the man who had called out: he was thirty yards away, standing in deep shadow at the edge of the wood. For an instant – until he heard the rasping local dialect – Kane thought he might in some way be connected with Fischer. As soon as he realised that he was not, Kane decided on attack as the best means of defence. 'Who the hell wants to know?' he shouted truculently, in a voice loud enough to warn the others to keep quiet.

'I think you had better step this way, friend,' the other replied, advancing out of the shadows. Kane saw moonlight glint on the twin barrels of a shotgun.

He walked back towards the wood. Since the success of the mission depended on their remaining undetected, on their keeping a low profile at all times, the only weapons they had brought with them were small German automatic pistols. These – Walther PPK models with eight-round, 7.65mm magazines – were little more than six and a half inches long and could be concealed in a large pocket. They were to be used only in emergencies – and although this could turn out to be an emergency, Kane dared not use his now, lest it drew attention to their arrival. Nevertheless he grasped the butt with a feeling of confidence as he approached the man with the shotgun.

He was wearing a uniform with which Kane was not familiar. The barrels of the shotgun came up as Kane drew near. Was he part of some kind of patrol? Had he seen the parachutes against the moonlit sky?

'You people have been warned against this time and again,' the man said (he was in fact a Czech country policeman). 'In times of shortages, illegal pursuit of game is a crime against the state. You know as well as I do that clandestine trapping is forbidden – even rabbits.'

With a rush of relief, Kane realised that he had been

61

mistaken for a poacher, that his scrabbling behind the briars had been taken for the laying of traps at the mouth of a warren. He determined to reinforce the error. 'A man has to eat,' he whined. 'With a family to feed and no ration cards . . .'

'No ration cards? You must be a gypsy then.' The policeman's tone hardened. 'You know the policy: you should not even be at liberty. You come with me, my lad. The camp at Hradec is the place for shiftless elements and asocials like you.' The gun was trained on Kane's belly. The man holding it jerked his head towards the road and the village. Obediently, Kane began shambling in front of him.

He was not worried at the thought of besting someone he imagined to be a hick gamekeeper; the problem was that it had at all costs to be done without the gun going off. In this initial stage of the mission, before they had a chance to go to ground, a shot in their landing zone would be disastrous: it could alert security forces and provoke a whole series of difficulties they would otherwise avoid.

To seize the gun and disarm his captor would be child's play to a man with Kane's experience. But if he adopted the usual tactic and jerked the barrels forward, the man's finger would automatically tighten on the triggers: Kane had to act rapidly, brutally, pushing the shotgun violently back in such a way that his hold was broken at once.

His opportunity came just before they emerged from the wood. A grassy track slanted down between steep banks to join the lane. The undergrowth was thick here, and the ground dipped unexpectedly a few yards before the track. Kane fell forward, momentarily losing his balance as his foot plunged into an unsuspected hole. The policeman, concentrating too much of his attention on his prisoner and not enough on where he was going, staggered abruptly forward too. In the dim light filtering through the trees, Kane saw the gun barrels tilted up as the man involuntarily flung his arms wide to prevent a fall.

He whirled around, still in a crouching position,

grabbing the cold metal with both hands, one at the muzzle, one at the breech. At the same time he twisted violently, continuing the upward swing of the barrels, like a rigger spinning the airscrew of a plane.

The policeman's index finger, caught between the forward trigger and the guard, snapped as loudly as one of the twigs they had stepped on during their passage through the wood. He gave a strangled cry, reaching for a holstered revolver with his free hand. But Kane had already wrested the shotgun from his grasp. Still holding it by the barrels, he swung it in a vicious arc so that the steel-tipped butt cracked against the side of the policeman's head. The man fell heavily into the undergrowth and lay still.

Kane bent over him and felt his pulse. He was unconscious, but still alive. Kane left the gun beside him. If he was discovered before he came to, those who found him might believe in some kind of accident. In any case, his story would simply be that he was surprised by a poacher who escaped. The fact that the shotgun was still there, Kane hoped, would support the idea of an amateur fleeing in panic. I clobbered the bastard. Great. Now let's get out before the next one comes, and the hell with the shooter.

He got out. Keeping to the shadowed side of the hedgerows, he walked away from the wood . . . and away from the village. It was essential to tread carefully now, while he was within earshot of the dogs who might bark and give the alarm. Once over the lane, he crossed a field of sleeping cows, stumbled through another, waist-high with some leafy crop, and finally found himself in a meadow. On the far side of this stretch of coarse grass and bramble clumps, the heath began.

Very quietly, lifting his leg over a stile that led from one to the other, he whistled the air of a Schubert *Lied* that had been agreed on as a recognition signal.

At once the tune was taken up, almost at his feet. Fischer and the other three parachutists were concealed in the bracken that grew along the lower edge of the moorland slope. The moon, lower down the sky now toward the west, disappeared once more behind the clouds. 'You took your time,' Fischer's voice said from the dark.

Chapter 6

The car was a 1937 Tatra, a bulbous, futuristic machine with a rear engine and a tail so streamlined that the back window was almost horizontal. It had been hidden behind a clump of acacia saplings on the far side of the sandpit – so well hidden that Kane had not noticed it when he was burying his parachute.

Before they drove away, the parachute was disinterred. It would be safer – in case the man Kane had knocked out came back to investigate the supposed traps – to dispose of it, with the others and the directional equipment, somewhere along the route.

A mile further on, the country road crossed a tributary stream running down to the Vltava. They stowed the tell-tale material in the culvert that carried it beneath the macadam. It was almost dawn. 'We don't have time to dig it in,' Fischer said. 'Not if we're going to cover the place up so that it won't be noticed; not if you want to be well into Prague before the workers' rush begins.'

'OK,' Kane said. 'You're the boss.'

Fischer slid behind the wheel of the Tatra. Hawkins,

Daventry and Zygmund sat on the broad back-seat. Kane resumed his place beside the driver. Some of the Bakelite mouldings on the dashboard were loose and the Bedford Cord upholstery was threadbare. Fischer pressed the starter button. 'I suppose,' he said over the clatter of the big six-cylinder motor, 'that you're another Princeton and West Pointer?'

'Not exactly,' Kane replied evasively. He had spent a year at Oxford after he left Heidelberg.

'Yale then? I simply cannot imagine why they . . .'

'Yes?'

'Nothing.' Fischer steered the car out onto a main road. 'I don't know. It's just that . . . I mean, why the hell should Staff planners imagine that men from monied families, with a certain kind of education, will automatically make a better job of our kind of work? Goddammit, they send them out all the time.'

'Perhaps,' Kane suggested mischievously, 'they feel the background gives them an automatic insight into the fascist mentality.'

In the dim light from the hooded instruments, Fischer's face wore a scowl – he was not a man who smiled often – afraid for the moment that Kane was taking the Mickey. Then he changed the subject, although not the grudging tone of voice. 'Your German's perfect,' he said. 'The sergeant's and Zygmund's too. Absolutely without accent. But don't think, once we get out there, that this will be enough to get you by in the field. There are points – '

'Look,' Kane interrupted. 'I'm a professional soldier. A professional saboteur and a professional spy too, right now. But in this kind of deal I'm an amateur: leading a small raiding party, that's my bag. Here, you're the expert. You're liaison-control for the whole of southern Germany and points east. You don't think I'm going to try and tell you how the cookie crumbles, do you? You don't imagine I'm going to try and tell you how to do your job? Until we are on site and able to start the search for this goddam letter, I'm under your orders. We all are, whatever nominal ranks we may have at home. Is that clear?'

'All right, all right,' Fischer said, slightly mollified. 'Half the guys the OSS send out here on special assignment think they know it all before they arrive. At least you have a reasonable attitude. But the way you say you're under my orders – shit, you make that sound like an order itself!'

Kane laughed. 'Come off that high horse, Fischer. Tell me the story of your life, huh?'

Fischer had plenty to tell. He was a naturalised citizen of Switzerland: he had been born in the German-speaking part of the country, so German was his mother tongue. Because of these advantages, and because of the excellent papers that Georgopoulous had been able to provide, he had, despite his American father and French mother, been able to move fairly freely in and out of the Reich under various aliases. Apart from acting as a case officer for OSS agents and settling in sleepers, he had also been instrumental in organising prisoner-of-war camp escapes and arranging for shot-down aviators to reach neutral territory. 'But this isn't really my manor, Prague,' he told Kane in a burst of confidence. 'Austria, Bavaria, Baden, Württemberg – those are my stamping grounds. I've been here before; I know my way around OK. But I don't have the feel of the place.'

There were apartment buildings and factory chimneys on the skyline when they saw the road block. From the top of a rise they looked down on soldiers in field-grey around a movable barrier that had been placed at an intersection. A personnel carrier was parked nearby, and there were two motorcycle combinations with machine-gunners in the sidecars drawn up at the side of the road.

'Is this routine? Is there normally a checkpoint here?' Kane asked Fischer as the Swiss lifted his foot momentarily from the throttle pedal.

'No,' Fischer replied. 'There isn't.'

'A panic then. Could be because of us. So what do we do?'

'Go through and bluff it out.' Fischer accelerated again. 'You've all been given Austrian ID papers, right? The stuff that Georgopoulous hands out is good. Practically foolproof. My papers are Czech. They're good too. And the guys on the road block are German. Ordinary Wehrmacht. They don't really know what goes in this country: they're foreigners here.'

'OK,' Kane said. They were half-way down the hill. 'But what's the story? Why are we here?'

'I'm a contractor. In the construction business. It says so on my papers. I've driven south to collect you guys: you're going to work clearing up the bomb damage in the city. Subcontracted from the Todt Organisation. It's difficult to find labour locally, with all able-bodied men in the army, fighting the Bolsheviks. Right?'

'Right,' Kane said. 'That's the way we'll play it.' He saw that there were already several vehicles halted at the checkpoint. A flatbed truck loaded with bedding and sticks of furniture, two or three private cars, an ancient Unic charabanc crowded with men in overalls, a delivery van carrying vegetables. The road ahead led to the city; that on the right looked as though it twisted up through fields to a group of farms on a ridge to the east. The left-hand road clearly took traffic to the Slapy Reservoir.

And it was this route that interested the Wehrmacht men.

Kane saw, before they rolled to a stop behind one of the cars, that drivers going north, south or to the farms were cursorily checked – a glance at the papers, a word with the officer in charge of the detail, and then the peremptory wave on. Travellers heading for the reservoir, however, were subjected to a much more rigorous examination. A man and woman taken from the cab of the truck, for instance, were searched and then ordered to off-load every single item from the vehicle. The workers in the charabanc, on the other hand, were not even asked to produce identification. The chauffeur showed the officer some kind of pass, and the entire crowd were motioned on

67

. . . towards Prague.

Fischer allowed the Tatra to roll up to the barrier. The officer, flanked by two soldiers with Schmeisser machine pistols, approached. He leaned down toward the driver's window and held out his hand. 'Papers?' he said curtly.

Fischer produced a grubby cardboard folder, greasy with use. The Wehrmacht man opened it, flicked over a page, shone a torch on Fischer's face, and handed it back. 'And the others?'

Wearily, Fischer held out his hand. Kane and his men placed their papers on it. Fischer handed them over. 'What is it this time, *Herr Leutnant*?' he asked. 'Black-market cigarettes? Smugglers of Jewish gold?'

The officer shone the beam of his torch on Kane and the others. 'We have a report that saboteurs are heading for the dam,' he said. 'Where are you going with these men?'

'Manpower shortage,' Fischer said. 'The Todt people want additional labour to put right the damage done by the damned Bolsheviks.'

'Very well.' The officer stood back and motioned him to continue. 'You would be wise to hurry. The Jiraskuv Bridge was touched last night, and there may be traffic jams on the outskirts.'

Fischer nodded and drove on.

'Blimey,' Sergeant Hawkins said from the back of the Tatra, 'I never held me breath for five fuckin' minutes before!'

'You should worry!' said Zygmund. 'A nice, big, strong, short-haired Aryan like you! Just pull in to the side, driver, while I empty the sweat from my boots.'

Daventry said nothing.

Now that it was full daylight, they could see the surrounding countryside beyond the immediate confines of the road. Once below the Bohemian highlands, the undulating landscape with its woods and fields could have been almost anywhere – Wiltshire, New England, the plateau of Langres in eastern France: only the timbered houses, their overhanging upper storeys, the square-towered churches and their spire-topped onion domes, gave away the fact that this was the Central Europe of romance, on the borders of Ruritania and the realm of Count Dracula. Until you saw the coal-scuttle helmets and jackboots, Kane reflected, it was difficult to remember that for six years the country had been subjected to a tyranny far more sinister than that of the vampires, rendering the people more soulless than the zombies.

The approach to the city was less romantic. Mist that had been lying in the hollows dissolved in the heat of the sun, but there was a haze of industrial smoke veiling the blue sky above the outer suburbs, where foundries, chemical works, an engineering complex, fought for space with the ugly workers' homes. 'Disney must have been on vacation when they designed this set,' Zygmund said. 'Can we go to the movies and come back after dark?'

'You'll be in bleedin' jail, mate, if you go on talking English,' Hawkins said. 'Unless they fuckin' shoot you right away.' He pointed to a crossroads ahead, where military police were waving some drivers to the side of the street and allowing others to proceed. The traffic, which had been getting more dense for some time, slowed to a crawl.

Kane glanced to right and left. A textile factory enclosed by a high wall on one side; a row of small, shuttered shops on the other. 'You think maybe we should split up?' he asked Fischer. 'Can we risk getting five civilians in a car past a second checkpoint? Or would it be pushing our luck too far?'

The Swiss shook his head. 'You forget their damned efficiency,' he said. 'It's precisely because they want to check that there are still five men in this car – and thirty in that coach – that they've set up this second block. That's my guess. They probably phoned ahead with numbers and descriptions of all vehicles heading this way from the Zivohost area. We said we were heading for the city centre: if we're really going there, we can't be on the way to sabotage the reservoir, can we?'

'You figure there really are saboteurs around? Or have

they gotten on to us but misinterpreted the situation?'

Fischer shrugged. 'You tell me,' he said.

Judging from what they could see as the queue of cars, trucks, buses and delivery vans approached the checkpoint, Fischer had been right. Vehicles carrying nobody but the driver, Kane noticed, were allowed to go straight through or waved on after only a brief examination of their papers. Those with two, three or more passengers were scrutinised carefully. Some were called to the side of the street, some were not. The charabanc they had seen at the first road block was stopped, and all the workers made to get out.

'That's it: they're on the look-out for specific travellers,' Kane said. 'They must have passed on the descriptions, as you say.'

'Or the registration numbers. Whichever way, it's bad news,' Fischer replied.

An MP with a baton was staring at each car as it came near. When the Tatra drew level, he motioned it brusquely toward the kerb. An officer flanked by two men carrying Schmeissers walked up to Fischer's window. He did not salute. 'Where are you going? What are you doing with these men?' he asked.

'Oh, look,' Fischer complained with a well-simulated show of irritation, 'I already told them all that at the checkpoint a couple of miles down the road. Why should you want – ?'

'Tell me.'

Sighing, Fischer repeated his story.

'Very well, let us see these brave, sinewy Austrians whose muscles we need so badly,' the officer said. 'Get out, all of you, and line up by the car.'

As they stood by the factory wall, Kane felt as vulnerable as he ever had in his military career, more so than at any time during his life as an ace Hollywood stunt man. The attaché case with Zygmund's forgery materials packed inside was beneath the Tatra's front passenger seat. If the cops should decide on a body search,

Daventry's safe-breaking instruments and skeleton keys were in a canvas belt strapped around his waist. All of them were carrying guns. Admittedly the guns were current German models, but what would a detail of unskilled labourers be doing with 7.65mm automatics in their pockets?

'Where do you come from?' the officer asked Kane when their papers had been examined.

'Linz.' That was what it said on the ID card.

'Why are you coming here to do this work?'

'A man must do what little he can to advance the sacred cause of the Fatherland.'

'You would do better to help the Fatherland with a gun in your hand. Why are you not in uniform?'

'Because I am a diabetic. It is marked on the card.'

The officer grunted. He turned to Sergeant Hawkins. 'And you? A great, strong fellow like you! Why are you not carrying arms for the *Führer*?'

Hawkins shifted his feet. Kane could have sworn that he actually blushed. Perhaps he was thinking of the gun that he *was* carrying. 'With the *Herr Hauptmann's* permission . . .' He cleared his throat. 'I was with our glorious German army. The 19th Army, General von Blaskowitz, in the south of France. Unhappily, there was a . . . a little misunderstanding over mess funds that had been – '

'A jailbird. I see.' The officer turned away. 'You,' he said to Zygmund, 'can explain to me exactly why you are neither fabricating munitions nor in one of the fighting services. You cannot be more than thirty-five years old. Clearly' – the tone became sarcastic – 'the intellectual genius you possess has not been commandeered in the interests of secret weapon design. You look healthy enough, although a period of disciplinary training might hive off some of that excess fat. And so?'

Zygmund refused to be cowed, even by a Nazi officer who had the power to arrest, imprison and shoot him as a spy. He decided on overt familiarity as his defence. He contrived a loud, braying laugh. 'The answer,' he said, 'is that I am a Swiss by birth. An Austrian by naturalisation only. I volunteered for this work.'

The officer frowned. 'But if you are naturalised, surely the call-up laws apply? You are able-bodied.'

Zygmund laughed again. 'For that, too, I volunteered. But they didn't want me. Not even as a clerk. Just because I had wrongly been committed to a psychiatric – '

'Enough.' The German was staring at him. 'A Swiss, eh? You look more like a Jew to me.'

'I can't help my looks,' Zygmund said daringly. 'Do you want me to take my trousers down and prove it?'

'Spare me the sight.' The officer stabbed a forefinger at Daventry. 'What is your story?'

Kane froze. The safe-breaker not only spoke no German; he wouldn't even understand the question he was being asked.

Daventry was gazing woodenly at a point behind the officer's left shoulder. 'Answer me, do you hear,' the Nazi rapped.

Fischer stepped forward. He cleared his throat. 'With respect, *Herr Hauptmann*, that is just the point. He does not hear.'

'What do you mean?'

'He is deaf. He has been stone deaf from birth. He comes from my own village – Losenstein, in the Sengsengebirge.'

The officer repeated his question in a shout. Daventry uttered a noise in his throat that reminded Kane of the voice given to the Walt Disney cartoon character, Goofy.

'Also a little simple, you understand,' Fischer said. He tapped his forehead. 'But strong? You ought to see him strain when he puts his shoulder to a block of masonry! A real demolition expert!'

The officer fell back a pace. 'But . . . Good God! Are you asking me to believe that all five of these fools are defective in one way or another? That all of them are either sick men or crackpots? Do you bring nothing but misfits to do this work?'

'Well of course,' Fischer said calmly. 'If they were not misfits – as you yourself rightly say – they would be in uniform, wouldn't they?'

The officer shook his head. 'Get them the hell out of here,' he shouted. 'And hurry. We want that damned bridge working again before dark.'

When the checkpoint was two hundred yards behind them, Daventry spoke for the first time since they had hidden their parachutes. 'What was that all about?' he said.

Kane laughed. 'Maybe Fischer's story wasn't so far out after all,' he said.

Later that morning, the German officer who had been in charge of the checkpoint detail phoned a colleague in the Abwehr (military intelligence). 'Schmidt-Valk here,' he said. 'I am just going off duty, and . . . well, it's probably nothing really, but I have had second thoughts about an incident early today. Perhaps, to make absolutely sure, you could run a quick check for me?'

'What incident? What check?' The Abwehr officer was harassed. There were reports that the partisans were being supplied with Russian arms smuggled through the Lusace mountains near Jablonec. 'What are you talking about?'

'The report that enemy parachutists may have been dropped with orders to sabotage the Slapy Dam. You know about that, of course? . . . Yes, well, we were manning the road block on the outskirts – not that they thought the saboteurs were coming this way: simply to check that those who had passed an earlier control were in fact heading the way they said they were.'

'Well?'

'It did not occur to me at the time. It may of course be nothing, but . . .'

'Get on with it, man.'

'. . . we had passed through a coachload of Todt workers, labourers drafted in to clear up the bomb damage. Normal routine. And, just afterwards, there was a car bringing four more. From Austria. Nothing unusual in that – except that, with the fuel shortage, one wonders, as there were so few, why they did not cram them into the coach with the others. It's just a thought.'

'I see. What do you want me to do?'

'I wondered if you could contact the Todt personnel chief in Prague, and ask him . . .'

Schmidt-Valk produced a notebook and flipped over the pages.

'. . . and ask him has he in fact subcontracted any labour hire to a man named Franz Schiller? And, if so, whether Schiller was expected to produce four Austrians today? Schiller is driving a Tatra sedan, registration number 513-7269.'

Chapter 7

By noon on Friday, 18 August, British, French, American and Canadian troops in Normandy were fanning out towards the Seine and Paris; Patton's 3rd Army was racing south-east through the Château country; near Argentan, units of the 2nd and 15th Canadian Corps linked up to trap the whole of the German VII Army and much of the V Panzers in the Falaise pocket. In Provence, Allied troops broke out from their bridge-head and advanced on Aix and Marseille. Field Marshal von Kluge, relieved of his command in Normandy, committed suicide rather than return to the Reich and face a 'people's court'. One hundred miles east of the Czech frontier, Marshal

Malinovsky was poised to launch the offensive that would sweep through the Balkans and decimate 44 German and Rumanian divisions investing the southern Ukraine.

In Prague, drably dressed housewives queued outside the few stores that were open, in the hope of obtaining the meagre allowance of bread or cheese indicated on their ration tickets, or perhaps coaxing a pound of free-sale potatoes from a surly shopkeeper. The wider spectrum of the war in Europe was invisible here: the gossip in the queues was parochial. Country folk bringing vegetables to town had spoken of a partisan insurrection near Zilina. Forty hostages had been shot in reprisal. A Russian plane shot down during the raid the previous night had been carrying cannisters of poison gas. The Jews had thrown arsenic into a tributary of the Vltava: the water was no longer fit to drink. Two thousand American paratroopers had captured the Slapy Reservoir and blown up the dam. There would be a flood. The fat ration was to be reduced yet again.

Fischer drove the Tatra down the whole length of the Vaclaveske Namesti, the city's principal artery – past the grey museum and the cracked fountains of its neglected garden, past the six- and seven-storey nineteenth-century façades, past the great statue of Wenceslas on his iron horse. At the top of the wide avenue, where the central tram-lines divided around a pedestrian refuge, there was a T-junction: Prikopy to the right, the Narodni Trida to the left. Fischer turned left, narrowly avoiding a collision with one of the articulated, single-deck, three-car trams that was shuddering around the curve into Prikopy. The tram driver shouted. A police whistle blew some way off to the right. Fischer shifted down and pressed hard on the accelerator. The clapped-out engine bellowed; the Tatra's worn tyres screeched on the polished cobbles. 'We'll have to junk the car and make the rest of the way on foot,' Fischer said.

'Couldn't we at least go on, as far as the river?' Kane argued as they lurched into a side street. 'I don't see any patrol car behind us yet.'

'I know what I'm doing,' Fischer snapped. 'They have

radios. They're very hot on traffic offences. There'll be a police car and cops strung across the road at the next red light. Failure to stop when the whistle blows is a serious crime.' He jerked up the handbrake and stopped the Tatra in a cul-de-sac.

At the end of the cul-de-sac, a steep stairway zigzagged up between stone balusters to the oldest part of the city. 'Three parts, actually,' Fischer said in a burst of pomposity. 'The Stare Mesto, built as a fortress by the Dukes of Bohemia in the ninth century; the Mala Strana, which was in fact a German ghetto, four hundred years later; and the Nove Mesto – the Czechs' answer to the Teutons – founded in 1348.'

'And five gets you ten the railroad station isn't in any of them,' Zygmund said.

'No,' Fischer said humourlessly, 'the tracks run near the river. The place is a bit like Perugia, where you came from: the old part on what they call The Heights; the modern, industrial city laid out below.'

'How do we get there from here?' Kane asked. They had reached the top of the stone staircase and were facing a small cobbled square. An outsize ash tree grew in the centre of the square, and there was a small *kavarna* selling beer and hot *parkys* beneath one of the tall, shuttered houses.

'We should split up,' Fischer said. Police whistles and sirens were shrilling and braying below. 'They'll be looking for a group of five.'

'I agree. How do you want to play it?'

'I'll make it on my own. You go in two pairs.'

'Right,' Kane agreed. 'You want to give us a rendezvous?'

'Sure. You won't be able to get into the sorting office until after dark; it would be safer not to case it until later this afternoon. So we have time. Let's use it. Wait until the hue and cry over a traffic violation is over. Make our way to the yards slow and easy. OK?'

'OK. And the meet?'

'Three o'clock. Let's say three o'clock. On the embankment by the Smetanov Bridge. There are eleven bridges over the river, but that's the only one with three islands just before it. You go down on the far side of this hill, and turn left. There are linden trees along the embankment, so you'll be shaded from the sun if you get there early.'

'Check,' Kane said. 'Daventry: you come with me. You two' – turning to Hawkins and Zygmund – 'don't get into any fights in bars!'

Kane and the safe-breaker made their way north and west through the narrow, mediaeval streets. Zygmund and the sergeant went to the *kavarna* on the far side of the square. Fischer had already vanished from sight down a twisting alleyway.

Beyond the ancient enclave, the Vltava curled wide and blue below them. Opposite, on the left bank, the spires and turrets and pinnacles of the Hradcany Palace rose into a cloudless sky from the crest of those heights which also supported the cathedral, a romanesque basilica, and a number of baroque museums and public buildings. From many of the façades, Kane could see, long scarlet banners ornamented with swastikas in white circles moved lazily in a breeze blowing still from the east. It was already quite hot in the sun.

'We'd better grab a drink and make for a shady place,' Kane said. 'There are slopes leading down to the *quais*, like the Seine in Paris. There are even guys down there with rods and lines! You feel like supplementing the rations, Daventry, with a couple of casts?'

'Fishing?' Daventry said. 'Not blooming likely! You never know if you're going to get a bite or not.'

As well as the anglers, the tree-lined embankment offered shelter to a large number of men in field-grey. Some were promenading German girls in blue *Helferinnen* uniforms; some were on patrol; some walked alone. Between the bridges, starved-looking semi-pro whores leaned against the lindens, offering themselves for

77

cigarettes, a bar of chocolate, extra ration tickets, silk stockings. There was very little civilian traffic, but Wehrmacht trucks, scout cars and Mercedes Staff convertibles crossed and re-crossed the bridges, sharing the roadway with the crowded red trams.

Kane and Daventry had time before the rendezvous to walk to the central station and back, working out the best route and noting possible avenues of escape in case of pursuit. The concourse was crammed with travellers, most of them in uniform, and the few Skoda and Mercedes taxis outside were besieged by an arm-waving mob. Most of the glass from the great hooped canopy above the platforms had been blown out by blast. At the far end of the goods yard, the front of a bombed apartment block had collapsed and blocked the lines with a huge slant of rubble.

The post office headquarters was on the far side of the tracks – a saffron-yellow building with a flat roof and barbed wire protecting the outer wall and gates. So far as Kane could see, the only entrance led off a road that crossed the main line via an iron bridge. There were delivery vans parked near an open loading bay, and Wehrmacht men in fatigues – presumably APO personnel – mingled with the blue-overalled postal workers.

'The important thing,' Kane said, 'is to find out if there are night watchmen. And it the place is guarded by the military when there is no shift on duty.'

'There are two sentries on the gate,' Daventry pointed out.

'Sure there are. There would be when the place is open for business. But I'm hoping, even in wartime, that maybe they knock off at sundown on a Saturday.'

'Today's only Friday,' the safe-breaker objected.

'Yeah. I know. So that gives us twenty-four hours to stake the place out, make notes on the schedules of the guard details if there are any, and check ways and means of breaking in. After all, if that Kraut who was on the strafed train knows his onions, the consignment we have to sift through only leaves Linz this evening. In which case the sacks won't even arrive here until tomorrow.'

'If that's true – if he's right and they do leave them here over the weekend – maybe they'll be, as late arrivals, on the outside edge of all that?' Daventry gestured toward a mountain of mail sacks visible through the open loading bay.

'I hope so,' Kane said.

After the meeting by the bridge, they split again into different pairings. Kane and Hawkins returned to the station to keep watch on the sorting office. Fischer took Daventry to a small public garden on the far side of the bridge, from where they could establish the pattern of postal arrivals and departures. Finally Zygmund went away along the embankment until he could see the sloping, wedged roofs of the towers on either side of the horse-shoe arch that led to the Karlsbrücke, the oldest bridge in the city. He crossed the river, passed below the blind stare of the huge stone statues on their plinths, walked under the arch and climbed the steep slope of the Mostecka. From The Heights – on a belvedere beneath the turrets of the Hradcany Palace – he looked out over trees at a panorama of Prague: from here he could see where the bomb damage was at its most severe, stock up enough background information to support the story that they were salvage workers if they were questioned by a patrol.

'You are to warn all patrols,' the Abwehr colonel instructed the military police area commander, 'to keep a special watch for Austrian labourers, in particular those claiming to have been drafted in for salvage work. Double the number of civilian checks. Pay special attention to groups of four or five men.'

'Very well, *Herr Oberst*. Is this in connection with the dam saboteurs we were briefed about this morning?'

'Possibly.' The colonel was unwilling to pursue the subject; he was more concerned about reports of arms supplies to the partisans in the north-east.

'But is it true enemy agents were parachuted – ?'

'So far as we know,' the military intelligence officer cut in irritably. 'An unidentified aircraft approached from the south before dawn, and then flew away again. A junior officer *thought* he saw parachutists. A country policeman was attacked. Four foreigners and a supposed labour contractor named Schiller entered Prague from the south not long afterwards. They said they were employed by Todt. The Todt personnel people know nothing about them – or about the contractor. As you see, there is nothing here but supposition: these events may be in no way connected. The only hard fact is that there are in the city five men in a Tatra automobile who are not what they say they are.'

'A Tatra? That is curious,' the MP chief said. 'It was a car of such a make that disobeyed traffic instructions and was later found abandoned at the foot of the old town this morning. There were said to be four or five persons in that.'

'Doubtless the same vehicle. But men travelling under a false identity are not necessarily saboteurs. They could be enemy spies – not necessarily dropped by parachute – with orders to report on our military installations.'

'Or black marketeers? Or common criminals anxious to avoid detection?'

'Precisely. Or even foreign deserters from the Wehrmacht. It is because we can answer none of these questions that it is essential – absolutely essential – that these five men be traced and caught. Rigorous interrogation will then show whether or not we have enemy agents to deal with.'

'Very good, *Herr Oberst*. I will see to it personally that the patrols carry out their questioning with the utmost efficiency.'

Rudi Halder unstrapped his artificial leg and stretched out on the bed in his requisitioned room. It had been an exhausting day. He had been grilled by his company commander, by an Abwehr colonel, by an intelligence officer from the Prague *Flugwachkommando*, and finally by some civilian connected with the *Propaganda Abteilung*. By the time they had finished, he almost wished that he had never bothered to report his suspicions about the mysterious aircraft he had taken for a Dakota. Because he had in the end to admit that they were nothing but suspicions: he was convinced that he was right about the plane . . . but the parachutists were no more than an extrapolation, an inference based on the assumption that he had indeed seen a DC-3. And, no – this too had to be admitted – he had in fact not actually seen any parachutes.

There was, it seemed, a small band of strangers loose in the area. But they had headed for the city and not the dam. Halder's hunch that there were saboteurs in his sector was therefore characterised as 'premature', and instead of being praised for his zealousness and initiative, the young man found himself, if only by implication, criticised as a time-waster, a nuisance. His relief at the reservoir had nevertheless been ordered to keep a specially close watch on the barrage.

A closer watch still had been kept throughout the day by the man billeted in the next room to Halder's. His name was Viktor Turderer, and he was an Austrian. As education officer attached to Halder's company, he had been in on all the discussions during the morning and afternoon following Halder's original report . . . and he had in addition accompanied the Abwehr experts on their inspection tour of the dam and its defences. Now, as the sun sank behind the hills on the far side of the valley, he was engaged in an activity that would have interested Halder's interrogators far more than any inspired guesses about the purpose of a single enemy overflight.

Turderer was sitting on his bed turning the pages of an English language edition of Liam O'Flaherty's book, *The Informer*. Since the novel dealt with the private life of Irish republicans, it could be said to be anti-British – and therefore acceptable as reading matter for a German army education officer desirous of improving his languages. But Turderer was not reading. From time to time he held the book open – it was a Penguin paperback reprint published in 1936 – and transferred figures to a cigarette paper smoothed out on his bedside table.

When he had finished – the task had taken him over an hour – there were twelve five-figure groups pencilled on the paper, four groups to a line. Turderer had written:

22123	11721	11106	24705
02433	08108	12935	10505
13001	22829	11123	07611

These cypher groups were in fact a book code. For in spite of the fact that he was commissioned in the German army, Viktor Turderer was a sleeper, an agent working for Britain's Special Operations Executive. And later that night he would leave the cigarette paper, folded again and again, in a crack between two bricks in the outer wall of the village beer garden. From there another operative – Turderer would never know who it was – would collect the message and radio it to London.

Because of the speed with which Gestapo radio-detection vans could home in on clandestine emissions, messages were limited to twelve words. The book code was used because it was simple. And because, even with a full transcript of the numerals tapped out on the morse key, such a code is unbreakable unless the book being used is known. No cryptologist, no sophisticated machine can deduce the code from the frequency of letters used, or the language from group patterns: each five-figure group represents a word, the first three figures indicating a page number in the book, the last two the line on the page. As an extra precaution, the relevant word in that line was changed at fixed intervals. In the message that Turderer sent, the text was composed alternately of first and last words. But the two final groups always referred to first words: that was Turderer's personal

Chapter 8

Once the target was within reach, Martin Kane took a firm hold of the expedition's leadership. He had remained inconspicuously in the background while Colbert and Georgopoulous were outlining the mission and the reasons for its importance; in the Dakota, clearly he had had to leave the decisions to the crew: all he had to do was jump when they gave him the signal. Having just arrived in Czechoslovakia, he had, as he explained to Fischer, been content to leave the travel organisation to the Swiss – for if it wasn't his normal stamping ground, he was at least familiar with the routines of life inside wartime Greater Germany. Now, however, Kane's natural flair for leadership, his daring, his judgement, and all those other qualities which made him a brilliant cloak-and-dagger operative and a bad subordinate, were allowed to surface and show the man in his true light.

Kane was an undercover agent, but although secrecy and stealth were part of his tradecraft, it was the lightning hit-and-run raid that followed at which he excelled. He had the master tactician's ability to size up a situation at a glance, profit from its weaknesses, and formulate a plan to exploit them without any second thoughts. His decisions were quick, viable, and seldom wrong.

After their mid-afternoon meeting on the embankment, he led his team on a discreet reconnaissance of the station area. From the iron bridge over the railway tracks, an overall view of the postal centre was possible. Even in the role of idle workmen watching a train arrive, it was impossible to loiter there long without attracting attention, but Kane had already made a mental note of his dispositions.

'Get a load of this fast,' he told the four men when they had engineered an apparently casual meeting half-way across the bridge. 'You may not get another chance in daylight.'

He gestured toward the ten-foot wire fence that bounded the post office area on the side nearest the station. The fence was on top of a steep embankment that rose straight from the tracks. 'No point trying to get in there,' he said. 'Too many MPs around . . . and too much risk of being spotted, even at night. Same goes for the far side: a service road leading to a lumber yard runs along outside the wire.'

'And there could be perishin' sentries on the main gates, the way they are now,' Sergeant Hawkins said, nodding at the two guards seventy yards away beyond the bridge. 'What are we supposed to fuckin' do? Tunnel in from the bleedin' river?'

Kane grinned. 'You could try. It might be easier. There's a six-storey warehouse immediately behind the centre, and the wire runs right up to a blank wall.'

'No alley or lane between the warehouse and the centre?' Zygmund asked. 'As if I didn't know!'

Kane shook his head. 'And some derelict property backing on to the far side of the warehouse. But there is an alley between that and the lumber yard.'

'Big deal!' Zygmund said. 'So what do we do then?'

'We take the alleyway and we go in over the roofs,' Kane said.

'Over the roofs?' Daventry echoed. 'What, all of us?'

'Probably. But I'll check out the exact route tonight. I'll take the sergeant as back-up and go in myself alone. When I've found the best way, we can repeat the dose after the sacks arrive tomorrow. OK?'

'What do the rest of us do?' Zygmund asked. 'Tonight, I mean. Feed on pretzels and olives maybe, while we drink a Manhattan in some nice bar?'

'Exactly that,' Kane said.

The Pole stared at him. 'The more we can change our image the better,' Kane explained. 'There's a chance there might be a call out for five guys in working clothes: it was unfortunate that we had to abandon the car like that.'

'All right, all right,' Fischer said angrily. 'I made a mistake; it's all my fault.'

'Nobody's blaming you, Fischer. It could have happened to any of us. You happened to be driving, that's all. But we have to take it into account. So I figure a smart bar's as good a place as any to sit out the waiting time. You'll need to liberate suitable clothes, you three.' He nodded at Daventry, Zygmund and the Swiss. 'And make the right alterations to your ID papers. That's up to you, Ziggie. Daventry can get you into a clothing store once it's dark. I'll leave the choice of bar to Fischer. He knows the score here.'

'What are you going to do?' Fischer asked.

'I figure it's time the Wehrmacht had two new recruits,' Kane said. 'Hawkins and me, like the guy on the road block said, we should be in uniform. Sergeant, there's an army barracks on the far side of the freight yard, beyond that bombed apartment building. See what you can do.'

'Very good, sir.'

'I'll meet you as soon as it's dark in the men's room off the station concourse. In the meantime I'll recce the timber yard and the alleyway.'

'That splits five into two and three,' Fischer said. 'But when do we meet up again? And where do we spend the night?'

'I leave that to you. You know the options: a museum or library after it's closed; department store stockrooms; freight cars in a siding; underneath a river bridge. Too risky to use the station here. I would think the best bet would be some bomb-damaged premises. Can you eat in a restaurant?'

Fischer shook his head. 'The ration tickets keep changing. Too many civilian police checks too.'

'Then buy food and eat it where you sleep. But there's no reason why you shouldn't pub-crawl first. I don't want to see you until this time tomorrow. We'll meet by the newspaper kiosk in the station entrance. After that, believe me, you'll have things to do!'

A long-distance express had just pulled into the main arrivals bay. The platform was black with people: men in uniform, shabbily dressed workers, women. Beneath the bridge, a locomotive hauling a long line of box cars waited for a signal to change, belching black smoke up through the girders. 'OK,' Kane said, 'the sappers laid us a smokescreen. Let's take advantage of it and split.'

Hawkins strode away on his own. Fischer led Zygmund and Daventry towards the river. Kane followed them at a distance: he did not want to prospect the service road and the alley until the day shifts at the postal centre and the lumber yard came off duty, when a solitary person in the street would have plenty of cover.

They were nearing the damaged Jiraskuv Bridge when Kane passed a half-track Type 251 *Panzerkampfwagen* disgorging a platoon of military policemen onto the sidewalk.

'. . . and remember,' an MP officer was saying, 'that you are looking for men in workers' clothes; possibly a group of five, although they may have split up. In any case they are claiming to be Austrians working for the Todt Organisation. Forget about the other controls for the moment: the arrest of these spies is top priority.'

As the MPs themselves split up into pairs and marched off to their planned dispersal points, Kane lowered his head and increased his pace. Fischer and the others were almost at the bridge. Presumably they intended to cross the river and go either into the botanical gardens or through the wide Mezibranska Square and then past the museum and up the Vaclaveske Namesti. In either case they risked being stopped – and they would not know that their cover as Austrian Todt workers, God knew how, had been blown.

The MPs were some way behind. Kane began to run: he must warn the three men at all costs.

The bomb-damaged bridge was closed to road traffic, but a temporary boardwalk for pedestrians spanned the crater that had been blasted during the previous night's raid. A Czech policeman was waving the walkers through.

Fischer and his companions turned on to the bridge.

Kane panted in pursuit, not daring to call out. The three men were almost at the boardwalk when Kane saw that he was too late. An MP patrol was already installed on the embankment at the far end of the bridge. He glanced over his shoulder. Two of the men from the half-track had taken up position behind him and were questioning civilians about to cross the river. The were blocked at both ends.

The policeman motioned Fischer and the others onto the temporary span. He held up Kane to allow a party of Hitler Youth children going in the opposite direction to walk off it. By the time Kane had crossed the gap, Fischer was showing his papers to one of the MPs ahead.

'*Fischer!*' Kane yelled in German. '*You're blown! This way, man . . .*'

The MP was beckoning his two comrades with the hand holding Fischer's papers; with the other he reached for the gun holstered at his waist. Kane's hand was already in his pocket. He shot the man through the coarse wool of his jacket. As the MP staggered and fell, Kane leaped for the other two.

Fischer might have been cussed and argumentative, but he thought and acted quickly . . . and, as Kane had been told, he was immensely strong. The warning was scarcely out of Kane's mouth before he had ducked and plunged for the ankles of one of the MPs running up. He straightened, whirling the soldier around as easily as a baseball player with a bat, and slammed him against the stone balustrade at the side of the bridge. The MP crumpled and slid to the ground. At the same time Kane's leap had taken him to the remaining man. A stiff-arm elbow jolt beneath the chin, a knee in the groin and a blow with rigid fingers to the solar plexus dropped him gasping.

A hundred yards along the embankment, a whistle blew. More Wehrmacht men were running toward the bridge.

Zygmund and Daventry, obeying orders without

question, were already half-way to the boardwalk. Fischer followed. Kane saw that the man he had shot was on his hands and knees, groping for his fallen gun. He kicked him expertly on the jaw and sprinted after the others.

Pedestrians on the bridge had frozen at the sound of the shot. Now they scattered as the four fugitives sped toward them. The Czech policeman was standing with his mouth open. He made no attempt to draw his gun.

'Shit! We're done for!' Fischer gasped, seeing the second patrol blocking the exit from the bridge. He halted on the edge of the gap. Kane shook his head. He pointed downwards.

Through the ragged hole blown by the Russian bomb, a tug towing three empty coal barges was visible beyond the mangled steelwork of the damaged span. The drop to the well decks of the barges was about twenty feet.

Kane called back Daventry and Zygmund, shouting, 'Jump!'

Daventry plummeted straight through, landing with a crash on the decking of the second barge. Zygmund crouched, leaned down to grasp one of the twisted girders, lowered himself until he was hanging at arm's length, and then dropped. He landed, sprawling on all fours, two feet from the stern of the barge. Fischer, using the same technique, waited for the third barge to pass underneath.

Kane was the last to go. By this time the crowd had fallen back and the advancing soldiers were near enough to fire their pistols. There was a fusillade of shots, and heavy 9mm Parabellum slugs thunked into the boards and screeched off the ironwork as the leader of the mission dropped from sight.

He landed catlike some way behind Fischer, and the two of them dived for the shelter of the gunwale. The patrols continued to fire from the parapet of the bridge. But, however deadly they seem when fired from the saddle of a galloping horse in Western movies, handguns, even when steadied and aimed, are rarely accurate at more than fifty feet and quite useless at anything over fifty yards. By the time reinforcements arrived with Bergmann-Schmeisser machine pistols, the barges, which were travelling with the current, were beyond their 200-yard range also. A few splinters of wood were gouged from the decks, but none of the four men was ever in any real danger.

The danger arrived from a different direction. Kane saw personnel carriers and soldiers clinging to commandeered private cars careering along the embankments on either side of the river. Some of them had already passed the tug and were racing for the next bridge downstream. If he and his men were still aboard the barges when they passed underneath, they would be sitting ducks. If they swam for the shore on the other hand they would fare little better: one detail on either bank was keeping pace with the barges to guard against just such a possibility.

Kane bit his lip. It seemed as if he had led them from one trap into another.

He had reckoned without the skipper of the tugboat.

Two hundred yards before the next bridge, the roadway that followed the left bank of the Vltava curved away from the river to circumvent a factory attached to a complex of wharves, warehouses, and a small refinery. Approaching the quayside, the tug slackened speed and veered to starboard, allowing the string of barges to swing wide and nudge against the wooden wharf.

Kane yelled orders and leaped ashore. The skipper of the tug was standing aft of his tiny wheelhouse. 'It's all I can do for you,' he shouted. 'I don't know who or what you are . . . but any enemy of the Boche is a friend of mine.' He increased speed as the last man – it was Zygmund – hauled himself up onto the jetty, adding: 'So far as I'm concerned, I never saw a damned one of you!'

Before the last barge drew level with the continuation of the embankment, Kane and his companions were indeed invisible behind a stack of crates at one side of a self-propelled crane.

Chapter 9

Sergeant Hawkins was two hours late for his rendezvous with Kane at the central station. Kane was in a quandry. What should he do? Was the man in difficulties? Had he fallen foul of a patrol and unknowingly shown the Austrian papers, not realising that his identity was blown? Was he blocked someplace in the barracks, trapped during his attempt to steal the uniforms? Was he in jail, perhaps suffering torture in some Gestapo cellar?

There was no way of knowing. Kane decided at once that it was useless speculating: the only one of those questions that he could answer was the first.

There was nothing he could do.

The army barracks were too scattered, too diffuse, for it to be feasible for him to go in and search for the big sergeant – who, even if he was still there, would probably be in hiding. If Hawkins had been taken prisoner, Fischer was the only person who might know in what part of the city he would be kept. And Fischer wasn't due to reappear until late the following afternoon; Kane had no idea where he and the other two aimed to pass the night.

They had parted as speedily as possible after their escape from the coal barges. In a characteristic decision, Kane had led them, at the double, straight through the warehouse, past astonished dockers and donkeymen and loaders, out into the street.

The patrol that had lost the tug from sight when the road swung behind the warehouse and the factory might not know that the skipper had offloaded his human cargo there until they reached the next bridge. Unless they were in radio contact with their colleagues on the far side of the river, and Kane figured that the chase was too much an off-the-cuff action for that to be likely. Even if they were able to see inside the empty barges from their vehicles, and realised then what must have happened, it would take them a moment to turn back and cordon off the factory complex.

Rather than play hide-and-seek like heroes in the last reel of a movie, Kane wanted to be off the premises and over the road before that happened.

They found themselves in a poor area, where the narrow, twisting streets were lined with drab two-storey houses and run-down shops, most of them boarded up and closed. It was here, nevertheless, that they had their first piece of good luck. On the far side of a square, behind a row of dusty and dispirited plane trees, the doors of what might once have been used as a garage stood open. And in the shed beyond, women sat working at a double line of old-fashioned treadle sewing machines. They were piecing together the cut-out parts of dungarees and cheap alpaca suits.

'A sweat-shop with felling hands already!' Zygmund breathed. 'You could almost be in the garment district of New York. Maybe this was the Jewish quarter before the jackboot boys moved in?'

Beyond the square, a lane choked with rubbish led past a yard at the rear of the shed. And from this yard, starved-looking young girls in brown overalls were loading rails of completed garments into a special truck.

Kane whistled. 'Those suits,' he said. 'They might not get you into the local Ritz or the crush bar of the Prague Opera – but, by God, they'd take you out of the Todt class!' He looked expectantly at Daventry.

The safe-breaker nodded. 'Leave it to me,' he said.

Grimy, barefoot children were playing some complex game around the truck. When it moved off, they followed it down the lane, cat-calling and screaming. Zygmund and Fischer removed their caps and jackets, stuffing them behind one of the bulging trash cans. Bareheaded, in trousers and singlets, they walked around the corner and installed themselves in a workmen's *kavarna*. Zygmund's attaché case was concealed now, like an artisan's tool-box, in a carpet bag. Later he would have to find a quiet place where he could get to work with bleaching agents and inks, altering their ID papers.

Daventry fished a set of skeleton keys out from his body belt and sauntered toward the locked door in the wall behind the shed. Kane left the deserted lane and worked his way, by a roundabout route, back to the station. There were whistles blowing over by the river, but no patrols had penetrated the area where the sweat-shop was situated.

Now, after a two-hour wait, the leader of the mission was beginning to feel conspicuous among the travellers thronging the platforms and concourse. Soon, the arrivals and departures would become less frequent, and he would be more noticeable still. He decided to remain for one more hour. After that, reluctantly, he would leave and reconnoitre the postal centre on his own.

When at last Hawkins did arrive, Kane was unable at first to recognize him.

The big man was resplendent in the dress uniform of a major in the Luftwaffe, complete with Iron Cross, the winged propellers of a pilot, and a gold cap-badge representing a diving hawk surrounded by a laurel wreath. Over the right breast pocket, to balance the Iron Cross on the other side, there was a plain yellow cross with a small fleur-de-lis sprouting from the end of each arm. 'Good Christ!' Kane exclaimed when finally he had realised that the gorgeous apparition with the blue hide suitcase really was Hawkins. 'Where the devil did you raise that gear? What happened to you? . . . and what the hell is that yellow thing on your pocket?'

'That's me Baltic Cross, guv,' Hawkins said complacently. 'Shows I fought against the soddin' reds up in the north. As to the rest – well, it was too much of a bleedin' chore, penetrating them barracks as you told me to get into. Too many Krauts left an' right. I found this lot in an officers' mess up in the old town. Kind of a hotel been taken over to keep the top brass happy, see. One room per man. I hear this geezer saying as how he's off to the fuckin' opera with some skirt, so I reckoned it safe to wear his spare set for two or three hours.'

'Astonishing!' Kane said admiringly.

Hawkins shuffled his feet in their highly polished boots. 'Nothing really,' he said. 'Piece of cake. I got your duds in this bag.' He cleared his throat. ''fraid you're only a *Hauptmann* – a captain,' he said. 'I couldn't do no better. They was comin' out of the canteen, finished noshin' and all: I had to take what I could fuckin' get and leg it before I was rumbled.'

Kane shook his head. 'Ten out of ten, *Herr Major*,' he said. 'Just give me your orders!'

'If I was you,' Hawkins said, 'I'd nip off down the lavvy and change into this clobber.' He placed the hide valise on the ground at this feet. Suddenly he grinned. 'Otherwise folks'll be askin' what the hell I'm doing, chattin' up a type like you, sir.'

Kane picked up the valise. 'You're right,' he said. 'I'll lock myself in one of the johns and indulge my schizophrenia.'

'Sir?'

'I'll change clothes,' Kane said. 'And identities.'

Hawkins nodded. 'I'll take a shufti left and right, and give you the all-clear when it's safe to come out,' he said.

The uniform fitted Kane tolerably well, although the boots were a little too big and the cap, with its sharply dipping peak, sat uneasily on his head. He checked the valise, with his labourer's clothes inside, in at the station cloakroom: it was likely that the officers' uniforms would be missed before morning, and it might be tempting providence to promenade in them the following day, especially as they had no Luftwaffe papers. 'We'll buy you a rollneck sweater as soon as the stores are open,' Kane told the sergeant. 'That way, without cap and tunic, in sweater, boots and breeches, you could be some kind of civilian overseer.'

It was after nine o'clock when they walked smartly over the bridge and passed the closed gates of the postal centre.

The day shift were long gone, and the gates were locked. There were still two sentries on guard, nevertheless.

They sprang to attention and saluted as Kane and Hawkins drew level. The sergeant snapped into a text-book acknowledgement, only remembering at the last moment to tilt his wrist backward in the Nazi manner. Kane raised a languid hand. 'And with respect, *Herr Major*,' he said in German as they turned the corner into the service road, 'I have to say that, in my own experience, the fuel injection used in the latest Heinkels avoids all that carburetter icing that has plagued us so much with our Dorniers . . .'

The service road was deserted. Beyond the high walls of the sorting centre and the warehouse adjoining it, a Skoda sedan and an Adler touring car with the hood down were parked in a cobbled yard fronting the derelict property Kane had seen before. There were in fact three separate buildings joined together here, two and three storeys high, with steeply slanted roofs. Judging from the wide doors at ground level, they might once have been stores, dispatch departments or even small workshops, with office accomodation above. But now the lower levels were unused, although at least one of the upper floors must have been 'converted' into some kind of bohemian living quarters: small trees in tubs stood outside a door at the top of an exterior staircase, and the sound of music drifted faintly from somewhere inside. Immediately after these buildings, the road turned and ran along beside the wooden fencing of the lumber yard, until it reached the top of the embankment above the railway, where it stopped.

No lights showed through the black-out screens of any of the buildings. So far as Kane and Hawkins could tell, there was no night shift working in the postal centre. No rumble of machinery, no sound of voices penetrated the walls; the yard was empty and the loading bay closed. The only illumination visible in the whole block was the faint pool of radiance thrown by a hooded street lamp above the sentries, and another, even more dim, where the

96

service road turned into the alley by the entrance to the lumber yard.

'All right,' Kane said, 'I'm sorry about the captain's uniform, but I'm afraid it may get slightly sooty: somehow or other, I have to find my way over those roofs and into the sorting centre.'

'You don't think the perishin' sentries'll suss us out – walking round that corner bold as bloody brass, and then not comin' back?' Hawkins asked. 'They must know it's a bleedin' cul-de-sac.'

'We're lucky at least one of these places is lived in,' Kane said. 'Let's hope they think we're just two of the capitalist class knocking up a bit of crumpet on the side. Or two eager and zealous party members keeping watch on suspected premises.'

'You're the boss,' Hawkins said. 'What you want me to do? Give you a leg up from roof to bloody roof?'

'Stay out of the light, but keep watch from this corner,' Kane replied. 'If anyone comes into the street, blow this whistle once – but keep hidden. If it's a patrol, blow it twice and take a powder until they go. If they look as if they're on to me, blow it three times and . . . well, in that case, you'll have to play it by ear.' He handed the sergeant a high-pitch whistle on a lanyard.

The building that faced the timber yard was unused. Judging by the rubbish stacked outside the peeling double doors, it had once served both as carpenter's shop and paint store. Dented painters' cans and fragments of planking still littered the weed-grown cobbles in front of a stack of weathered trestles.

Kane and Hawkins carried one of the trestles to an angle of the wall where a slope of roof swept down to within fifteen feet of the ground. The sergeant then climbed onto the trestle and hoisted Kane up on his shoulders. From there, Kane was able to reach up and grasp the guttering that ran along below the edge of the roof.

As soon as he transferred his weight to his hands and

began to haul himself up, the rusted guttering gave way and a whole length clattered to the ground. Teetering and swaying, the two men managed to keep their balance, waiting with pounding hearts to see if the noise would have alerted the sentries on the gate.

They heard nothing but the distant rumble of night-time traffic. A siren bleated on the river. Some way off, a dog was barking and, barely audible now, music still pulsed from one of the buildings between them and the warehouse. When it was clear that nobody was coming to investigate the noise, they moved the trestle further along, to a place where a stackpipe supported the gutter.

This time Kane was able to pull himself up onto the tiles. Hawkins heard the scrape of his boots on the steep slant of roof, and then his dim silhouette vanished over the ridgepole and he was gone.

Hawkins stole back to the corner and lit a cigarette, shielding the glowing end with a cupped hand. Time passed. The sound of traffic faded. He smoked a second cigarette. A man on a bicycle pedalled into the pool of lamplight at the corner and turned into the service road.

Hawkins blew one short, shrill blast on the whistle. He ran across the road, moving lightly and surprisingly fast for a man of his size. He ducked down in the shadows behind the trestles.

The cyclist was whistling the refrain of 'Lili Marlene'. He coasted to a halt by the parked cars, dismounted, and wheeled his machine to the double doors at the end of the yard. Leaning it there, he climbed the outside staircase and rapped on the door of the apartment above.

Kane was standing on a four-inch ledge, spreadeagled against the blank wall of the warehouse, when he heard Hawkins's warning. He froze, pressing himself against the wall. The ledge spanned the gap between the last of the derelict buildings and a coping that ran around the warehouse façade. The distance it covered was no more than twelve feet, but it was an awkward place to stop: there were no handholds, and beneath it yawned a forty-foot drop into an airshaft between the two buildings.

Until then, the climb had been difficult but not dangerous. Once he had negotiated the steep roofs surmounting the paint store, there had been a gentler slope studded with chimney stacks and ventilation shafts, which lay, he imagined, over the apartment from which the music was coming. There followed a chaos of dormers and mansarded surfaces capping the last house before the warehouse. The disadvantage here was that, to gain the ledge traversing the air shaft, it was necessary to cross a slanting area that was glassed in. Presumably there was some kind of studio or workshop beneath.

The large opaque panes, encrusted with soot, were reinforced with a layer of chickenwire. Kane hesitated nevertheless to put his weight on the slope, with the whole of his 175 pounds pressing on the area covered by a single boot. To spread the load, he lowered himself to a prone position and worked his way slowly, face down, to the far side. Once he fancied he heard the glass creak in protest, but nothing cracked and nothing gave way.

Now, spread flylike against the warehouse wall, he wished he had taken a little more time over the traverse: it would have been more comfortable to wait face down, even on a glass roof, than to cling, muscles trembling, to a sheer wall with the heels projecting over a void.

It was with a sigh of relief that he heard the knocking on the apartment door. Seconds later, the volume of the music swelled, he was aware of a babble of voices, and then, as the cyclist went indoors and the door was closed, the night became quiet again.

Kane completed his passage along the ledge, grasped the coping, and hauled himself thankfully up onto the roof of the warehouse.

So far as he could see with the light from the pencil torch that he carried, it was a large flat area, broken here and there by chimneys, hydraulic-lift housings, greenhouse-style skylights and the cowled shafts of ventilators. He rose cautiously to his feet. The moon was not yet up, but he could conceivably present a blurred silhouette against the sky to anyone staring up at the parapet from the station or the yard below.

Crouching low, he sped across the asphalt and jumped down to the roof of the sorting centre, which was about five feet below.

The formula here was much the same: only the slanting skylight frames, arranged like a double row of dog kennels across the flat roof, rose above the surface between the stacks.

Kane moved to the nearest one and shone the thin beam of the flashlight through the grimed glass. So far as he could see, the room below was an office. He made out filing cabinets, a swivel chair, papers littering a wooden desk. He gripped the edge of the skylight and pulled. It was locked on the inside.

The second housing was above a PBX telephone switchboard. This one too was locked. It was not until he tried to lift the fifth that Kane struck lucky. He propped open the glass in its heavy iron frame, and dropped silently through into a corridor that ran below.

Forty-five minutes later, he whistled softly for Hawkins to help him down from the corner of the paint store roof.

'We should be able to get you all in OK tomorrow,' he panted, 'but, Jesus, the work we're going to have, finding one sack among the stuff they have in there!'

PART THREE

An Inside Job

Chapter 10

Brigadier Terence Honeywell stared at the flimsy that the RAF orderly had just placed on his desk. Below the second floor windows of his office in the Albergo Posta, excited Latin voices, the squeal of tyres and a continuous high-pitched staccato of motor horns witnessed the fact that life in Perugia, now that the tides of war had passed, was returning to normal.

Honeywell called through the open door into an anteroom where a tall blonde girl in the light blue uniform of a WAAF sat typing at a Renaissance desk: 'Patience! Can you spare a minute? Bring in the O'Flaherty book when you come, will you?'

'Right-ho, sir,' the blonde replied. 'Be with you in a tick.' She finished tapping a line, rolled the paper out of the machine, and laid it in an overflowing out-tray. Then, sliding open one of the shallow drawers in the desk, she took out the orange-and-white paperback and carried it through to the brigadier.

'Got a signal from CZ-17,' Honeywell said. 'Damned thing's really for SOE, but it's been routed through us because the blasted booster relay copped a packet from Jerry last night.' He held up the flimsy. 'Shove this into clear for me, will you? There's a good girl.'

'Right-ho, sir,' the blonde said again. She took the semi-transparent sheet of paper to an occasional table by the window and laid it down beside the book. The brigadier had underlined five of the teletyped cypher groups so that the message now read:

22123	<u>11721</u>	11106	<u>24705</u>
02433	<u>08108</u>	12935	<u>10505</u>
13001	<u>22829</u>	11123	07611.

'You know the drill?' Honeywell said. 'First three are the page number, last two the line.'

'Yes, sir.'

'I've underscored the groups where it's the word at the end that counts; the others are first words. Unless the first word is an "a" or a "the", of course. In that case ignore 'em and take the next one.'

The blonde nodded and opened the book. 'And, Patience,' the brigadier added gently, 'slip a magazine or something under the flimsy when you're decoding and writin' in the words, eh? Don't want to mark that quattrocento rosewood, do we?'

'No, sir.' The WAAF picked a copy of *Picture Post* from a magazine rack and laid it on the desk. The cover showed a photograph of Winston Churchill and General Alexander regarding the Gothic Line from a Polish observation post. The premier was wearing a pith helmet.

Patience propped up the book and began to turn the pages, pausing every now and then to write a word above one of the cypher groups.

In a little over ten minutes she had completed the job. She went back to her typewriter, rolled in a fresh sheet of paper, and copied out the decoded message. She laid the sheet on the desk in front of the brigadier. The message read:

> INITIAL SUSPICIONS MISTAKEN BUT
> SUGGEST ATTACK RESERVOIR AIR
> BURST DAM PANIC POPULATION

'By Jove!' the brigadier said. 'Fighting words, eh? We'd better get on to the skytrain wallahs right away.'

'You want me to contact Colonel Georgopoulous, sir, and fill him in at the same time?'

'Good God, no!' Honeywell sounded scandalised. 'We don't even have to liaise with Colbert, not strictly. CZ-17 is an SOE plant. I may tell Colbert later, as a matter of courtesy, but we're not obliged to row in the OSS at all. This signal is aimed at the RAF.'

'Shall I put you through to the AOC's office at Follonica, then? That's the nearest combined-ops airstrip.'

'Yes, yes. Ask for Air Commodore Chapelow and tell them it's urgent.' The brigadier drummed his fingers on the desk until the connection was made, and then he said, 'Ken? Honeywell here. Very well, thanks. Mustn't complain. And you? . . . Look, Ken, here's a bit of a problem. One of the SOE bods staked out in Czechoslovakia has sent us a signal asking for action . . . Yes, there was a spot of confusion earlier, when a team we sent in on a private deal was thought to be a sabotage squad targeted on one of the dams south of Prague. That particular panic is over now, according to our man out there. But the rumour has given him an idea: attack the bloody dam anyway, he says – but from the air. Like the Möhne show. You know? . . . Well, this SOE johnnie feels that a burst dam in that area would be just the job to sow a modicum of alarm and despondency among the locals. What do you think, old bean? Can do?'

He listened for a moment and then said: 'All right, old chap, I'll hold . . .' With the receiver clamped between his ear and a hunched shoulder, he settled his spectacles on his nose and picked up the message. He squinted across the desk at the blonde. Beneath the pleated breast pockets and the sack-like tunic she had a good figure; the calves in their grey lisle stockings were slender and shapely. He said, 'What do you do when you go off duty in this town, Patience?'

'Sit on a monument, smiling at grief, sir.'

'What?'

'It's Shakespeare, sir. From *Twelfth Night*,' the blonde explained. She had been at Cheltenham Ladies' College.

Honeywell cleared his throat. 'I was wondering if you'd care . . . that is, I wondered if you'd fancy a spot of grub at the – Hallo? What? Ken? . . . They did? Good show. Splendid! . . . Mosquitoes, I should think. I'll send a runner down with the co-ordinates PDQ . . . Yes, I'll come back to you on that later today. Thanks very much.'

He replaced the receiver. The blonde was looking expectant.

'Better raise old Colbert on the blower and brief him, just the same,' Honeywell said. 'I shouldn't think a spot of flooding would affect his postmen: they'd be on their way home before the Mossies went in. In any case, that's a combined-ops job, initiated by the Yanks; this is strictly a British show. None of their business, really. Still . . . you never know. Mustn't put up a black, what?'

'Do you want me to ring Colonel Colbert, sir?'

'What? Yes, yes. Get him now. Might as well have at least that one off our plate, hey? That's the trouble with this damnfool liaison: keeping tabs on the OSS, SOE and MI5, putting the army, the navy and the Raf and the Yanks into the picture – the right hand don't know what the blasted left is doing!'

The brigadier grumbled for several minutes about the difficulties of his desk job. He spoke at length to Colbert. He picked up the decoded message and glared at it. 'When will these fellers in the field learn?' he said. 'Brevity's the thing: saves time, saves lives. I mean, look at this!' He waved the paper in the air. 'That "but" at the end of the first line's completely unnecessary.'

The blonde was straightening the seam of her stocking. She looked up and smiled. 'Was there something else, sir?'

'Something else?' Honeywell cleared his throat once more. 'Oh yes. Now about tonight, me dear . . .'

Chapter 11

Just before dawn on Saturday, a fine drizzle began to fall, misting the windows of the early-morning worker's trains and setting a halo around each dim lamp beneath the cavernous roof of the central station. By eight o'clock the sky was covered with low cloud and it was raining steadily. Hawkins and Kane mingled with the throng of pale-faced Czechs and German military, waiting for a chance to change their clothes in the washroom. They had already recovered the blue valise from the baggage check, but a constant flow of men, banging in and out of the cubicles, queueing for the urinals, shaving in cold water at the grimy basins, killed any chance of effecting a transformation unobserved.

Hawkins had removed the decorations and the pilot's insignia from his Luftwaffe uniform, but he was still a splendid figure and Kane thought it best for him to buy a newspaper and retire behind it on a bench near the main departure plaform, as though waiting for a train that was delayed. There was plenty of evidence to support this stratagem: munitions trains and troop transports heading north had been passing through at intervals of a few minutes ever since daybreak. The headlines in Hawkins's paper spoke in glowing terms of a Nazi counterattack in Lithuania that had stopped Riga from falling into Russian hands, but every snatch of conversation that the big sergeant heard was concerned with the impending offensive by Petrov and Malinovsky, whose armies were poised in the Ukraine, only a few dozen miles from Czechoslovakia's eastern frontier.

Kane himself was obliged to spend some time in the washroom, even though he was unable to discard the uniform. His face and hands were filthy, the boots were scuffed, and streaks of dirt from the rooftops stained the knee of his breeches.

'What mishap befell you, *Herr Hauptmann*?' a jovial voice enquired at his side while he was sluicing water onto his face at one of the basins. 'A night on the tiles, eh?'

Kane looked up. A fat, pink-faced artillery captain was washing his hands at the adjoining basin. 'Something like that,' he answered truthfully. 'To tell you the . . . well, to be honest, I think the Slivovitz was stronger than I had bargained for! The lady was willing, but afterwards – well, you know how steep the streets are up on The Heights.'

The artilleryman laughed. 'Yes,' he said. 'I know! Just so long as the hangover doesn't spoil your aim when you're gunning for those Bolshevik planes.'

'No fear of that,' said Kane. He nodded and climbed the stairs to the station concourse. The familiar railway smell of soot, fish and cheap cigarettes was a relief after the odour of carbolic and unwashed bodies below.

Hawkins was no longer sitting on the bench. He reappeared some ten minutes later, minus the uniform jacket, wearing a fatigue cap with a long peak and a shapeless grey wool cardigan that covered his uniform shirt and reached almost to his knees.

'You keep on surprising me,' Kane said, trying to look as though he was an officer new to the district asking directions from a member of the station staff.

'No problem, cock,' Hawkins said. 'Sir, that is to say. This cove hangs up the woolly in kind of a broom cupboard off the stationmaster's office, and scarpers to the canteen to sink a cuppa. Well . . . no skin orf me nose, but it didn't take but a minute to nip in there and lift the stuff. I lost the jacket in a trash can. Couldn't find nothing for you, but I'd say we got twenty minutes, a half-hour, before the geezer finds he's been robbed.'

'Swell,' Kane said. 'So how do we spend the rest of the day until we meet Fischer and the others at dusk? Got any ideas?'

Hawkins scratched his jaw. 'How about . . . yes, how about takin' a bleedin' train, seeing as how we're on the spot as you might say? How about takin' a train to . . .

well, anywhere out of this? We could get off at some country place and lower a couple of beers, and then steam back in time for the meet.'

'It's an idea,' Kane said. 'But the timetables are all shot to hell. As you see. We couldn't rely on returning in time. Also, there's this uniform: an officer travelling would never buy a ticket; he'd have a railway warrant, destination marked, and all that. Apart from which, they probably control ID papers at the gates. Let's take a look and see.'

Walking separately, they sauntered across to the barriers closing off the departure platforms. Kane was right. MPs at each barrier were standing by the ticket collectors, examining papers and sometimes even demanding that travellers empty their wallets or billfolds. On the main departure platforms, men in plain clothes stood beside the police scrutinising everything, comparing faces and photos, flicking over the pages of passports.

'Gestapo,' Kane said. 'I think, my dear Major, seeing that we have no papers at all for the clothes we are wearing – and that those we do have in this valise are like tickets to jail – I think, as your countrymen so elegantly say, that we should piss off.'

'I should've thought you'd say take a soddin' powder,' Hawkins remarked. 'They told us you was half English anyway.' He pulled the peak of the cap lower down over his eyes. 'You think the Gestapo are looking for us in particular? Or would the buggers be there anyway?'

Kane shrugged. 'You tell me. I guess they're around everyplace. But this could be special – after that routine with the barges yesterday afternoon. There's one good thing, though: you're the most noticeable among us, on account of your size – and you were the only one not playing a role in the barge scenario. So, in theory at any rate, you should be the freest to move about: no description circulated, see.'

'I see all right,' Hawkins said mournfully. 'Put the bleedin' other ranks up in the front line, and if they don't catch a packet, the orficers can finish their gin and fuckin' limes and join in.'

'I love you too,' Kane said, smiling. 'C'mon. Let's go.'

The problem was: go where? It was still raining. They could hardly walk the streets all day or sit in public parks without attracting attention. In Kane's case, it was unlikely that an officer would be promenading without a greatcoat or a waterproof on a day when it had been wet since dawn. In addition, they were both unshaven, hungry, and in need of rest after a sleepless night.

It was the kind of puzzle in which Kane revelled. Luckily, they had been provided with plenty of zlotys – and Reichsmarks too, which were also legal tender in Czechoslovakia. The main difficulty was the fact that, until they met Zygmund again, they had no papers they could use and no chance of obtaining any. 'We'll organise the day in order of importance,' Kane decided while they drank ersatz coffee beneath the awning of a stall outside the station. 'Number one: we must at all costs avoid running into a patrol or police check. That means, two, that we have to be suitably dressed for a wet day.' He grinned. 'There are so many goddam boots in Germany and parts east that anything covering us as far down as the knee should do the trick. I'll give you the zlotys, and you can go into the local five-and-ten and invest in a couple of raincoats that button up to the neck. That way I'll hide my uniform . . . and the guy you robbed won't recognise his sweater.'

'What about this?' Hawkins asked, kicking his foot against the blue hide valise that stood on the wet sidewalk between them.

'Junk it,' Kane said. 'With the clobber inside. We'll just keep the papers, in case Ziggy can doctor them to go with the raincoats.'

'And if I get the raincoats without bein' nabbed?'

'Number three, we go – separately – to barber shops and get cleaned up. After that, it's a question of filling in time. I reckon our first priority is to catch a couple of hours sleep. Maybe one of the museums? After that we'll plan the day hour by hour – a streetcar ride from one end of the tracks to the other; a coffee here and a beer with a slice of sausage there; a visit to a department store to buy stuff we don't need; you name it, we'll do it.'

In fact the plan had to be modified. The museum at the lower end of the Vaclaveske Namesti, the Sternberg Palace, the galleries at the Czerninsky, the Loreta and the Hradcany on The Heights were all closed or requisitioned by the military. Police were checking streetcar passengers at some of the main fare stages. Hawkins found the raincoats easily enough – at one of the many second-hand clothes stalls in the old town; the wash, brush-up and shave was no problem; but the need for rest was becoming urgent – until Kane had an inspiration. They were tramping past a hospital, heads bent and collars fastened against the rain. Ahead of them, poorly dressed men and women hurried through the gates to queue outside the double doors of an annexe. As Kane watched, the doors were opened by a woman in a white smock, and the crowd began to troop inside. 'That's it!' he exclaimed. 'Just what we need: we should be good for the rest of the morning in there.'

Hawkins stared at him, frowning. 'Out-patients,' Kane explained. 'Public Health Department, people on what you call the panel, guys and dames who can't afford their own doctor. The poor bastards are treated like cattle. There must be damned near a hundred there; if we tag on at the end of the line, it'll be hours before our turn comes up.'

'And when it does? What are *you* goin' to say when the quack holds your balls in one hand and tells you, "Cough!"?'

'Be your age,' Kane said. 'We get cheesed off, waiting, and walk out before they get to us.'

The woman at the door was handing out greasy, dog-eared rectangles of pasteboard with numbers printed on them. The cards given to Kane and the sergeant were numbered 77 and 78. 'Hand in the cards with your stamped forms when your numbers are called,' the woman said mechanically.

Kane nodded and they went inside. The waiting-room was huge. It smelled of sweat and disinfectant and wet cloth. Wooden benches along each wall, and back-to-back in the centre, were already crammed with patients, but they were able to find space near a window where they could sit on the floor with their backs against a cold radiator. A PA loudspeaker above an inner door called out numbers from time to time as the old, the sick and the infirm shuffled through into the consultation cubicles. Keeping watch alternately, Hawkins and Kane were able to doze there half an hour at a time. It was past midday when the sergeant tapped Kane on the arm and whispered. 'They just got into the seventies, squire. Think we should scarper now?'

Kane nodded. He looked at the clock above the loudspeaker, shook his head, sighed audibly, and then rose to his feet and strode out. Hawkins, concealing his number, went through a similar can't-stand-it-any longer routine and followed him five minutes later.

Back in the city centre, they parted. Hawkins went into a department store; Kane strode down the Narodni Trida to the river. On the way he saw Daventry and Fischer. The safe-breaker's eyes were hidden behind smoked glasses. He was tapping the edge of the pavement with a white stick. Fischer held his arm solicitously as they prepared to cross the street. Kane smiled inwardly. He supposed it was as smart a way as any to keep official attention off a man who didn't speak any Czech or German. He strode past the couple with no sign of recognition.

He was walking on the embankment, beneath the linden trees near the Karlsbrücke, when he saw the girl. She was on the quay below, leaning against a buttress that supported the embankment wall, a tall, slender girl with straw-coloured hair and a red beret pulled down over one eye.

Kane stopped and leaned on the parapet. The rain had

slackened off and, apart from an occasional scatter of drops from the trees, was now little more than drizzle. A German soldier strolled along the quay. The girl spoke as he passed. The soldier halted, approached her, replied. She pushed herself upright and pointed across the river. The soldier shook his head and walked away. The girl shrugged, lit a cigarette, and leaned back against the buttress.

Another man, a *Feldwebel*, stopped and talked. And Kane saw now that there were a number of girls along the quay and promenading the embankment above. The first soldier had been accosted by a heavy brunette at the foot of the steps that led up to the bridge. After a minute they left together and crossed the river.

The *Feldwebel* too had refused the girl below. Kane looked at her more closely. She was wearing a tightly belted trench-coat with shoulder flaps and a storm collar. So far as he could see, she had large eyes in a lean, racy face. Her smile was wide and bright.

His pulses quickened. That was an idea all right, a way to pass the time until dusk without messing around department stores or fooling with museums! A civilian in a poorly fitting overcoat approached the girl. She turned haughtily away and walked a few steps along the quay.

Kane made up his mind: she was too expensive for the rank and file . . . and she was choosy. A high-class operator, then. If she had her own apartment, and was not obliged to rent some sleazy hotel room by the hour, he was her man. He ran down the nearest flight of steps, fearful now that the girl would have found a suitable client.

She was still by the buttress.

He walked up to her. 'I wondered when you were coming down,' she said. 'What took you so long?'

Kane smiled. They had eyes everywhere. 'I wanted to check that you were officer material,' he said rudely.

'You're not an officer,' the girl said. 'At least not a German officer.' She had a deep voice, slightly husky. The face, he saw now, was older than he thought, with hollows beneath the wide blue eyes and lines of tension around the mouth. She was pretty, though, and the figure beneath the belted raincoat was generous. He opened his own waterproof to show the uniform jacket that he still wore.

The girl smiled, brushing a lock of the straw-coloured hair from her eyes. 'Clothes don't make the man! Are you coming home with me or not? The . . . terms are reasonable, and it is not far.'

'How far?'

She pointed again across the river. 'In the Mala Strana. We climb the Mostecka a little way and then turn right. It is not far.'

Kane looked over the water at the jumble of ancient roofs surrounding the baroque buildings below the Hradcany Heights. It would take no more than ten minutes to walk there. 'And it is home?' he asked. 'I'm allergic to hotels.'

'I live there,' the girl said simply. 'But yes, of course.'

'How much?'

She quoted a figure. Kane could understand why enlisted men would find it too expensive. 'I'll give you three times that,' he said, 'if you will allow me to stay with you until dusk.'

She took his arm. '*Milacek*,' she said, 'we will go.'

'*Milacek*?'

They had been speaking German. '*Liebchen*,' she explained. '*Chéri*, sugar, *caro mio*, *favorito*, darling.'

'You speak all those languages?'

'In my profession it is an aid. To avoid misunderstanding.'

'No Russian, though?'

'I cannot conceive of a situation where I would wish to say such a thing to a Russian. Come – it is beginning to rain more heavily again,' the girl said.

Kane re-fastened his waterproof as they mounted the stairs to the bridge. She glanced at him sideways. 'You're on the run, aren't you?' she murmured. 'I can always tell. You want somewhere to hide because it is safer for you to move after dark, yes?'

Kane made no reply.

'If you were really an officer, you would not be without a hat. Also that raincoat is not an army issue.'

'In your profession,' Kane said, 'the more languages you speak, the better. In mine it is best not to talk at all.'

'Ah. I understand. Do not be afraid: I have no more love for the police than I have for the occupiers.'

'The . . . occupiers? You still use that term after almost six years? Do you mean by this that you think I am not myself a German?'

'Of course not,' she said scornfully. 'You do not have the manners of a Nazi. I would say that you came, perhaps, from Moravia. No – more likely Upper Austria.' She stopped suddenly and turned to face him, a strand of hair blown over her eyes by the wind. They were half-way across the bridge. Squalls of rain gusted from one side of the river to the other, flattening the ripples on the grey water. 'I know!' the girl exclaimed. 'The East-Central Experts!'

'Come again?'

'That's what the newspapers call you, isn't it? They said the leader of the gang was usually disguised as a German army captain! You're the brains behind those bank robberies in Brno and Ostrava and Zilina, isn't that right?'

'Not in Ostrava and Zilina,' said Kane. What the hell – he wouldn't be able to support the fiction that he was the gang leader she supposed him to be, but if she imagined that he was *some* kind of underworld figure, then, sure, he'd play along for all it was worth. It was better than being a spy. He figured he could trust her not to turn him in if she thought he was a crook; he'd back his hunch that she was no stoolpigeon, no paid performer working for the Gestapo anyway.

The apartment was at the far end of a cobbled yard off a quiet side street. It was on the top floor of a six-storey building, slotted in like the letter E between two eighteenth-century gable ends and the dormers punctuating the mansard that linked them. The central

114

arm of the E comprised a tiny entrance hall, a shower room and a kitchenette; the bedroom formed the top arm and a salon that at the bottom. At the rear of the apartment, a passage – the 'upright' of the E – connected the three areas.

Automatically, Kane noted the details: like any undercover agent, it was his invariable habit to check on possible exits before he permitted himself to relax in a strange building. Between half-drawn drapes in the bedroom, he looked straight down through low windows crisscrossed with anti-blast tape to the yard. But there was a rusted iron fire-escape outside the kitchenette, and from this a man could reach an alleyway running behind the building – or jump to a complex of chimney stacks and asphalt and tiles roofing smaller houses in the adjoining street.

Below the slanting ceiling of the bedroom, the gloom was accentuated rather than diminished by the light from a bedside lamp veiled in a tasselled red silk shawl.

It was as typical a whore's room as Kane had seen, and he had seen plenty. A kewpie doll and a life-size scottie in black plush stared at each other across the purple quilted bedcover. On one damask wall, gilt framed, a Spanish senorita flaunted bare breasts over the scarlet flounces of a flamenco skirt. There was a coffee table near the bed. On the glass protecting its highly polished veneer, five gold-rimmed Moravian cocktail goblets had been arranged around an empty decanter. No books or magazines were visible.

The girl's name, she told him, was Hilde Finnemann. She was Austrian by birth; her parents had owned a curio shop in the Vorarlberg and she herself had been a mountaineer and ski-instructor before the Anschluss in 1938. 'But you know how it is, darling,' she said, sighing. 'There is not a great deal of winter sports during a total war, and a girl has to live. For living, there is not enough food on the official ration, and so one is obliged to go to the black market. The black market is dear. And so . . .' She shrugged. 'You understand?'

She unbuckled the wet trench-coat, stripped it off, and hung it behind the door. Beneath it she wore a grey pleated skirt and a cotton blouse the same colour as her beret. Her breasts, Kane saw with relish, were full and firm, but her hips were slim and almost boyish. The calves above her rubber overshoes were muscular. He could believe that she had been a mountain climber.

'Because you are in hiding,' she said, 'this does not mean that you cannot relax, no?' She began to unbutton her blouse.

'Shit, no,' Kane thought to himself. He was no movie hero with a Hays Code to satisfy, no novelist's prude whose sex life was restricted to a row of asterisks. The girl was attractive; he wanted her. The fact that she was a pro had nothing to do with it. He was keyed up, tense as a coiled spring, the way he always was before the action started . . . only this time the action was all negative: keep out of sight, don't mix it, stay quiet, don't let the enemy know you were there. The spring was tensed all right, but there was no way the energy could be released. A fuck (Kane thought, to put it at its crudest) would do him good.

'What do you think?' he said aloud. He peeled banknotes from a roll, laid them on the coffee table and stood one of the cocktail goblets on the pile. He wondered what had happened to the sixth glass. A drunken client? A jealous ponce? A fit of temper when the girl – Hilde, wasn't it? – had thrown it at some guy taking too many liberties? He started to undress. Beneath her street clothes, Hilde wore the regulation, obligatory seductress's set as defined by *Esquire* magazine, *La Vie Parisienne* and *Privat*: black silk stockings, black satin garter belt with ruched suspenders, see-through panties, and a black lace brassière with cut-outs to expose the nipples. Kane was no sexual sophisticate: he thought she looked great.

He was no sophisticate, but he was a man of wide experience. In his varied and eventful life he had whored, alone or with buddies, in half the major cities in the western world. As a drinking man and a fighting man, a daredevil whose very existence was precarious, he had neither formed nor wished to form any permanent alliance, but he was a good lover and a considerate one: none of his mistresses, paid or unpaid, had complained.

So far as the paid ones were concerned, Kane had formed, as the result of his experiences, his own personal valuation. He believed that the courtesans of Tokyo, Singapore and Bangkok were the most inventive, those of Amsterdam and The Hague the most homely, the sexiest from Munich. Parisiennes offered most, gave least, and were the worst value for money. The crudest girls came from Glasgow, the coarsest from Hamburg, the most decadent from San Francisco, the friendliest from Vienna. Which was lucky for him at this moment in time because the blonde letting her breasts spring free from the lacy bra was at least Austrian, even if she didn't come from the capital.

'What do you like to drink?' she asked. 'Baracz? Schnapps? Slivovitz?'

'Schnapps. Do you have Steinhaegger?'

'Of course. With a Pils to wash it down?'

'That would be fine,' Kane said. He stretched out on the bed, brushing the doll and the dog to the floor.

Hilde came back from the kitchenette with the liquor in shot glasses and the beer in a tankard. She eyed his compact, muscled body, with the down on the shoulders and the crisscross of old scars approvingly. 'I always did go for the predatory type,' she murmured. 'I hope you are going to enjoy this afternoon as much as I am.'

Kane thought he might. He sipped the fiery spirit as her cool fingers wrapped around him. Her breast shifted under his free hand, the nipple hard and hot under his palm. He set his glass down on the floor and reached for her.

He wanted those slim hips beneath him, the springy hair that shadowed the base of the belly grinding against him, the muscular legs locked behind his knees. Her red-lipped

117

mouth was open and moist. her breathing fast. Kane lowered his head.

The rain fell more heavily toward the end of the afternoon, beating against the leaded windows, gurgling in stackpipes and guttering. At five o'clock the drumming on the roof rose to a crescendo, there was a livid flash of lightning, and a summer storm burst over the city. After that the rain ceased altogether. In the dimly lit room the silence was broken only by the drip of water from the eaves and a distant rumble of traffic. The Germans were still moving reinforcements up to the Russian front.

Kane and Hilde lay on their backs, smoking. Kane was finishing his third schnapps. 'I guess I'll have to re-think the categories of Tokyo and Singapore,' he mused.

'What did you say, darling?'

He shook his head. 'Forget it. It was just a thought.'

She propped herself on one elbow and looked into his eyes. 'If you should . . . if it would help that you remained in hiding for several days . . . there is plenty of room here for two.'

Kane stared at the elbow. He saw with a pang of compassion that the flesh in the crook of her arm had begun to wrinkle and lose its elasticity. She must have been very beautiful, tanned and smiling, teaching the pre-war playboys to ski on the slopes between Innsbruck and Bregenz. 'You are very kind,' he said. 'Unfortunately, I have . . . commitments.'

'You are married?'

He shook his head again.

'There would be no question of money: it would be for me a pleasure, an indulgence. This is a lonely profession. You see many people but you are always alone – especially if, like me, you refuse to have a protector. I would be happy if you were my guest.'

'It's not that,' Kane said. 'I have . . . work to do. I cannot postpone it.'

'Ah. I understand. And the other members of your . . . that is to say, confederates who await you?'

'Something like that. I appreciate your offer, it touches me deeply,' Kane said sincerely, 'and I too would be happy if it were possible. Another time perhaps? In the meantime, I have been very happy today. The most important thing about sex is that it should be fun. And we had fun here, didn't we?'

Hilde lay back and stretched her arms above her head. The straw-coloured hair was spread like a fan on the pillow. She shifted her hips slightly, the triangle between her thighs tawny in the dim red light. 'Fun?' she repeated. 'Yes, we did. I am not laughing very often. Perhaps before you leave you can amuse me once more?'

Kane leaned over until his lips were close to her ear. 'Have you heard this one?' he whispered.

It was after six and they were drinking again when a thunderous knocking on the entrance doors below echoed up the stairwell. At the same time a klaxon rasped and a voice shouted something unintelligible out in the yard. The girl gave a smothered exclamation and ran to the window. Kane got up from the bed and looked over her shoulder.

A black Horsch touring car with the hood up and side curtains in place stood on the wet cobbles. The driver was still at the wheel but three men were grouped in front of the hooped radiator, staring up at the apartment – two black-uniformed SS officers and a civilian in an ankle-length green leather coat and Tyrolean hat.

'Jesus!' Kane said. 'I'm getting – '

'Do not worry,' Hilde interrupted. 'They are not here because of you. They are here because of me. The man in the leather coat is Gestapo, certainly – but his business is private.'

Kane scowled. 'I don't get it.' He stared down at the Gestapo agent. The man was heavily built, with pig-bristle hair and small eyes in a meaty face. It was he who had been shouting. He called again now: '*Fräulein* Finnemann! Open the doors at once! Have you no time to offer an aperitif to old friends? Open, I say!'

Hilde bit her lip. 'I will have to go down,' she said. 'You had better leave by the fire escape after all. It will be quite safe. But of course you must not be found here.'

'What goes on?' Kane asked suspiciously.

She sighed. 'An old story. That man, the fat one, wishes me to become his mistress, his kept woman, to see nobody but him. For weeks now he has been bothering me.'

'But you don't want to know?'

'Certainly not. He is a pig, a pervert. He wants me to corrupt children, little girls of ten or eleven, to beat him with a riding crop. It is disgusting.'

'Christ! The bastard! Don't you run a risk, though, turning him down?' Kane was hastily pulling on his clothes.

'Not so far. There are some things you cannot order people to do, or make them do; they have to be willing. In the meantime, he permits himself to call on me any time he desires a free drink, sometimes with friends, even if I myself am . . . occupied.'

'Bastard!' Kane repeated. He scooped up the overflowing ashtray and the two glasses and followed the girl into the hallway. She took them from him, placed them in the sink in the kitchenette, and opened the window. 'Now you must go,' she said. 'Think of me sometimes. Come back if you can. Here is my telephone number.' She pressed a card into his hand.

Kane kissed her. The last he saw of her, as he swung his leg over the windowsill, she was wrapping her naked body in a scarlet silk robe and heading for the stairs.

Before he dropped to the fire escape, he scanned the alley below. So far as he could see, it was deserted. It was best, nevertheless, with Gestapo and SS around the corner, to take no chances. At the foot of the second zigzag flight, he leaped nimbly across a five-foot gap to the flat roof of a building on the far side of the alley. From here, via tiled slopes and ridgepoles and dormers and stackpipes, it was no sweat for a stunt man to regain ground level a block away.

The rain was still holding off, but the light was fading fast because of the low cloud cover. It would take him

120

between twenty and twenty-five minutes to make the station for his rendezvous with Hawkins and the others. The timing was just about right.

Kane's hawk face was thoughtful as he hurried across the bridge. He felt great, it was true; he had been telling no lies when he said he was happy, that the afternoon was a success. The fact that he was still at liberty, and not being tailed (he had already checked that out), proved that his hunch about the girl's honesty had been right. Just the same, there were one or two things that bothered him, things that didn't quite fit – or, rather, fitted maybe too perfectly, left the picture with no possibility of a flaw.

That apartment, for instance, wasn't it just a little too much the classic, textbook whore's den? Too much like a movie set that had been dressed by an over-talented art director? The doll, the dog, the unused cocktail glasses, the Spanish dancer and the shawl covering the light – sure, you could say that each of them was typical. But all of them together? At the same time, in the same place? Wasn't that perhaps a trifle too much to believe?

Again, if the girl was really as high-class an operator as her fees would suggest, why didn't she work by telephone instead of standing out in the rain with the common tarts? If money was as short as she said it was, how come she was prepared to sacrifice several days' takings for the pleasure – however exciting – of being with a man she had known only a couple of hours?

Even the excitement was suspect. Not because it wasn't genuine but precisely because it was: a working prostitute could never afford to let herself go, to give herself so completely as that.

Most significantly of all – and this gave the lie to that too-good-to-be-true apartment – was a discovery Kane had made while Hilde was in the shower room. Idly sliding open a drawer beneath the bedside table, he had seen copies of Rilke, Thomas Mann, Heine, Tolstoy and *The Good Soldier Schweik*, by the Czech novelist Jaroslav Hasek. Curiously adult reading for a supposedly dumb call-girl?

121

And then there was the leather overcoat and the SS men . . .

On the face of it, there was enough circumstantial evidence to suggest that the whole thing was some kind of plant. Yet it could not possibly be. Or if it was, it could have nothing to do with him.

Nobody had known he was going to be on the embankment at that time; he hadn't known himself until he was there. Nobody had known that he would pick up the girl – it had after all been an impulse – and thus nobody could know that he was going to her apartment. If, on the other hand, he had unwittingly stumbled on some kind of set-up stage-managed for a person or persons unconnected with him, why had he been allowed to stay for the whole afternoon? And, again, why the invitation, apparently genuine, to stay for some days?

The mystery was without solution. He could resolve none of those anomalies.

Of one thing, though, he was tolerably certain: even if, incredibly, the events of the afternoon could in some obscure fashion be associated with him personally, in no way could they be connected with his mission. Since they had no contacts, no safe-house, no possibility therefore of weak links in Czechoslovakia, the most any authorities, German of Czech, could know about him was that he had entered the city the previous morning under false pretences.

That was a cross, Kane felt in his new mood of exhilaration, that he was prepared to bear. For the moment, his first priority was to contact the rest of his team and set the plans for that night in motion.

It was to prove slightly more difficult than he expected. As he turned into the station yard, the rain started to fall once more. At the same time, the banshee howl of an air-raid siren wailed in the distance. It was echoed by another one, closer, and then a third so near that the ear-splitting racket made conversation impossible. Within seconds, the sirens were screaming all over the city.

And then came the far-off crump of anti-aircraft batteries and the uneven beat of approaching aero engines in the darkening sky.

Chapter 12

The bombs started to fall as workers on the late day-shift flooded out of the postal centre and hurried for their homes in streetcars, on bicycles and on foot. The panic made it easier for Kane and his team to mingle with the men and women milling around the gates and reach the lane between the timber yard and the buildings behind the centre, but conditions became a great deal more difficult once their hazardous journey across the roofs began.

The raiders' approach was nothing like the remorseless pattern bombing favoured by the Americans or the continuous stream of planes organised by the RAF. They attacked in waves of no more than three or four at a time, making their run-in from different directions. The targets seemed once again to be the bridges over the Vltava, a chemical complex and engineering works on the outskirts of the city, and two important railway junctions. At one of these, the southern lines from Linz and Plsen came together; the other separated the routes that led to Chemnitz, Dresden and the Russian front around Breslau. Together with the marshalling yards where the munitions trains and troop transports were made up, the latter was too close to the station for Kane's comfort.

Climbing up from the trestles to the paint store roof, he found the noise more hellish than the risk of death or injury from the explosions. Oerlikons, pom-poms and the big 75mm and 88mm anti-aircraft guns were flaming against the dark, all around the city. To the thunderous racket of these weapons and the roar of bursting bombs was added the scream of Soviet AR-2 dive-bombers and the bells and whistles of fire fighters and rescue teams.

Somewhere on the northern horizon, incendiaries had taken a hold, and the skyline was ringed with fire. Nearer at hand, stick after stick detonated with pulverising concussion around a blazing apartment block.

The rain, combining with soot on the roofs to form a slippery film, made progress difficult. For Kane, impatient at last to get to grips with the *raison d'être* of their mission, the obligation to school the others over a route that he already knew was an additional irritation. Fischer and – not surprisingly – Daventry were nimble climbers, sensing instinctively which parts of the slopes were safe and which to avoid. Hawkins found that his bulk was an impediment to swift progress, and Zygmund was just plain clumsy. Kane mastered his exasperation and shepherded them as far as the slant of reinforced glass that led up to the ledge and the air shaft behind the warehouse. It was here that their first setback occurred. Hawkins and Daventry had reached the air shaft. Kane was waiting to bring up the rear. Zygmund and Fischer were half-way up the slope, spreadeagled on their faces, when suddenly a bright light was switched on in the room below.

The effect was dramatic. Crucified in silhouette, the two men froze, as immobile – and as visible – as flies in amber. Anyone looking upward from beneath the glass would see them as clearly as specimens on a microscope slide.

And there was someone down there. Evidently Kane had been mistaken on his reconnaissance trip: far from being derelict, the building nearest the warehouse still contained a top-floor apartment; and the owners, since it would be invisible from anywhere on the ground, had ignored the rules and left the skylight-ceiling with no blackout.

Kane cursed under his breath. So long as that light was on, Zygmund and Fischer were marooned on the semi-transparent roof, he himself was forced to stay where he was, and the two men on the far side were stuck until he arrived and told them where to go next. He hoped fervently that the apartment was not a one-room studio. There were two people down there now, a man and a woman, and they were in the middle of a furious argument. Each time the clamour of the raid subsided, the intruders blocked on the roof could hear the angry voices.

The man: 'I told you we should have gone to the country for the weekend; I told you there'd be another raid. But no, you wouldn't listen; you had to have your own way as usual.'

The woman: 'My own way? That's good, that's really good! Who was it who *insisted* yesterday that we – '

'Be quiet, you stupid bitch. You know perfectly well – '

'Oh, pack it in, Heini. You're just scared of the bombs!'

'Me? Scared? Would I be a commandant in the Defence Corps if I was scared of a few lousy red bombs? The trouble with you – '

'Your hands are trembling.'

'That's anger, you cow. Why, I ought to slap you . . .'

Three heavy explosions shook the building, and there was an express-train screech as a fourth erupted on the far side of the road bridge beyond the sorting centre. Bricks, tiles, paving stones and fragments of hot metal clattered to the ground. Between the probing beams of the search-lights the sky flashed and twinkled with bursting anti-aircraft shells. Kane recognised the rasping engine note of Ilyushin Il-4 long-range bombers: once, briefly, he saw the slender, pointed, transparent nose of one of the twin-engined planes reflecting a searchlight. They were coming in low now, swooping over The Heights to deluge the industrial areas below with flame and fire.

Beneath the glass roof, the argument still raged.

'You're a pig, Heini, and a hypocrite too. You've such an inflated idea of your own damned importance that you can't stand even the slightest check – '

'Shut up, shut up, shut up! You're hysterical again.'

'Hysterical! I didn't come scuttling for cover the instant the siren sounded.'

'I don't know why I bother with you. You just don't know, do you? You'll never know. I might as well have picked up – '

'A whore from the embankment? Why don't you say it?'

'I'm saying it. It'd be easier, quicker, probably cleaner.'

'You insulting bastard . . .'

'You slut . . .'

Kane was thankful the quarrel was so violent. The couple were so busy hating each other, they didn't have time to look up at the ceiling. But how long, for God's sake, was it going to go on?

From time to time, pieces of shrapnel from the AA shells showered down onto the tiles. He offered up a silent prayer that the wire-covered glass should be spared.

The sky pulsed red with the flames from burning buildings. In the flickering light he could see Hawkins and Daventry standing helpless on the far side of the roof. From where he was, the station below its embankment was invisible, but he could hear a hubbub of voices – shouts, screams, calls for help? – and the shrill of wardens' whistles. There must have been a direct hit nearby.

In a lull between two waves of raiders it became clear that the couple in the apartment had switched from character assassination to personal abuse.

'Just because you've two tits and a cunt you think the whole world has to obey your slightest wish.'

'You're a weakling, Heini, a shiny belt with a big buckle and no guts underneath.'

Kane ground his teeth in impotent fury. Fischer and Zygmund lay motionless, huge spiders trapped in a web of light.

126

'. . . not only dumb, you're a rotten lay. I've had better – '

'You don't know how to treat a real woman. Poor, frightened Heini, afraid to stay out in the open when the guns start firing!'

'If I'm so scared, how come I stay under a glass roof – '

'Oh, shut *up*' – the light snapped out – 'and come to bed.'

The voices faded, died, A drone of approaching bombers grew louder. The anti-aircraft batteries opened up once more. Kane breathed a deep sigh of relief. 'Give them five minutes,' he whispered to the two men lying on the glass, 'and then press on. But for Christ's sake move carefully!'

When everyone was safely across, he allowed them to rest a moment before they tackled the ledge. Relief after the suspense took the form of army banter. 'Think he's getting it?' Daventry asked.

''Course,' Hawkins said. 'That's what she wanted, innit? Joshing him, eggin' him on the whole time to give her one across the chops. Rape complex, they call it. Who turned out the soddin' light?'

'How do you see her, the bird?' Daventry asked nobody in particular.

'Big tits,' Zygmund told him. 'An ass I should be so lucky to see the likes of. But small in the waist. About twenty-five.'

'Get away!' This was Hawkins again. 'Forty if she's a fuckin' day. And plain with it. Like the backside of a bleedin' bus. That's why she's so keen to get stuffed.'

'I dunno,' Daventry murmured. 'She could be a bit of class. The one with the money. What about him?'

'Little runt with no chin already,' Zygmund said decidedly.

'Nah!' Hawkins again. 'One of them big Kraut cunts. Blue eyes, sandy hair, red boat. Strong all right, but a beer belly and too big in the bum.'

Fischer had taken no part in the exchange. Now he said, 'Isn't it time we pushed on? It must be getting late.'

'Guess you're right,' said Kane. With the pencil torch he pointed out the ledge. 'On the far side of the shaft there's a coping. You grab hold of that and pull yourself up onto the roof.'

'You mean we have to walk across that ledge?' Fischer asked.

'It's not difficult. So long as you have confidence. You face the wall, spread your arms, put all your weight on the balls of your feet, and take it one step at a time.'

'But it's less than six inches wide!'

'Wide enough to take half your foot. You flex your muscles and press yourself inward against the wall. It's tough on the toes and calves, but it's only twelve small steps. Ten if you're brave!'

'It's not that. I . . . I suffer from vertigo.'

'Then you must overcome it. Just never look down, that's all.'

'There isn't some other way?' Fischer asked wretchedly.

'See for yourself,' said Kane. A star shell burst in the sky, splashing the rooftops with livid green. In the death's-head light, the wall of the warehouse rose sheer above them, broken only in the centre by the rectangular shaft. The ledge was the sole visible projection on the whole façade.

Sweat glistened on Fischer's forehead. 'I'll have a go,' Sergeant Hawkins said. He stepped cautiously onto the ledge with his right foot, stretched out his right arm, brought up the other foot, extended the left arm . . . and then, sliding out the leading foot again, moved crabwise along the ledge until he was on the far side of the gap. Before the light from the star shell faded, they saw him haul himself up onto the coping one storey above them.

Daventry made the crossing next. He reached the coping without incident. 'Your turn, Fischer,' Kane said briskly.

Fischer swallowed. 'I . . . I can't,' he muttered. 'I know I'd never make it. I can't.'

'Pull yourself together, man. You've bloody well got to,

and that's all there is to it,' Kane rapped. 'I'll cross over with you, so you won't be alone. I'll be immediately behind.'

Fischer's teeth were chattering. 'I don't . . .' he began.

'Get out there!' Kane's voice was a strangled shout. 'Look, I'll reach out; you can hold my hand; Hawkins or Daventry will stretch theirs from the other side. You'll only have a fucking yard when you're not literally in touch with someone.'

'Yes, but you won't be in a position to hold me if I . . . if I . . .' Fischer gulped, swallowed the rest of his sentence and placed one foot gingerly on the ledge. The authority in Kane's voice was enough to override his fear.

Inch by inch, his cheek to the cold, wet wall, Fischer moved out over the void. As soon as he was far enough away, Kane followed, his extended fingertips in contact with Fischer's trembling left hand. Hawkins and Daventry were leaning over the coping on the far side of the air shaft.

Fischer was more than half-way across when, somewhere above them, a raiding bomber touched by anti-aircraft fire burst abruptly into crimson flame and spiralled earthwards like a blazing torch. The wavering light threw into relief the stark geometry of the shaft and deepened by contrast the darkness of the abyss below the ledge. Fischer uttered a sound that was between a laugh and a sob. He stopped moving and remained plastered against the wall. 'I can't go on,' he said dully.

Kane was familiar with the syndrome. The clawing nausea of vertigo immobilised the limbs, forbidding them to obey the brain's instructions. 'Fischer,' he said urgently, 'don't give up, man. Above all, don't blame yourself. It's not funk; vertigo is a physiological condition. It's like an illness. It's not your fault!'

Fischer said nothing. His eyes were closed, his breathing fast and shallow.

Kane said, 'It's no more than a question of mechanics. If your centre of gravity lies outside the edge of the shelf, your own weight will tend to pull you backwards off it. On a narrow ledge like this, it *will* be outside, so what you have to do is thrust upwards and inwards hard enought to counterbalance that force. If the ledge was twelve inches above ground, there'd be no problem. It's only the idea of height that fazes you.'

Away to the east, a pillar of black smoke that rose above a ruptured oil-storage tank was tinged with scarlet from the fire below. As Fischer still had not moved, Kane decided on a shock tactic. '*Don't* move. I'm going to pass behind your back and go ahead,' he lied. He scraped his right foot along the ledge.

'*No!*' Fischer choked. 'You'll pull us both . . .'

He shuddered into motion, covering the last few feet in a frantic shuffle. Anchored by Hawkins, Daventry was leaning far out over the parapet to lend him a helping hand. Together, they pulled him up to safety. Fischer collapsed on the warehouse roof and vomited.

Kane had almost completed the traverse. Three more steps would do it. He moved his right foot . . . and the foot slid a little inside the oversize jackboot that Hawkins had found for him. The instep cramped, the ankle gave under his weight, and he lost his balance. If Daventry hadn't reached out a long arm and grabbed him by the collar he would have fallen. For a timeless moment he hung over the void, supported only by the cloth of his waterproof, and then, with the sergeant's powerful grip added, he too was dragged up over the coping.

Zygmund was the last to cross. The carpet-bag containing his precious attaché case had been fitted with a shoulder strap, and he adjusted this around his neck so that the bag hung down over his back before he eased himself onto the ledge. 'To think that my father, God rest his soul, puts me through commercial college I should graduate as a cat burglar!' he said mournfully. 'Just so as my gold watch doesn't get broken to pieces when I fall.'

When Zygmund had covered half of the twelve-foot span, a Russian plane dived low over the railway station and released a shower of incendiary bombs above the timber yard. The missiles streaked across the roofs of the postal centre and the warehouse with a noise like a huge flight of geese. Startled, the Polish-American jerked back his head to look up at the sky.

The carpet bag swung away from his back. He pressed suddenly, frantically, with his right foot to counter the upset to his balance. The stone lip of the ledge crumbled under his weight and gave way. Zygmund fell without a cry into the dark.

It seemed a long time afterwards that the horrified watchers above heard his body hit the floor of the shaft.

Chapter 13

He was unconscious but still breathing when they got to him. Kane, misled on his reconnaissance by the feeble radiance from his pencil torch, had assumed that the air shaft went down to ground level. In fact he was mistaken. The floor of the shaft was less than thirty feet from the ledge: they were able to reach it through a staircase window between the first and second floors.

Zygmund was nevertheless a heavy man. Daventry, who knew something about first aid, diagnosed a broken leg, a cracked elbow, and suspected a fracture of the pelvis. Fortunately, the carpet-bag had swung out behind him, so that he had not smashed his head against the asphalt-covered concrete when he hit the floor. He was probably suffering, just the same, from severe concussion.

On the third floor of the centre there was an emergency treatment room, doubtless installed with the victims of air-raids in mind more than workers injured handling sacks of mail. The door was locked. It took Daventry less than a minute to open it without damaging the frosted-glass panel that bore the red cross emblem. Inside there was a padlocked cabinet containing a surprisingly extensive assortment of medical equipment. Daventry required ninety seconds, plus a slender, stainless steel instrument from his body belt, to master this. Inside they found lint, gauze, disinfectants, alcohol, analgesic tablets, various ointments and bandages for patching up the abrasions on Zygmund's arm and leg. There was a hypodermic syringe and a phial of anti-tetanus vaccine. Daventry even unearthed in a drawer a pair of temporary splints. 'They have materials for a plaster cast,' he said, shaking his head. 'No good, though: I don't have the experience; I might set it wrong, and the bloke would be crippled for life.'

'Damned lucky he has any life left to be crippled in,' Fischer said. 'It's unfair: it should be me lying there, after my performance – '

'Cut it out, Fischer,' Kane interrupted brusquely. 'OK, you suffer from vertigo. You could have fucked up the whole deal – but you didn't. So forget it.'

'It's all very well for you. You didn't let down – '

'I said forget it. I don't want any of that sorry-to-be-alive shit, from you or anyone else. We have work to do. So let's get down to it, huh, and scrap the histrionics?'

Fischer's nondescript features had flushed dark red. His strong fingers flexed and unflexed, but he said no more.

They laid Zygmund on a stretcher taken from a rack in the first-aid room, and posted Daventry to keep watch beside it until he regained consciousness and the position could be explained to him. 'Christ knows how we're going to get him out of here,' Kane said. 'We'll worry about that when we're ready to leave. But get him out we fucking will. In the meantime, we'll take a preliminary look at the intake, and let you know if we run across any locks.'

'No problem,' Daventry said. He picked up Zygmund's limp wrist and felt for the pulse.

They had no trouble getting in to the centre once they had gained the warehouse roof. Kane had already told them that the upper floors were offices, an administration section, a large PBX telephone exchange, what appeared to be a teleprinter and typing pool, and a planning centre whose walls were hung with schematic maps of the entire Greater Germany rail network and complex schedules of the routing procedures available to the postal services in all the occupied countries.

The second floor, complete with moving belts, selector mechanisms and hundreds upon hundreds of wire pigeonholes, was devoted to the sorting of incoming mail destined for Prague and the rest of the country, and the routing of outgoing Czech material. The mail sacks, in and out, were stacked in the huge storage section that rose two storeys above the loading bay.

Below this, a freight lift communicated with a basement giving access to a spur that ran in underground from the station goods-yard.

'What we must have, before anything else,' Kane said to Hawkins and Fischer, 'is sight of the waybill duplicates, the day book, the logging forms, and the like. It's no fucking good starting a search for our one sack until we're one hundred percent certain the damned consignment has in fact arrived from Linz.'

There was a glassed-in timekeeper's box at one side of the loading bay. The books and papers and logging sheets that Kane wanted were all there – beneath the flap of the high, scarred desk behind the ticket window, or on clipboards hanging from wall hooks. It didn't take long to find out what he wanted to know. Special Consignment (delayed) BS-1323(2) from Bologna, routed via Klagenfurt and Linz, had been offloaded at 1605 hours that afternoon, from train No.251. Two further mail trains, one from Zilina and the Russian front, the other from Munich, had subsequently deposited their cargo at the centre. Each of the three was marked '*For attention earliest Monday*.'

'At least that confirms that we're safe here for the rest of tonight and all tomorrow,' Kane said. 'Thing is: do they stack in strict order of arrival – in which case our bag should be three loads in – or do the inefficient sons-of-bitches pile the stuff up at random?'

They could find no written indication in the time-keeper's box. Kane led them out into the main storage hall.

'Holy bleedin' mackerel!' Hawkins burst out. 'There's enough sacks there to keep fuckin' Santa Claus busy for a hundred years!'

Many of the incendiaries which were dropping when Zygmund fell from the ledge had set alight log piles, huts and stacks of planking in the timber yard. Reflected light from the blaze now sent waves of crimson radiance streaming through the tall windows of the centre, uncovered because the day shift had left before the black-out. On trolleys, along shelves and stacked ceiling high in the vast hall, the mountain of mail sacks loomed huge in the blood-red glare.

'They must be days, weeks behind,' Fischer said. 'Is there any way of telling one consignment from another?'

Kane shook his head. The bells and whistles of the fire-fighters directed to the burning yard echoed around the hall. 'Guess not,' he said. 'Not as consigments, that is. Individual sacks will each have identifying stencils. The sacks in each consignment should run in series. But they won't carry the consignment reference as well. Even the Krauts aren't that efficient. They wouldn't have the manpower to change the numbers on all the sacks every time they changed trains!'

'But all the bleeders from any one soddin' consignment should be together, eh?' Hawkins asked. 'Find one out of the series and you've found the bloody lot?'

'Let's hope so,' said Kane.

Fischer asked, 'What stencil numbers are we looking for?'

'The number on the sack we have to locate is 15AF/464/BG,' Kane replied. 'I reckon 15AF is the APO number and BG the code for Bologna, the railroad station where the consignment was made up. They tell me the series runs from 425 to somewhere in the 470s.'

'But our sack's a fake one, isn't it?' Fischer said. 'It wasn't put on the train in Bolgona: it was dropped on the strafed train?'

'Sure. And so?'

'What I mean – OK, all the fake sacks run in that series – but what about the genuine stuff, the mail that really was put aboard in Bolgona? Does that carry the same coding? Or will it be different?'

Kane scratched his lean jaw. 'I'm damned if I know,' he said frankly. 'I never thought to ask. I should have, too. If the OSS have spies behind the lines who can tip them off on specific departures, I would think they'd have access to the consignment indentification as well. But I don't know for sure. Why? You figure it's important?'

'Just that it would narrow down the search,' Fischer said, staring at the rampart of sacks. 'If both lots, the real and the fake, run in the same series, then there'll be a larger number of sacks that can tip us off that we're getting warm, that's all.'

'Yeah. That's good thinking. We must just hope they do,' Kane said again. 'In any case, everything on that train should terminate with the BG indicator – probably start with the APO code too. Any sack with either of those can be considered as a tip-off, I'd say.'

'Unless the fuckers that work here are so bleedin' lazy that there's a previous load from the same APO still waitin' to be cleared,' Hawkins said sourly.

'You,' Kane said, 'I can do without!'

They patrolled the storage area behind the loading bay. It was clear that their task would be Herculean. Some of the mounds of mail were fifteen or twenty feet high, reaching almost to the ceiling of the hall; many were ten or twelve rows wide at the base. 'The real bugger,' Kane told them, 'is that even when we've located the sack, and gotten the letter out of it, there has to be no sign that the sack's been tampered with – or that anyone's even been in here, fucking about with any of the sacks.'

'Jesus,' Fischer said. 'In effect that means everything, but everything, has to be put back exactly the way it was?'

Kane nodded. 'That's right. We have to act like real spies, searching a desk and then replacing all the papers so that nobody knows we've been there! And I'll tell you why,' raising a hand as Fischer was about to say something else. 'Quote. Because if there is evidence to be found, it could alert German counter-espionage experts to the fact that there was something suspicious connecting the particular postal delivery with the blitzed train, and thus lead to exposure of Operation Cornflakes as effectively as the letter itself. Unquote. Here endeth the lesson as composed by Colonel Colbert.'

'Bollocks!' said Hawkins.

Fischer said, 'That only applies if they knew we'd broken in . . . *and knew that the reason for the break-in was connected with that one Bologna consignment and nothing else.*'

'Exactly,' Kane said. 'I shall thus pursue my British approach and adopt a policy of compromise.'

'Meaning?'

'Meaning we'll follow the spirit of our instructions if not the goddam letter. Meaning any sacks with that 15AF designation will be replaced precisely where they were, as they were, but as for the rest' – Kane shrugged – 'if they are not re-stacked in quite the same order, too bad. Who's to know anyway?'

'How do you want us to tackle it?' Fischer asked.

'We'll divide it into sectors. The guy examining each sector will lamp the sacks on the outside of each pile first. If he doesn't hit pay dirt, he'll start stripping them off layer by layer. But he'll have to mark on a chart just where each bloody sack was in relation to every other one in the pile, if he wants to replace even our own little bird in its right nest. I'm not saying this is going to be easy,' Kane sighed. 'It's going to mean a lot of hard work, humping this shit around . . . and a whole heap of organization, logging the rejects so that they can be put back right.'

'Needle in a bleedin' haystack,' Hawkins commented.

Privately, Kane was inclined to agree. He made a rough division of the mail stacks. 'You take the pile behind the timekeeper's box,' he told Fischer. 'I'll handle Mount Everest here in the centre. The sergeant can take the Alps, over on the right. We'll leave out the parcels section altogether. Daventry can do the area between Hawkins and the parcels when he comes down.'

Daventry came down before they had even started: it took them over an hour to work out a system that ensured the correct replacement of each sack in its pile, and this involved the written notation of every serial number and a diagrammatic indication of the sacks' position. The safe-breaker was carrying waxed cartons of hot ersatz coffee that he had brewed in a small workers' canteen on the top floor. With them were slices of Wurst on stale bread. 'Let the canteen manageress suspect the blooming staff of pilfering!' Daventry said.

'And Ziggy?' Kane asked, gratefully chewing.

'Woke up. I told him what had happened. His breathing's all right, but he's in a lot of pain around the middle. I found some morphine tablets, and now he's sleeping again.'

When they started to examine the sacks, it was still several hours before dawn. The blaze in the timber yard had been mastered and the red glow penetrating the windows had subsided. To see the stencilled numbers on the sacks, some of which were faint or half-erased, was extremely difficult, even with the pencil flash-lights that had been concealed with Zygmund's forgery material. By

0415 hours, the tiny 1½-volt batteries had to be replaced with the single set of spares that they possessed. Fifteen minutes later, the last Russian plane – probably a photo reconnaissance aircraft, because no bombs had fallen for some time – flew back toward the east. The all-clear sounded shortly afterwards.

The outer layer of sacks had been removed with no luck. They lay neatly arranged in the loading bay and along the opposite wall, logged and docketed. The sky was paling and the second set of batteries was almost exhausted when Hawkins called suddenly: 'Got you, you bugger!'

Kane dropped the clipboard on which he was logging his latest reject. 'You found it?'

'Not your actual one, squire.' Hawkins was perched on top of his mound, crouched down beneath the ceiling, scrutinising the stencilled codes on the back row of the sacks. 'In the bloody running, though: one from the Linz train.'

'What have you got?'

'Four fifty-three. With 15AF before and BG after.'

'Fine. I'll come up and join you. You come too, Daventry – we'll really go over that section. Fischer, you might as well stick where you are, just in case.' Kane and the safe-breaker clambered up and over the sacks, forming a three-man chain with the sergeant, who passed each one down for stacking and logging after he had examined its number. But no more mail from the delayed Bologna consignment appeared. It was full daylight and a pale sun haloed the smoke pall hanging over the bombed areas of the city when the next sack was found. And it was in Fischer's sector, down at the other end of the hall. 'I've got one here!' the Swiss sang out. 'It's an early one in the series: 15AF/431.'

Once again, there were no others nearby. The next sack – it was number 447 – had fallen down at the rear of Fischer's stack, and 461, forty minutes later, was discovered on the far side of Hawkins's area. 'Shit!' Kane said. 'You know what?'

'Don't tell me, guv,' Hawkins growled. 'They ain't in no regular order at all. The load come in late in the afternoon, didn't it? So the buggers just chucked the bloody sacks anywhere – here, there, on top, down the fuckin' side – so's they could fuck off home quick and scoff their Sauerkraut and beer.'

'I guess you're right,' Kane said. 'And there are two more consignments that will have been flung on top after that. We'd best each work our own sector again: we'll have to sort through the whole damned lot.'

He himself discovered the fifth sack, and the sixth. The seventh was between Daventry's pile and the wire grille partitioning off the parcels section. By four o'clock in the afternoon, they had located, with two exceptions, every sack in the series from 425 to 472.

The exceptions were 463 and 464.

At sundown, every single sack in the whole huge area had been checked, and many of them carefully replaced in their original positions. But the two missing numbers had still not appeared.

Kane swore. 'They must have mis-routed into Parcels,' he said. 'I reckon we'll have to go through those too.'

The sacks in the parcels department had already been sorted. Now, ticketed and labelled with their final destination – Berlin, Warsaw, Gelsenkirchen, Düsseldorf, Bratislava, Bremen, Stuttgart – they lay ranked in orderly rows on shelves. They were a different size from the sacks filled only with letters and small packets, and the stencilled numbers followed a different pattern.

None of them bore the code 15AF/464/BG.

Kane was nonplussed – and furious. 'We must have missed the bastard,' he swore. 'There's nothing else for it: we'll have to go through the whole damned lot again.'

'Fuckin' 'ell,' Hawkins exploded. 'What do you think we are, chum: soddin' machines?'

'Oh, *no*!' Fischer began. 'That's too much. We can't – '

'It's not blooming possible!' Daventry groaned.

But it was.

'Quit bellyaching,' Kane snapped. 'I told you it would turn out to be a tough assignment. That sack has to be here someplace, and we're going to find it – if it means taking the goddam centre apart brick by brick. Now get cracking and move your asses, all of you.'

They switched sectors, so that each man was in effect double-checking the work of someone else. They toiled relentlessly on in the remainder of daylight, using the fading remnants of their torch batteries, and finally, greatly daring, with the black-out in place, by the light of candles that Daventry found in the commissary.

By midnight, the entire onerous, complex operation had been repeated. But neither of the missing numbers had been found.

Kane was forced to face it at last: wherever it was, the sack containing the vital letter, the sack they had come so far to find, was not in Prague.

Chapter 14

By one thirty all the possibilities had been exhausted. The mail from the blitzed train, held over in Linz, had arrived in Prague. Along with the genuine APO mail, all of the fake sacks dropped on the wreck by the Lightnings of the 464th Bombardment Group had been accounted for – all except two, one of which contained the German spy's letter exposing Operation Cornflakes.

Why should these two sacks – sacks with consecutive

code numbers – be missing from the consignment? Where were they now?

Kane sat with Fischer, Daventry and Hawkins in the timekeeper's box, checking off points on the fingers of one raised hand. There had been no air-raid alarm that night, but an oil storage tank was still burning north of the city, spilling streaks of crimson flame across the sky. 'If the sacks are not here,' Kane said, 'then they were not on the train from Linz. If they weren't on that train, then either they must be on another train, or still in Linz.'

'Maybe they split the consignment; maybe the Linz train was already overloaded?' Fischer suggested.

'Then why split it in the middle? It's not as if the missing numbers were at the beginning or end of the series.'

'But if the consignment had been salvaged from a wrecked train,' Daventry said, 'they wouldn't have been in order anyway.'

'Yeah. That's right.' Kane pinched his chin between forefinger and thumb. 'But in that case it's even crazier that the two missing numbers should be consecutive.'

'Couldn't we use the bleedin' switchboard?' Hawkins asked. 'I mean like phone the fuckers who made up the train in bloody Linz – pretend we was Krauts, and ask why wasn't this sack on the train, and was it on another.'

'They wouldn't have logged in the sacks one by one,' Fischer said. 'There'd be a consignment number, just like there is here. They might even note the number of sacks on it. But that wouldn't help because we don't know how many sacks there are in the genuine German consignment – or how many were destroyed in the raid.'

'Using the phone's a good idea, just the same,' said Kane. 'We could put out a query for those two sacks up and down the line.'

'I thought orders were that we mustn't draw attention to the sack we're looking for,' Daventry said.

'Fuck the orders,' Kane said. 'We've got to locate that goddam sack. In any case, the bastard's already drawn attention to itself by going missing.'

'Tell you what,' Hawkins began, 'why don't we – ?'

'Look,' Kane interrupted, 'if the sack's not here, as I said, it's on another train, still in Linz, or' – he paused and then added slowly – 'it's been expedited for some reason and gone ahead.' He looked at Fischer. 'What's the next main sorting centre, north?'

'On the way to Berlin? Dresden,' Fischer replied.

'Would there be a night staff on duty there? On a Sunday night?'

'At the centre? Could be. Dresden's a much more important junction than Prague – so far as the distribution of German mail is concerned.' Fischer, the expert on affairs inside the Reich, was looking dubious. 'But . . . why would anyone lift two sacks out of a whole trainload and send them on ahead?'

'You tell me.'

'Unless of course they knew this letter from the spy was in there . . . in which case we're wasting our time.'

'They couldn't know. But there's a limited number of possibilities; unless we eliminate some of them, we're never going to narrow down the search. That's why we must check out Dresden.'

Daventry said, 'What about the other sack that's missing? The one that doesn't have our letter? Could there be something important, something we don't know about, something the Boche would want to hurry along, in there?'

'Be your age,' Kane said impatiently. 'We know there isn't. Both the damned sacks are ours, man. There's nothing in the second one but phoney mail for Fritz.' He turned to the high desk by the timekeeper's window. 'Come on. Let's turn over all this bumph and see if we can locate a number for Dresden sorting.'

Protected by cellophane, they found the number along with several dozen others relating to the Reich postal system on a clip-board hanging from a hook above the antique telephone.

'Keep your fingers – all your fingers! – crossed, and

hope we can dial it out from the PBX upstairs,' Kane said, 'without calling an operator.'

They could. Seated in front of the top-floor exchange switchboard, Fischer studied the routing chart and made the connection while Kane prepared to act the part of an irate Czech post office functionary called from his bed by some idiot Staff major who wanted to trace part of an APO shipment.

There were night-shift workers staffing the Dresden sorting office. A sleepy supervisor told Kane that, no, no special forwarding instructions had been received from Prague or Linz during the past few days. They were overworked, understaffed, and the distribution was in chaos because of the war, but she was sure no such signal had been received. Because of the dislocation of schedules, the supervisor said, there had been no train bringing mail from Prague since Wednesday of the previous week.

'That's only the day the train was strafed,' Kane said when Fischer had pulled the plug from the switchboard. 'OK, so the sacks can't have gone ahead: now's the time, guys, to start looking behind us!'

Zygmund sat up painfully on the stretcher, his back propped against a pile of telephone directories and a leather cushion Daventry had found in the canteen manager's office. With the hand of his bandaged arm he turned the pages of the five passports resting on his lap. 'Names, occupations, addresses I can bleach out,' he said. 'Just tell me what you want instead. But you will still have four Austrian and one Czech: this I cannot alter.'

'We shall probably have to backtrack into Austria,' Kane said. He grinned. 'Tell you what: make two of them post office workers. That's Daventry and Fischer. With those suits you liberated, it's natural. Hawkins and me, we're telephone linesmen. That gives us an excuse to be around the tracks.'

'And Fischer's Czech ID? I throw that away?'

'You do not. That one's for you, Ziggy.'

'Ah, do me a favour,' Zygmund said weakly. 'You're not going to get me out of here. Not the way I am. Don't make yourself silly.'

'We certainly are,' Kane said with a conviction he was far from feeling. 'You make that one an inspector from the supply ministry. That way, they'll figure you for Gestapo.'

'An inspector with a busted leg, a damaged arm, and a middle he can't even cough it gives him such hell?'

'You got hurt in the raid. The ministry fell in on you. You were working late, and now your devotion to duty is being rewarded – you get sent to recuperate with your old auntie who lives in the Tyrol.'

Zygmund grunted. The tools of his illegal trade lay spread around the open attaché case by his side. With them were five blank Wehrmacht army pay books. 'What about these?' he asked. 'Did you decide what regiment you wanted to join yet?'

'Leave them until we know where we'll need them,' Kane said. 'Right now, I'd be happy if you could just doctor those five civvy IDs.'

'Get me some more rubber stamps then,' Zygmund said. 'There should be plenty someplace where they frank packages, cancel stamps, authorise waybills or whatever.'

'The cancellation and all that stuff is done in the post office, not the sorting centre,' Kane said. 'But we'll find you some stamps. Any particular kind?'

Zygmund shook his head, and winced. 'Those son-of-a-bitch incendiaries!' he complained. 'Any damn kind you like. Round, square, rectangular, octagonal. Just so there is a rubber head on them I can carve around and then ink up on this pad to make different visas from the ones I got here.'

'OK. Sure you feel up to it?'

'Oh, sure,' Zygmund said. 'There's all of half an hour before I am going to drop dead.'

*   *   *

The Gestapo man wore a zipped leather windcheater and a snap-brim felt hat with a feather sewn into the hatband. Orange and dirty white, the dog-eared copy of the Penguin paperback lay on the table between him and the military police area commander. 'If they are planning an air attack on the dam,' the MP chief said, 'it would seem most unlikely that they would send in a sabotage squad first with orders to attempt the same thing?'

'Not unlikely: ridiculous, out of the question.' The Abwehr colonel stood staring out of the window with his hands clasped behind his back. Below the baroque palace housing the intelligence headquarters, the roofs and spires of the old city had begun to assemble themselves against a sky that was lightening in the east. 'Out of the question,' he repeated.

'This man – the traitor Turderer – told you everything?' the MP asked.

The Gestapo man had tilted back his chair. He was picking his nose. 'Naturally,' he said indifferently.

'And he knew nothing of any saboteurs, any parachutists?'

'Nothing.'

'He had not been informed of the date of this . . . this projected raid on the dam?' the colonel said without turning round.

'No.'

'Presumably a signal will be sent? Which we can intercept?'

'We know about the code they use.' The Gestapo man glanced at the book. 'We know the same cypher groups are used for incoming messages. Unfortunately we were unable to keep him alive long enough to find out where he picked them up, or who was his cut-out.'

'A pity,' the military policeman said.

'It happens. He was not a very strong person.'

'In any case' – the colonel swung away from the window and faced the two men – 'it is clear that this fantasy about saboteurs is pure fiction. The five individuals for whom we are so diligently – and so fruitlessly – searching are no more than common criminals of a category yet to be determined.'

'Apparently.'

'The raid on the dam, if it materialises, will doubtless announce itself,' the colonel said, 'to our radar operators, who will have been alerted to keep a special watch on the south. Night-fighters, equally, will have been warned to stand by. In the meantime' – the fingers of his clasped hands were clenching and unclenching – 'I have enough to worry about with the Russian air raids, the threat of invasion, and the clandestine arming of terrorists in the north-east, without the added drain on our manpower caused by this search for illusory paratroopers. Do I make myself clear?'

'Yes, sir.'

'The affair of these five foreigners is therefore a matter for the civilian police. You will inform the Czech commissioner accordingly, and tell him that responsibility for the apprehension of these miscreants – if necessary with help from the Sipo and the SD – is from today entirely his. We wash our hands of the matter.'

'Yes, sir,' the MP area commander said again. The Gestapo man had transferred his attention from his nose to a hangnail that he was attempting to bite from his left index finger.

There had to be a reason. Kane sat by the silent telephone switchboard trying to concentrate. Daventry was with Zygmund; Hawkins and Fischer were raiding the canteen. There had to be a reason. Why would two sacks – just two out of almost fifty – have got themselves separated from the rest of the consignment? Why would a couple of sacks so separated both be from the phoney mail delivery dropped by the Lightnings? And why should one of those sacks be the very one he had come so far to find?

Of one thing he was fairly sure. The loss was not due to any deliberate action on the part of any person or persons.

There was no possible way it could be. If it had been, that would mean that whoever it was knew about the existence of the letter . . . and this in turn would imply that they must have found out through Colbert or Georgopoulous which (as Euclid used to say in the geometry problems) was absurd. Because then there would have been no reason to organise Kane's mission in the first place.

Unless, of course, it was some kind of double bluff, and the mission was meant to fail. . . ?

No. He shook his head. That made no sense at all. So OK, if the loss of the sacks was accidental, it followed that it was no more than a coincidence – if a bloody annoying one – that one of them was the one they were looking for.

What kind of accident could provoke the loss of two sacks from a trainload?

Kane started. A loud click from the far side of the room was followed by a mechanical whirring. A teleprinter began chuntering out a message. A line of white paper appeared above the Plexiglass viewing slit. The carriage banged to and fro, clacking out words. The paper jerked up a line, jerked once more. Kane rose to his feet and walked over to the machine.

The message was short. As he approached, the clacking ceased. Paper spewed suddenly up through the slit. The teleprinter hummed and then clicked into silence. Kane tore off the paper, read:

FLUGWACHKOMMANDO PRAHA (2) WARNS PAZ ZONES
A,C.E.
PAZ TO AZR ESTIMATED FIFTEEN.
NOTE AD/20 FOR WHOLE AREA SECTOR.
ENDS 0415/210844/FWK(P2)XXXXXXXX.

'Shit!' Kane said aloud. The message was an advance warning of an impending air raid from Prague anti-aircraft headquarters. PAZ was the sign for a pre-alert zone; AZR stood for full alert. They were in what the British would term a yellow warning zone, and it was expected

147

that this would change to red within a quarter of an hour. Meanwhile, zones not specified in the alert were notified they could be included within the next twenty minutes.

With half of his mind, Kane was still reasoning out the mystery of the sacks. What kind of accident, he had been thinking, could provoke the loss of two phoney sacks from a trainload?

With the other half, he was taking in the details of the teleprinter message, pondering the effect of another raid on his plans.

Abruptly – on his way back to the switchboard, Kane stopped in mid-stride – the two halves ran together and made a whole. Train, plane, air-raid, accident . . . surely he had been tackling the problem from the wrong direction? He was phrasing the most important question wrongly. He should be asking himself what kind of accident could account for the disappearance of sacks, not from a trainload but from a planeload. That would explain why only fake, not genuine, sacks were missing. If something had gone wrong with the delivery . . .

He remembered the debriefing report of the Lightning pilot who had dropped the sacks on the blitzed train, the transcript given him by the intelligence officer. Kane had an almost photographic memory. Now he closed his eyes, summoning up the words he had seen and then forgotten, words that could be all-important now. The young man had been complaining that his plane was difficult to control, that 'she was kind of capricious today'.

Kane saw the relevant passage of the transcript:

> *'I had to keep on feeding the crate a touch of left rudder . . . the Krauts were running from the wreck . . . some of them legged it for a belt of trees between the tracks and the river . . . goddamn, I almost zapped those guys with my first stick. She was still pulling to the right and I guess I over-corrected . . .'*

The German guards were running towards trees, the plane was veering towards them, the pilot reported that the first load of sacks he dropped almost fell on the soldiers . . . didn't that suggest something? Something that could account for an anomaly in the delivery of the sacks?

What if two of the sacks that 'almost' hit the Germans did in fact hit the trees?

Suppose they plunged into the summer foliage and became lodged in the upper branches?

And suppose they remained hidden there, unnoticed by the salvage crews when they picked up the pieces and sent them to Linz? Wouldn't that account for their absence from the rest of the consignment here in Prague?

Sure it would. And in that case, where would the sacks be now? In Linz, waiting to be put aboard the next mail train if they had been discovered subsequently; still in those trees if not.

Kane was on his feet, shouting. 'Fischer! Come here! You have work to do: I want you to get me the Linz centre on the blower.'

Fischer ran up the stairs with the clipboard. He sat down in front of the PBX console and settled the headset over his ears. 'Who shall I tell them?' he asked.

'Say that it's . . .' Kane frowned. 'Yes, tell them it's General Hunziger of the *Propaganda Abteilung*. General Klaus Hunziger.'

Fischer found that he was unable to dial out the Linz number directly: he was obliged to call the international operator at the Prague central exchange. 'I don't care if it's PAZ to AZR for the whole damned country,' he snapped when at last the operator replied. 'This is a priority call from Army Group D . . . Yes, priority, if you know what that means . . . I can't help that: the war doesn't stop just because it's dark . . . You put through this call. At once. Is that clear?'

He looked up and grinned at Kane. It was the first time Kane had ever seen him smile. 'Got to beat them over the head with an iron bar if you want some action,' he said. 'You know what switchboard girls are like!'

'I just hope there's a night staff on duty in Linz,' Kane said. 'We don't have much time: according to the work sheets downstairs, the day shift here come on at 0600 hours, and we have to be away the hell and out before then.'

Fischer looked at his watch. It was almost four-thirty.

A series of clicks, followed by a burbling noise sounded in the earphones. Kane looked expectant. 'Hallo?' Fischer said. 'Hallo?'

He heard a screech, and then a louder click. On the switchboard, a tumbler fell. 'It's ringing out,' the operator said curtly, and immediately went off the line. Fischer listened to the repeated burring for what seemed a long time. When at last a voice answered, it was very faint and its owner sounded angry.

No regular personnel were on duty in Linz on Sunday nights, Fischer was told. Only a logging clerk who acted as night watchman and firewatcher while he caught up with some of the paperwork left over from the previous week. If the caller wanted any information about shipments he must call again after eight, when the day supervisor would be there.

'The information must be obtained at once,' Fischer rasped in his best Prussian manner. 'Immediately. If you are a logging clerk you must have access to the relevant sheets.' He cut short the protests quacking in the earpiece and shouted: 'Silence! Keep your wretched excuses for the civilians. This is General Hunziger of the *Propaganda Abteilung* calling. Do you understand? . . . Yes, General. You had better answer him efficiently or it will be the worse for you.'

Kane nodded. He picked up the handset at one end of the console and held the receiver to his ear. Another tumbler fell on the switchboard as a buzzer sounded. Fischer pulled up a lead and jammed the plug into a socket. The tumbler tilted up out of sight and the buzzing stopped. 'Listen to me,' Kane barked with parade-ground force. 'A consignment of mail that had been salvaged from a train wreck was forwarded from your centre to Prague last Friday. Its serial number was BS-1323(2), origin Bologna, in Italy, and it was loaded onto train number 251. Have you got that? . . . Well, write it down, you dolt, and be quick about it.' Kane paused for a moment, listening to the wail of sirens that were now audible in the distance.

'Two of the sacks from that consignment are missing,' Kane said accusingly when the clerk came back on the line. 'They must be found at once or there will be trouble.'

Again he listened impatiently, before cutting in: 'I am not interested in protestations or excuses . . . I will not wait until your supervisor comes in; you are quite capable of investigating yourself. Very well. The shipment number is BS-1323(2). I assume, when it left Italy, before the train was cravenly attacked, that it was 1323(1). What you are to do now, at once, is examine your centre's charts and logs and see whether any 1323(3) is on record. If so, you will check that the sacks numbered 15AF/463 and 464/BG are included . . . Not a word. There are important official papers in those sacks and I intend to have them located immediately . . . That is no concern of mine: neither your health nor your conditions of work interest me. And I warn you, I shall expect a written report on the reasons for this gross incompetence by midday – a report that assigns the blame to those responsible . . . You will do as I say, or I shall make it my personal business to have you put in uniform and sent to the Russian front. Now get started.'

Kane winked, holding the receiver to his chest while he waited. Hawkins and Daventry had come into the room. They could hear the thwack of anti-aircraft guns in the distance. 'Fuckin' sergeant-major!' Hawkins said admiringly. 'Trust a bloody Kraut!'

Kane spoke to Daventry. 'Is there a safe or any kind of strong-room in this dump? We may have to leave in a hurry, and I want an alibi, an excuse for our being here, if we don't have time to clear up every trace. They can't tie us in with the sacks, if they're not here, so let's make it look like a robbery, huh?'

'There's an old safe in the supervisor's office on the floor below. Meissen & Albrecht. A G-2 or G-3. Been there years.'

'Can you crack it?'

Daventry opened his cheap Czech jacket and patted the slight bulge of his body belt. 'Piece of cake, guv.'

'Anything else?'

'Kind of a strong room. On the first floor. Looks like one of those bank places where they keep safe-deposit boxes. I guess it's for special registered mail – gems, *objets d'art*, stuff like that.'

'Can you do that one?'

The safe-breaker shook his head. 'Do you the outer grille, but not the big steel door inside. Not without jelly.'

'Make it look as though you'd tried.'

Daventry's saturnine face split into a grin. 'Be a pleasure,' he said. He turned and strode from the room. Somewhere out in the dark, the engines of an aircraft droned.

Fischer looked up from the switchboard and nodded.

Kane held the receiver to his ear again. 'Yes?' he said brusquely. '*Ach, so?* Proceed.'

He listened, motioning to Fischer, who took up a pencil and began to write on a notepad beside the console dial. After a while the expression on his hawk face softened. He smiled, although the voice, when he spoke again, was as hectoring and imperious as ever. 'Continue. Don't prevaricate, man. I want all the details. All.'

Alternately whining and protesting, the clerk in Linz went on with his monologue. Finally, Kane snapped. 'I am not interested in whose fault it was; I am interested in results. Others will assign the blame later. Train 243, you say? Very well. Tell your superiors to make sure that it does.'

He slammed the receiver back on its hook. Fischer pulled the plug from the switchboard and allowed the lead to snap back into its hole. He tore the top page from the notepad and handed it to Kane. '*Yippee!*' Kane crowed. 'We got the bugger at last!'

He read through the notes on the paper. His hunch had paid off. The missing sacks had fallen among the trees. Lodged in the top branches of an alder, they had been overlooked by salvage men who had the entire wreck to deal with and the track to repair. Noticed by a linesman checking out the signals controls the following day, they had been handed over to a patrol, assumed to be the victims of a freak blast effect. The patrol had taken them by road to Klagenfurt, and from there they had been sent to Linz by train.

It was all there in writing, logged with Teutonic efficiency in the Linz day book, complete with explanatory notes, waybills and dockets signed by the man in charge at each stage of the journey. The train bringing the sacks onto Prague was due to leave between 1100 hours and midday.

'Could we make it to Linz by then?' Fischer asked.

'Not a chance,' Kane told him. 'It's between 120 and 130 miles, a lot of it through mountains, with a frontier to cross. Plus we don't have any transport yet. Plus how the hell could we bust into a busy GPO on a Monday morning? And there's Ziggy to think of.'

'But if we wait until the bleeders land here. . . ?' Hawkins began.

'Of course we can't do that,' Kane said. 'We can't just wait here all day, hoping nobody notices five strangers in the centre! Nor could we hope to bust in again and have the place to ourselves, not on a week-night. Too much of a bloody risk. Anyway, who the hell wants to go through all that humping of sacks for a third time?'

'You can say that again,' Fischer agreed fervently.

'The Krauts'll know we're interested – somebody's interested – in them sacks anyway,' Hawkins said. 'I mean after that phone call, like. It'll all be written down somewhere.'

'Is there a General Klaus Hunziger?' Fischer asked.

Kane nodded. 'The kind of guy to make just that kind of fuss. But they can't check with him – he was captured last Tuesday at St Tropez, when we made the first bridgehead in the south of France. But you're right, Sergeant: attention will have been drawn to those two sacks in particular, so we'll have to switch plans some.'

Hawkins and Fischer looked enquiring. Kane explained. 'We were told to close up the target sack once we had the letter, so that nobody would know it had been tampered with. Ditto the break-in here. We already decided to ignore the latter. Now the first point won't apply either. So we have to cover our interest in those two sacks by bringing it out in the open . . . and making it part of something bigger. Then, with luck, they'll figure the enquiry about those sacks as a blind – a way of checking on that particular trainload as a whole.'

Hawkins stared at him. 'Just how do we manage that?' Fischer asked.

Kane smiled crookedly. 'We follow the example of the sacks: we take the train.'

Before he could explain further, a heavy knocking on the entrance door resounded through the building.

Kane swore. Pinching out the candle, he strode to the window and tweaked aside the black-out. In the dim pre-dawn light, he could see that the gates were open. The two guards stood by a Hanomag scout car. The knocking was repeated, louder than before.

Kane pressed his face to the glass and squinted down at the forecourt. Three steel-helmeted figures, machine pistols slung over their shoulders, stood at the top of the steps outside the doors.

Chapter 15

Kane catapulted down the stairs two at a time, shrugging on the uniform jacket as he ran. His boots were scuffed and his breeches filthy, but the waterproof had protected the jacket from the dirt on the rooftops. Behind him, Hawkins clattered from step to step. He had stripped off the stolen sweater and was dressed simply in boots, his Luftwaffe trousers, and an army issue shirt.

Kane flung open the main doors as the knocking resumed for the third time. A young Wehrmacht officer in a greatcoat stood with two hardbitten enlisted men in their late thirties. 'What the devil is going on here?' the officer demanded. He had heavy-lidded, insolent eyes and an out-thrust lower lip.

'I could ask you the same. What do you think you're doing?' Kane said in his haughtiest manner.

The beam of a powerful torch sprang from the officer's hand. 'Oh,' he said, seeing the uniform, '*Herr Hauptmann* . . . the guards on the gate reported a light behind one of the black-outs. As this building is empty at night, we decided to investigate. There was a chance that incendiaries from the raid might have started a fire.'

'The building is not empty at night,' Kane said. 'As you see.'

The young officer – he was an *Oberleutnant* – shone the flashlight beam on a duplicated sheet. 'This is among the public and official buildings listed as unoccupied. Saturday and Sunday nights only, in this case.'

'As a rule,' Kane agreed. 'But not this weekend.'

'This bulletin is dated yesterday midday. There is no mention of any change in the arrangements.'

'How very inefficient.'

'May one ask precisely what a captain in the air defence corps is doing, at night, in a deserted postal sorting centre?'

'One may not. Not when that captain has been seconded for intelligence duties. There is no fire in this building. No bombs fell on it. Now, will you be good enough to withdraw and allow us to continue with our work?'

It was worth trying, but it didn't work. The *Oberleutnant's* voice was perceptibly harder as he drawled: 'I am afraid, *Herr Hauptmann* – purely as a formality, of course – that I must ask you for your papers.' The beam swept over Hawkins, lingering on the Luftwaffe trousers. 'And yours too.'

'Of course,' Kane said. 'They are upstairs, where we are working.'

'You do not carry them on your person?'

'Look,' Kane said, with an exasperation that was not entirely simulated, 'it is not yet five o'clock. We were only half-dressed' – he gestured at Hawkins – 'when your thundering at the door disturbed us. If you must see the papers, wait here and we will fetch them.'

'They include, naturally, an authorisation permitting you to enter listed buildings?' The young German's voice was becoming progessively more disagreeable.

'Naturally,' Kane said.

'How odd, then, that the sentries at the gate have not been shown this – or any other – document: they swear that nobody has come in or out.'

'Possibly.' Kane was bored. 'It is conceivable, however, that this might be because my colleagues and I arrived before those two men were on duty. You should have asked the men they relieved.' He shrugged disdainfully, thrust his hands into the pockets of his jacket, and turned toward the inside of the building.

'I should prefer to accompany you.'

'As you wish.'

Kane and Hawkins moved toward the stairs. The officer and his two escorts followed, their footsteps echoing on the wooden floors. 'If you are, as you claim, working here, why is this part of the centre in darkness?' the *Oberleutnant* demanded.

'You yourself pointed out that the black-out is inefficient.'

'I must inform you . . . *Herr Hauptmann*' – the voice was a definite sneer now – 'that as duty security officer I have the right, irrespective of rank, to require a full explanation of your actions here.' The German unfastened the flap of his holster and withdrew his revolver.

'You will get it,' Kane said. He began to climb the stairs.

On the first floor, Hawkins pressed a switch. The yellow light threw into relief the dusty corridor, the cream and green walls, a succession of office doors.

'And these famous papers?' the Oberleutnant queried.

'The papers you will see. My work remains secret,' Kane said shortly. 'And I would advise you that I have superiors, to whom your attitude – and your manners – may be reported.'

'Big words, *Herr Hauptmann*. When I have seen the papers, I will decide whether or not my attitude requires to be modified.' It was clear that the young officer was suspicious, but that the uniform, plus Kane's apparent rank, had so far inhibited him from following through his doubts.

'The papers are on the top floor,' Kane said.

Approaching the second staircase, the procession passed an open door. Hawkins was in the lead, followed by Kane, the officer, and the two Wehrmacht men. Daventry had managed to extinguish the candles by the light of which he had been working, but reflected radiance from the passageway illuminated only too clearly the iron bars of the grille hanging open, the scarred steel door of the strong-room beyond.

Before anyone reacted, a door behind them opened and Fischer moved silently up behind the two soldiers. He reached out with his powerful hands and slammed the two helmeted heads together with such force that the impact sounded like a gunshot in the confined space of the corridor.

After that, things moved with bewildering speed. The soldiers, dazed and half-stunned, staggered against the walls; one reeled to his knees. Fischer leaped in tigerishly and struck him across the throat with the flat of his hand. At the same time, the young officer swung around with an exclamation.

'What the devil. . . ?' His gun was raised to line up with Fischer's chest. Kane shot him through the pocket of his jacket. The muffled report of the short-barrelled PPK was lost in the tramp of feet as Hawkins sprang back to grapple with the second soldier.

Hurled forward by the punch of the 9mm slug, the officer crashed to the floor. Fischer, too, was holding his Walther now. He fired twice at the man on his knees. Kane had moved in to help the big sergeant: he wrestled the machine pistol away and lent his wiry strength to the struggle; the heel of a huge hand was under the German's jaw, forcing his head back; Kane kicked him in the groin and then trapped his ankles in a leg lock, jamming a knee in the small of the man's back. He was choking. His breath gargled in his throat. His arms flailed the air as helplessly as the legs of a fly on its back.

There was a sudden crack, loud and definite as a dead branch snapping in a wood. Kane and Hawkins allowed the body to slump to the floor. 'All right,' Kane panted, 'there's the driver and two guards still below. Hawkins and I will deal with them; you two go fetch Ziggy. Like fast – we have to get out of here.'

As Fischer and Daventry pounded up the stairs, Kane and the sergeant took the weapons from the fallen men. In a life punctuated by violence, Kane never ceased to be amazed by the difference in the amount of blood voided by the dead. The *Oberleutnant* and the soldier shot by Fischer, for instance, had both been killed by bullets of the same calibre, yet apart from two small black holes haloed by crimson in the back of his coat the soldier could have been sleeping. Kane's slug. on the other hand, had smashed an exit wound so extensive that the young officer lay in a red puddle eighteen inches across, from which thin fingers of blood fanned out to grasp the stair head and stain the top few steps.

'Did you have to kill them all?' Daventry, surprisingly, asked later.

'It's not pretty,' Kane agreed, 'but think what they would do to us if we were caught.'

'Think of Auschwitz,' Fischer said.

'Think of what? Never heard of it,' said the safe-breaker.

'You will,' Fischer told him.

In the forecourt, between the entrance and the loading bay, Kane and Hawkins could hear shouts and the thudding of booted feet. 'It's all right,' Kane yelled in a voice as near the *Oberleutnant's* as he could contrive. 'There were robbers here, but we've got them!'

For a moment there was silence below. Then a voice called up something unintelligible. Kane snapped off the light. 'Get their helmets,' he whispered to Hawkins. 'Greatcoats too, if you can.' The shuffling sounds of Daventry and Fischer and Zygmund's stretcher were now audible on the floors above. 'We're coming down with the prisoners,' Kane shouted.

Holding the Schmeisser MP-38 across his chest, he trod warily down the stairs. But his talents as a film stunt man were clearly not equalled by his gift for mimicry. The guard who had called up was not fooled. From the doorway, once again a flashlight beam lanced the dark before he was half-way down. An instant before the guard's machine pistol spat fire, Kane put his palm on the wooden handrail and vaulted into the stairwell. He hit the floor below while the ripping detonations of the Schmeisser's initial burst still rang in his ears, rolled over, and came up supported on his elbows with his own gun at the ready.

He squeezed the trigger long enough to loose off half a dozen rounds at the gun's cyclic rate of 520rpm, and then hurled himself into the shelter of a reception counter just inside the doors. The guard fired again while he was still moving. Wood splintered behind him. Glass shattered by his shots tinkled to the ground.

Kane's next burst, over the top of the counter, matched a longer one from the guard. The hallway of the centre leaped in and out of focus with the muzzle flashes of the two guns. Beside Kane, panels from the counter were ripped into matchwood. But the German had been unwise enough to stand silhouetted against the half-light of the approaching dawn, and a stream of 9mm shells from Kane's MP-38 smashed across his chest like a leaden whip.

Before he hit the ground, Kane had dived headfirst over the counter and somersaulted to the doorway. He was prone on the top step before the second guard realised that his mate was out of the fight – for good. The man was holding his Schmeisser with the wire stock retracted. He fired from the hip, hosing the steps and the doorway with a stream of death. Kane felt a slug stir the hairs on the top of his head. Another thudded into the boards beside his elbow, and a third gouged from the wood a long splinter that slashed his cheek. But Kane sighted properly, lining up foresight and backsight just above the flame belching from the MP's flashguard.

The second guard hit the ground and his weapon clattered away across the macadam. Now there was only the driver of the scout car to deal with. Kane raced down the steps and out into the open, swinging his gun in a wide arc from right to left.

What Kane didn't know was that the driver had coasted the Hanomag up level with the loading bay. He was using it as cover, crouched down behind the sloping bonnet, and at first Kane did not see him. The man was armed only with a standard service P-38 pistol, but he fired first and the shot was a lucky one, hitting the breech of Kane's gun and knocking it spinning from his grasp.

With his hands momentarily numbed, Kane hesitated before he reached for the Walther in his pocket. He was a sitting duck.

The driver rose upright, drawing a bead on him with a two-handed grip. Glass exploded outward from a first-floor window. Daventry leaped through and landed feet first on the German's shoulders, knocking him face down across the Hanomag's bonnet with all the breath startled from his lungs. Before he could recover, Daventry had scrambled upright and clubbed him twice with the butt of his own Walther. The driver slid unconscious to the ground.

Kane ran across and clapped the safe-breaker on the shoulder. 'Thanks,' he said briefly. 'But what's with this feet-first routine? Here you jump fifteen or twenty feet, and the same at the bridge: you didn't even bother to hang by your hands and reduce the drop!'

'I'm used to it,' Daventry said modestly. 'I left Wandsworth that way a couple of times, and the walls there are high.'

Kane laughed. 'Did you make it with the small safe?'

''Course I did.'

'Anything of value?'

'Between thirty and forty thousand Marks; one or two registered packages that might contain jewels.'

'You brought them with you?'

'You bet!' Daventry said, patting the bulging front of his jacket.

'Swell. So far as the Krauts are concerned, we're burglars, then, who killed to escape capture. Now we have to get the hell out of here.'

'How do we. . . ?'

Kane slapped the Hanomag with his open hand. 'We drive out, of course. Take the greatcoat and helmet of the guy you clobbered, and put them on. Then get the two guards' helmets: I guess the coats will be too stained to use.'

Hawkins staggered down the steps carrying three steel helmets, a Schmeisser and the two greatcoats he had taken from the patrol soldiers. A moment later, Fischer called Daventry to help him carry Zygmund's stretcher down the last flight of stairs.

'I reckon that's torn it an' all,' Hawkins observed, staring at the three supine bodies on the tarmac. 'What do we do about the inside, guv?'

'Leave everything the way it is. Just get the attaché case with Ziggy's toys, and leave the rest. Hold-up men don't shut drawers,' Kane said.

Between them they now had three long greatcoats and six steel helmets – one more than they needed. Hastily, Kane organised the Hanomag's new crew. Since he was still wearing officer's uniform, he took the navigator's seat on the right of the driver. Fischer was behind the wheel, leaning back against the squab to hide the two bullet holes in his greatcoat. The garment, like the one Hawkins had taken from the man he killed, bore the scarlet edged shoulder strap and double red collar bar of an *Oberschütze* (or private first-class) in the *Feldgendarmerie*. Daventry's shoulder strap had a white border with a single star: the original driver of the scout car had been a transport *Feldwebel*.

There was no way a stretcher could be stowed aboard the stubby, soft-top, open-sided vehicle. Zygmund, swathed in bandages, with a steel helmet on his head, sat propped between Hawkins and the safe-breaker in the rear seat. After his work on the ID papers, he was now suffering from delayed shock and had sunk into a state that was almost comatose.

'OK, let her go,' Kane told Fischer. 'This little party won't have gone unnoticed, even at five o'clock in the morning in a country at war!'

The anti-aircraft guns had stopped firing some time before, and so far as they knew no bombs had been dropped. Perhaps the Russians had sent a single reconnaissance plane to take infra-red photographs of the previous night's bomb damage. Certainly the fusillade of shots had alerted the neighbourhood, for they could hear a babble of voices from the station and the service road on the far side of the sorting centre, although as yet nobody had dared to come near enough to investigate.

Fischer thumbed the starter. The four-cylinder motor

burst into life with a roar. As they careered out through the open gates and past a knot of scared citizens huddled on the railway bridge, sirens all over the city started to sound the all-clear.

PART FOUR

On the Run

Chapter 16

'I thought,' Fischer said, shooting a red traffic light on the road that led southward out of the city, 'that you told me we'd be taking the train?'

'That's right,' said Kane.

'But . . . I mean, what station could we – ?'

'No station.' Kane was smiling. It was growing lighter every minute. 'We take it between stations.'

'Perhaps I'm just dumb,' Fischer said angrily, 'as well as suffering from vertigo and being a drag in general. But I don't see – '

'No need to lose your cool,' Kane said. 'When I say the train, I mean *the* train – the one with our sacks aboard. And when I say take it, I don't mean what the British mean when they say "catch a train": I mean take it militarily.'

Fischer took his eyes off the road long enough to flash a sideways glance at his leader. He waited for Kane to continue.

'We couldn't make Linz in time,' Kane explained, 'even if we could get into the GPO sorting office there. We dare not stay here in Prague and wait for the stuff to arrive. So we have to liberate those goddam sacks somewhere between the two. And to do that we must take control of the train. Obviously.'

'You mean . . . ambush it? Hijack it? Shoot our way aboard?'

'Something like that.' Kane at last was in his element. His eyes shone with the light of battle; his lips were twisted into a reckless smile. 'I pinched a chart of the railway system from the sorting centre. We have maps. We know the number of the train. All we need is a suitable place not too near civilisation. And we've got plenty of time to sniff one out: the train doesn't leave Linz for another five or six hours.'

'Yes, but . . . Even if we find one, how are we going to know when train 243 is due to arrive? I mean, it won't be the only train on the line. Like the man said, it'll be low priority. And there will be a lot of traffic, with the build-up of reinforcements and supplies to meet this Russian attack they're all talking about.'

'No problem,' Kane said cheerfully. 'We'll find a nice lonely signal cabin and persuade the brakeman to tip us off when the train's expected. We'll already have the site staked out: it's just a question of knowing when to attack.'

The rooftops to the east were silhouetted now against a bar of orange light, and the sky above it was a limpid green, shading to violet overhead. It was going to be a fine day. 'We've got to get out of town and find a secluded place pretty damned quick,' Kane said. 'The nights are chilly now, but we can't believably steam around in greatcoats once the sun's up. Not in August. In any case, there'll be an all-stations alert out for this buggy – and five guys in steel helmets – before we're much older.'

'I'm doing the best I can,' Fischer said. 'About this attack: we have five Walther PPK automatics, that officer's service pistol, the driver's gun, and four Schmeissers with partially discharged magazines. Plus two cartridge belts of 9mm ammunition and a couple of stick grenades we took from the infantrymen guarding the gates. There are four of us in a condition to use this stuff. I know the sacks we are looking for won't be on an armoured train protected by a 75mm anti-tank gun, but I still can't quite see. . . ?'

'How we're going to make it?' Kane was suddenly in an

167

expansive mood. 'Well, clearly four guys standing by the track can't expect to stop a whole train, however many guns they have. So we have to stop the train by other means and attack once it's come to a halt. I looked at that railway chart: there's a certain viaduct that carries the line across a valley not too far away. We'll blow one span of the viaduct and stop the train there.'

'With two grenades?'

'No,' Kane said. 'Not with two grenades. We have to find a quarry first and lift some dynamite before the workers arrive.'

'And before it's so soddin' hot that we have to junk these coats and show we ain't real soldiers,' Hawkins said from the back seat.

'Right,' said Kane. 'According to the map, there are quarries on the way to the Slapy Dam. I guess they used the stuff to build up the barrage. We'll head that way as soon as we can.'

This was to prove a great deal more difficult than Kane expected. They were leaving Prague by the same road they had taken when they arrived four days before. Just beyond the textile factory where they had run into the second roadblock that morning, the road divided, the right fork leading toward Zbraslav and the Slapy Dam, the left in the direction of Benesov. Two hundred yards down each road there was a police checkpoint – and Kane saw at once that, while that on the left was almost perfunctory, vehicles being waved on as soon as the officers had glanced inside, the one on the right involved a full ID check and the examination of papers. There was a movable barrier there, and it was only lifted after each vehicle had been cleared. 'Bear left . . . and don't slacken speed,' Kane told Fischer.

Soon after dawn, with the sun not yet risen, there was little traffic on the way to town. Industrial workers would not be crowding the streetcars for another hour; commercial traffic was mainly heading in. Fischer pulled out to overtake an empty farm lorry, a delivery truck, two private cars and a horse-drawn brewer's dray as they slowed for the checkpoint.

A policeman stepped out into the middle of the road and waved them down, but Kane motioned him angrily out of the way and Fischer kept his foot pressing hard on the throttle pedal. The Hanomag sped past and raced up a long, straight hill towards a skyline of chimneys. 'Bloody nerve!' Kane said. 'A civilian cop flagging down a scout car from the Reich's victorious army!'

'He don't look very pleased.' Hawkins was staring over the Hanomag's high back. 'Dancing about, he is, waving to his mates, an' all.'

'We can always bluff our way past ordinary cops,' Kane said. 'At any rate, until they know about the party at the sorting centre. But if we run into a regular military roadblock, we're cooked.'

Just beyond the top of the rise, a second road branched off toward the dam. There was a police check at the entrance to this one too, although the main road was clear. Within the next three miles, they passed two more turnings signposted *Zbraslav, Vrane, Jilowe, Slapy Lake Reservoir*. There were police stationed in each of them.

'They're certainly anxious to check anyone heading for that dam,' Kane said. 'I don't get it. They can't know we want to go that way: I only decided a couple of hours ago, and I certainly told nobody but you guys. If they were after us on account of the sorting centre, on the other hand, surely they'd be checking all roads – not just those leading to the dam?'

'Maybe it's some other panic altogether,' Daventry said, 'something that's got nothing to do with us at all?'

'I'll keep crossed fingers on that one,' Kane said.

Veering steadily to the east, the road passed a steelworks, the serrated roofs of an engineering factory, gasometers, a farming co-operative around a yard stacked high with milk churns. The sun was ten degrees above the horizon. Concrete poles carrying high-tension and telegraph wires cast long shadows across the road.

'Humming, those bleedin' wires will be,' Hawkins said, 'with orders to arrest the sods who knocked orf five of our brave soldiers and put a sixth out for the fuckin' count.'

Allotments planted with strips of cabbage, potatoes, beet, were visible now between the half-timbered houses with their steep gables. They passed fields golden with stubble, bare earth porcupined with hop poles. The next police check was in the main street of a village that was being sucked into the outer suburbs. A Skoda police car was parked with its nearside wheels on the sidewalk. In the centre of the narrow, cobbled roadway, an officer flanked by two gendarmes held up his hand. The only vehicle in sight was a tractor pulling a mechanical hay rake.

The gendarmes' automatic carbines were still slung, and Kane breathed a sigh of relief. Evidently they had not yet been warned that five hold-up men in a stolen Hanomag were at large. Maybe, he thought, Daventry was right: they would not be the only thorns in the flesh of the Czech authorities. The controls could be on the look-out for Russian spies, partisans or some other band of criminals. Perhaps the bank robbers the girl Hilde had mentioned? Crime did not stop paying just because there was a war on.

It was odd that the roadblocks were manned by civil police and not the military, but that was a point in favour of Daventry's argument. In any case, it would be crazy to act guilty and assume that they were blown: too many agents had been caught that way already.

Kane determined to act on the assumption that the safe-breaker had reasoned correctly. At the entrance to the village he had noticed two German army transport signposts, each marked with a red cross. One announced: *Deutsches Rotes Kreuz – Sanitätspark 672, Modrany*; the other read: *Krankenverteilungs u. Unfallmeldstelle* – patient distribution and accident report centre. Modrany was a small town a few miles ahead.

The information on those signs, Kane decided, could be

exploited to their advantage. 'Pull up beside them,' he told Fischer. 'But keep the revs up, okay?' He climbed out onto the scout car's footboard and stood up holding the windscreen pillar, making urgent sweeping motions with his right arm as they approached the police.

Fischer braked hard to bring the Hanomag squealing to a halt inches from the three men. He held the clutch out but kept the car in gear. 'What is this nonsense?' Kane shouted angrily, still waving the policemen out of the way. 'Clear the road at once and let us through: we are in a hurry.'

'With respect, *Herr Hauptmann*' – the officer was beside the car – 'we have orders, very strict orders from the *Kommandantura* in Prague, to examine all papers. Without exception.'

'Not German military papers, you dolt!'

'Without exception, *Herr Hauptmann*,' the policeman said firmly. He held out his hand.

'Get out of my way,' Kane yelled. 'Can't you see there's a seriously injured man here? He was almost killed in a terrorist attack in the city. He must be hospitalised at once.' He gestured toward Zygmund.

The policeman peered into the rear of the scout car. The Pole certainly looked as though he needed medical attention. His eyes were closed, he was deathly white, and his head lolled forward on his chest, bobbing slightly with the pulsations of the engine. In several places, dark spots of blood had seeped through his bandages. 'Well . . .' The officer bit his lip. He looked dubiously at the police car. The driver was at the wheel, listening to the voice of his Divisional Controller gargling in the shortwave radio speaker. 'I suppose . . . it's irregular, but in this case . . .'

'We have to get him to Modrany: every minute counts,' Kane insisted. 'Thank you for your understanding.' He tapped Fischer on the shoulder. Fischer let in the clutch and stamped on the accelerator, wrenching on the wheel at the same time to swerve around the two gendarmes. The Hanomag leaped forward, its rear wheels spinning on the cobbles.

As they passed the police car, Kane saw from the corner of his eye that the driver had erupted from his seat and was signalling frantically to his superior. He swung back into his place beside Fischer. 'I think our friends just got the message,' said. 'I mean like literally: at all costs, stop five men in German uniforms. Keep your foot down.'

Daventry was looking out of the rear window in the soft top. 'They're following us,' he reported.

Outside the village, the road wound along beside a stream in a shallow valley. Cattle knee-deep in a water meadow swished their tails among buttercups on the far side of the river. The Skoda was three hundred yards behind them, and gaining, when Fischer swung left at an intersection, rattled across a wooden bridge, and sent the scout car streaking up a hill. Dipping over the crest, he swore and lifted his foot momentarily from the pedal. A quarter of a mile ahead, the road was blocked by a farm cart piled high with a towering load of hay. And advancing from the other direction, an army convoy stretched as far as the eye could see along the undulating route.

Kane took in the scene at a glance: personnel carriers, half-track troop transports, main battle tanks, heavy trucks with gun-slit windows, trailers with angular cargoes shrouded in canvas. They hadn't a chance of overtaking the cart before it was reached by the motor cycle combinations at the head of the convoy. 'Take the track,' he ordered tersely. 'We'll make a stand when we reach the trees.'

Away to the right, a coverlet of dark woods draped the sunlit hillside. A grass-grown trail arrowed up there from the road.

'Christ, we can't hold off the whole blooming Boche army!' Daventry complained as Fischer skated the Hanomag off the road and sent it bumping along the track.

'Don't worry,' Kane said. 'They're not going to stop to lend a hand to some piddling local cops: those guys are on their way to the Eastern Front.'

172

The four unwounded members of Kane's team piled out of the Hanomag when Fischer stopped the scout car broadside on to the trail a hundred yards into the wood. Carrying the Schmeissers, they ran to a screen of bushes emerging from the undergrowth beneath the first row of trees. The Skoda was two hundred yards away, at the limit of the machine pistols' range.

'All right,' Kane said. 'Let them have it. I don't particularly want to kill Czech policemen: concentrate short bursts on the car.'

The eruption of the Schmeissers was alarmingly loud in the shade beneath the tree. There was an angry flapping and cawing as a colony of rooks floated up above the wood. A fountain of bright light played momentarily in the sun as the Skoda's windscreen shattered. The car stopped. Three figures darted out and lay prone in the hedgerows. Kane heard the sharp crack of carbines. Slugs thwacked through the branches; one or two leaves spiralled to the ground.

'Right,' Kane said. 'Now they won't dare advance uphill across open ground so long as they believe there's someone here with a gun. We haven't too much ammo to spare but we'll make 'em keep their heads down for a few minutes. Then, before they've had time to call up reinforcements and surround us, we'll push off through the wood, leaving one guy – and the car, which they can probably see – to hold the fort a little longer. It'll probably be another five minutes after he's quit before they catch on and risk an advance. By which time we should all be clear away.'

'Leave me behind,' Zygmund's weak voice called suddenly from the Hanomag. 'I can shoot one-handed and keep them off longer than that. You're not going to get me out of here anyway – and you're bitched speedwise as long as you have a passenger.'

'Not on your bloody life,' Kane replied. He fired a short burst down the hill in the direction of the Skoda. 'You're coming with us, Ziggy: you'll have work to do with those rubber stamps.' He fired again, followed by Hawkins and Fischer. 'I'll play end-stop myself while you guys forge on through the wood,' Kane said.

'Don't be bleedin' daft, cock,' Hawkins said. 'The orficer's supposed to lead, isn't he? You'll be needed on the far side of the wood, to decide which way to go an' all. I got long fuckin' legs; I can catch up quick. You let me hold the fort then.'

Kane had to admit that this made sense. 'OK,' he agreed. 'Fischer: you and Daventry make a chair lift and start off with Ziggy right away. Take your pistols and the two spare handguns, junk the greatcoats and helmets, and leave the Schmeissers with us.'

The police below were shooting again. Two of them had crawled away across a field in an attempt to enfilade. As Daventry and Fischer moved off down the forest trail with their human cargo, Kane and the sergeant fired the four machine pistols alternately, changing their position with each volley. Then, once the concept of a group of men firing from different places had been established, Kane took two of the guns, and the two stick grenades, and hurried after the others. 'Five minutes would do,' he said to Hawkins. 'Seven and a half would be better. If you could make ten, that would be jake.'

'I'll play it by ear,' Hawkins said.

For some time, as he traversed the wood, Kane heard the rasp of Schmeissers and the sharper crack of the police rifles. Then – sounds were curiously muffled in the sunless shade beneath those thickly planted trees – they merged and became one with the deep hum of insects, the snapping of twigs as he crisped through last year's dead leaves at the side of the track, and the puttering of a tractor on the far side of the hill. Once he imagined he could hear the whine of a car in low gear somewhere behind him, but when he stopped to listen the noise was no longer there.

Sunlight dappled the rutted earth of the track when he came within sight of the open country beyond the wood.

174

The tractor was working at the foot of a great slope of harvested corn. Daventry and Fischer had transported their burden half-way down the slope toward a road bordering the field. On the far side, the land rose again to a line of low, wooded hills in the south-east.

In their cheap, wide-trousered, off-the-peg Czech suits, Daventry and Fischer could have been any locals helping a friend who had met with an accident. Kane, wearing his grimy Wehrmacht uniform, was less likely to remain unnoticed. He stripped off the jacket and dropped it behind a furze bush at the exit from the wood.

There was a hedge at the side of the road. Beyond it, the black roof of a large motor car glittered in the sun. By the time Kane reached the hedge, his two companions had manoeuvred Zygmund over a stile and set him down on the grass verge. They were talking to the driver of the car – a huge Minerva taxi-cab with the bonnet propped open.

Kane glanced back up the slope toward the wood. There was no sign of Hawkins yet. He set down the two machine pistols and the grenades and climbed over the stile himself. The driver of the taxi was a woman. 'If I could only find out what was wrong,' she complained, 'I could probably fix it and get the thing going again.'

She looked up as Kane approached the group. 'My God,' she said, 'of all people!'

It was Hilde Finnemann, the good-time girl he had met on the embankment.

Chapter 17

'It was that bastard from the Gestapo,' she told Kane. 'Because I wouldn't play his game, because I refused to throw over all my other friends and satisfy the depraved tastes of him and his two SS friends, he planted dope and stolen jewels in my apartment and then tipped off the Czech police. Luckily one of the girls knew about it and put me wise, so I was able to get out before they came for me.'

Kane indicated the stalled Minerva. 'And this?'

'Back-scratching.' She smiled, tossing a lock of straw-coloured hair from her eyes in a gesture he remembered well. 'A cab driver friend of mine wanted it taken to Ceske Budejovice as soon as possible. I think it may be just a little bit hot. I wanted to get out of town as soon as possible. So . . . we're doing each other a favour.'

'What's the matter with it?'

She shrugged. 'I don't know. It just stopped.'

'Let's have a look,' Kane said. He bent over the wing, scrutinising the huge motor. Checking, he found that the ignition was in good shape, the plugs were clean, the carburetter jets were clear, and the fuel pump diaphragm was working. But no petrol was being delivered. 'Sure there's plenty of gas?' Kane enquired.

'It was full when I started.'

'OK.' He moved around the back of the car and unscrewed the filler cap, shaking the great limousine body. The tank was still almost full. He slid into the driving seat and pressed the starter. The engine started at once, purring softly and evenly.

Hilde stared at him. 'What did you do? I don't understand.'

Kane grinned. He held up the filler cap. 'Got a hairpin?'

Frowning, she plucked one from her hair and handed it over. Kane bent it straight and pushed one end into the

176

cap. The end pierced the cap and emerged pushing a speck of dirt before it. He held up the cap again. Light showed now through a tiny hole in the centre. 'When the engine draws fuel from the tank,' he explained, 'air has to flow in to replace it, or there'd be a vacuum created which would hold the petrol back. That's what this little hole is for: to let in your air. It was blocked, so you were getting no gas. It's as simple as that.'

'Well,' Hilde said, 'that's two favours I've been done today, and it's not even nine o'clock. What can I do for you in return?'

'Give us a ride,' Kane said at once. 'We're heading south too – for the moment. And we're as anxious as you to get out of town.' He turned to his men and murmured in English: 'This broad figures us for ordinary crooks – the homegrown variety. Don't let her think any different. She's all right, though: I met her before.'

'Surprise, surprise!' Zygmund said weakly from where he was sitting. 'I should be so lucky a girl like that she meets *me* in the middle of a mission!'

If Hilde was surprised to hear the foreign language, she made no sign. She was wearing no make-up today, and the lived-in face was a little haggard, but her figure was still remarkable in a neat dark grey suit and a cream silk blouse. 'Shall we go then?' she asked.

'If you don't mind waiting a few minutes,' Kane said, 'a friend of ours should be along soon.'

She shook her head. 'No problem. If it hadn't been for you, I'd be stuck here anyway.'

They made Zygmund as comfortable as they could on the spacious rear seat of the Minerva. Daventry and Fischer climbed into the tonneau with him. Kane recuperated the grenades and the Schmeisser machine pistols, stowing them beneath a valise of the girl's in the vast trunk fixed to the back of the coachwork. A quarter of an hour passed. Although he glanced frequently up the slant of hillside toward the wood, Kane saw no sign of Hawkins.

'If it's not indiscreet,' Hilde said, 'what are you planning this time? Another bank? Or are you on your way out after a heist?'

'No secrets between friends,' Kane replied, holding her gaze. He decided to back a hunch. 'Actually it's a mail train,' he said. 'We plan to blow a bridge later today and hold it up.'

'For the registered packages? You must be well briefed.'

'We are,' Kane said truthfully. 'You want to come in with us, Hilde? For a split of course. With Ziggy out of the race, we're a pair of hands short – and frankly we could use the car.' He paused. 'That is, unless all those police checks are for you, and you want out right away?'

'God, no!' She laughed. 'I'm not important enough for a general. They won't bother about me beyond the city limits – at least not until the next Wanted bulletin arrives by mail. So far as the car's concerned, Ferenc – my taxi driver – won't lose too much sleep if we arrive a day late. After all, I had broken down. And there's nothing he can do about it anyway.' She put a hand on his arm. 'I'd love to come in with you.'

'Swell,' Kane said. He looked once more up the empty slope of grassland. A breeze stirred the top branches of the trees in the wood. Bees hummed between cow parsley and clumps of valerian in the hedgerow. It was becoming uncomfortably hot in the sun.

Another fifteen minutes passed. There was still no sign of the big sergeant, no sounds of battle in the wood. At last Kane said: 'I'm going on up there and take a look around. Fischer – if I'm not back in, say, twenty minutes, abort the mission and get these guys out any way you can.' He turned, vaulted over the stile, and hurried away up the hill, thrusting his Walther PPK into his waistband.

The three men and the girl waited silently in the stuffy interior of the limousine. There was virtually no traffic on the country road. A tractor passed, towing a slatted trailer packed with live pigs. A bespectacled man in a smart blue two-seater drove by in the other direction. 'A doctor,' Fischer said.

'A local resident had failure of the heart due to over-excitement,' Zygmund said.

Eighteen minutes passed before they saw Kane once more. He strode quickly out of the wood and into the bright sunlight – alone. 'A mystery,' he said breathlessly when he reached the car. The shoulders of his shirt were dark with sweat and there were damp crescents beneath his arms. 'There's no sign of him anywhere – just a lot of spent shells on the ground. No sign of the cops either. Or their car.'

'So they took him,' said Fischer.

'I don't know. You see . . . the scout car's gone too.'

'So what? If they'd killed him with a lucky shot, or come up and captured him somehow, they'd have driven it away in convoy with their own, wouldn't they?'

'I guess so.' Kane sighed. 'In any case, there's nothing we can do. If they had taken him alive, we wouldn't know where to start looking for him.'

'What's the form then?' Daventry asked.

'We push on. The operation goes ahead.' Kane got in beside the girl and slammed the car door. 'I don't think anyone could make Hawkins talk, not even the Gestapo – but it's just as well I hadn't outlined our change of plan.'

'The Gestapo can make anyone talk,' Hilde said soberly. She drove the big car back on the road and accelerated away.

The silence lasted for some minutes. The road skirted farms, a belt of trees, a small lake. 'You said something about a change of plans?' Fischer said at last.

'Yeah.' Kane turned around, laying an arm along the mahogany frame housing the glass partition that could be wound up to separate the front of the Minerva from the rear. 'The original site I chose for the hold-up is out. It's too near the bloody dam. With all those cops on every road going that way, we'd never get near it.'

'So what do we do?'

Kane answered the question in a roundabout way. 'Because they're shit scared about this Russian attack,' he said, 'they're keeping the direct line from Linz to Prague free for munitions and troop trains. Low priority stuff is now routed north-west from Budejovice on the Plzen line, and then it swings around on the far side of the Vltava reservoirs and approaches the city from the west.'

'And that's the way our train will be coming?'

'That's what the guy in Linz told me.' Kane reached for one of the maps and shook it open. He held it out for Fischer and Daventry to see, tracing routes with a forefinger. 'Look – here's the direct line; here's the branch. Here are the reservoirs: Slapy, Kamyk, Orlik. I'd planned to attack between Slapy and the city . . . here, where the line crosses the valley. OK, that's out now. But see here, on the far side of Orlik: there's a confluence of two rivers, the Vltava and the Otava.' Kane tapped the map. 'And there's a fourth dam a few miles up the Otava, near a place called Pisek.'

'You're telling us the tracks bridge the valley below that dam too?' Fischer squinted at the map.

'Sure they do.' Kane opened one of the railway charts. 'And it says right here that there's a nine-arch viaduct there.'

'I know that bridge,' Hilde said suddenly. 'We used to picnic there in vacations. It's about 150 feet high in the centre, built on a curve. There's scrub on the valley floor, and woods on either side. I'd say it was a good place for an ambush.'

'Are you sure we can make it in time?' Fischer asked.

'I don't see why not,' Kane said. 'We have to take a wide sweep to clear the southern end of Orlik. But even allowing for detours to avoid patrols it's no more than fifty or sixty miles. The train won't be there until the end of the afternoon.'

'It's too bad about the sergeant,' Daventry said.

'It's always too bad,' Kane said shortly. 'But that's the way it goes. The mission comes first: you know that.'

For half an hour they travelled south-east, and then south through a network of minor roads, past small villages to a different world of wooden houses little more than chalets, goats and chickens behind picket fences, washing in the arms of wide women dressed in sweaters and gumboots, cows crossing the road, and then over a ridge to a bus terminus, trucks rusting on waste ground pitted with pools of stagnant yellow water, the drab grey of workers' tenements on the outskirts of a town. Steel-coloured smoke stained the blue sky above a factory chimney somewhere ahead.

There was an intersection ten miles short of Tabor, where a new concrete road led up toward wooded hills in the west. At one side of the crossing, a hoarding was filled with a giant poster showing three young men standing in front of a Nazi flag – a Brownshirt, an industrial worker, and a youth in Bavarian national costume. They had their arms around each other's shoulders, and beneath the square-jawed, unsmiling faces, gothic lettering spelled out the phrase: *Und Ihr Habt Doch Gesiegt*! – And nevertheless you won!

'Optimists already!' Zygmund said from the back seat. 'Why "nevertheless", I wonder? You think those are Jewish boys?'

Hilde swung the Minerva right up the new road. A mile further on – the road was curving through a dense pinewood – a small vehicle lay overturned in the ditch, its wheels as vulnerable as the legs of a dead bird. Beyond it, a large, heavily built man wearing blue dungarees and a fatigue cap held out a thumb in the internationally recognised hitch-hiker's plea. In his other hand, he held a bulging carpet-bag.

'*Hawkins, by God*!' Kane shouted, opening his door and leaping to the ground as Hilde braked the car. 'You old bastard! What the hell are you doing here?' he called joyfully, sprinting up and punching the big sergeant on the shoulder.

'Run out of juice, didn't I?' Hawkins replied, jerking

the thumb now toward the ditch. 'Thought it might take 'em longer to catch up if the heap was upside down, half-hidden in the bloody grass.'

'Yes, but . . .' Kane shook his head. 'Hell! I mean how . . . I told you before, now I'll say it again: you amaze me! How come you find yourself here? What happened in that wood? Spill it, for Christ's sake!'

'As to that,' Hawkins said, 'there was another track leading away through the trees. I said to meself, if I can get those coppers to follow me down there, I said, kind of draw them off like, then there'll be more time for the rest of 'em to scarper, I said. So I hopped in the scout car and away we went.' He chuckled. 'I meant to lose the buggers and then circle round and join you lot on the other side of the hill. Well, I lorst 'em all right. I think we must have bust the radiator as well as the screen, because they was steamin' like a bleedin' kettle when they ran orf the road! After that . . . well, I had to change me plans because I got caught up in that soddin' convoy. That was a bit of a barney, that was – gettin' shot of them!'

'But how come you happen to run out of gas and land up here, right here, smack in the middle of our revised route?'

'I could ask you the same, cock,' Hawkins said. 'Coincidence, that's what that is. They call it the long arm.'

'There's also the long arm of the law. How did you shake the convoy?'

Hawkins shuffled his feet. ''Fraid that was a bit noisy,' he said evasively. 'I couldn't keep out of trouble, the way you said we must. Tell you the truth, there was some shootin'. I had to run down a couple of fences and churn up a field of fuckin' cabbages before I . . . well, anyway, I drove through the plate-glass window of a chemist's and left everybody behind.'

'What about the Schmeissers?'

The sergeant coughed. 'I was out of the car with 'em at one time, and they . . . well, they got broke. A matter of a grenade,' he said. 'But I still got me pistol.'

'There were two cartridge belts.'

'They got left too. I packed all the ammo, though – what was left of it – along with Ziggy's 'tachy-case in this here carpet-bag.' Hawkins grinned. 'You want any cough mixture, aspirins, toothpaste? There's enough for a year underneath that old bus in the fuckin' ditch.'

'You're just not true, Sergeant,' Kane said.

A crafty smile illuminated the weathered façade of Hawkins's face. 'I thought you might be shirty,' he confessed, 'so I brought you a present.' He held up the carpet-bag – it was obviously very heavy – and pulled apart the handles to reveal the contents.

Packed around the attaché case, on a glittering bed of 9mm shells, a dozen bundles of what could have been fat candles stuffed the bag.

'Dynamite!' Kane breathed. 'Now *that* could excuse anything!'

'I found 'em lyin' around in a quarry, when I dropped in to borrow these overalls,' Hawkins said nonchalantly.

'In the circumstances, sir,' Kane told him, 'the least I can do – the very least – is to offer you a lift in our automobile.'

'Thanks very much. I don't mind if I do,' said the sergeant.

It was outside a village called Zahori, only a few miles short of Pisek, that the Minerva was flagged down for a routine check by a *Feldgendarmerie* patrol.

There were two motorcycle combinations, each with a machine gunner in the sidecar, plus an officer, an NCO and two more men standing beside a Hanomag scout car with a spare wheel mounted on the sloping bonnet. The officer and the NCO strode up to the driver's window while the soldiers unslung their carbines and the two gunners manoeuvred their weapons on rails so that the car was covered. 'Papers,' the officer demanded, holding out his hand. Hilde thrust out her own ID and documents relating to the car.

The officer flicked through them and then handed them

to the NCO. 'What are you doing so far from Prague? A taxi?' he asked.

She had been well briefed on that. 'This gentleman' – she indicated Zygmund behind the glass partition – 'has hired us to take him to Austria. An inspector from the supply ministry. He was injured in a terrorist attack in the city, and he has permission to convalesce in the Tyrol. As you see, he is in no state to travel by train.'

The German looked at Zygmund. He was comatose again. Daventry had fed him the last shot of morphine: a long car journey is not the most comfortable treatment for a man with a fractured pelvis. 'You have his papers?'

She opened the walnut lid of the glove compartment and handed over the passport, once Fischer's, that Zygmund had doctored for himself. With it there was an orange *Durchlassschein* – a special pass supposedly issued by the German authorities in Prague permitting the holder to make one round trip from Czechoslovakia to Austria, with a validity of one month.

The officer handed it back without comment. 'And for yourself and the car? You have the necessary *Ausweis*?'

'Naturally.' She produced a larger card, pale green, with her own *Personalangaben* – physical details – on the right, and a printed *laissez-passer* for herself and the Minerva on the left. Zygmund had concocted both cards from blanks in his forgery equipment during a stop earlier in the afternoon, before the rigours of the journey had sapped his strength again. The official stamps had been the least of the difficulties, since all the *Feldkommandantura* headquarters validated documents with the same logo: a circle surrounding a winged eagle with a swastika in its claws. Neither date nor office of origin was incorporated within the stamp.

The officer mouthed the wording on the pass aloud. '*Dieser Ausweis ist nicht übertragbar . . . im kleinen Grenzverkehr . . . Die besonders genehmigten Grenzübertrittsstellen . . .*'

Finally he handed them back and motioned the NCO

to return the other papers. 'And who are these men, these others?'

'I have no idea. They were walking. I picked them up a half hour ago. There are few buses in the region and it was far from the railway.'

Fischer was already holding his new papers and Daventry's out through the rear window. 'We missed the train. After a weekend in the country . . . you know how it is, *Herr Hauptmann*,' he said ingratiatingly. 'We have to be on duty at six . . . at the postal centre in Pisek, you understand . . . This lady kindly . . .'

The officer handed the papers to his NCO without looking at them. 'And you?' he asked Kane, glancing also at Hawkins.

'We work for the post office too,' Kane said. 'Telephone Service. Linesmen. We're not late, but there's work to do: faults in the signalling near Trebkov. With all this extra traffic, the whole sector's overloaded. And as for us, we're overworked, so it was kind of the lady to stop and offer us – '

'I thought,' Hilde said quickly, 'as I was coming this way, if I give one a lift, I might as well give them all. If it's a matter of the fifth passenger, when the taxi is only licensed for four, I can explain – '

'That is a matter for the Czech authorities,' the officer said in a bored voice. 'It does not interest me. You' – to Kane – 'do you know these other two?'

'Never saw them before,' Kane replied. 'We work the same sub-station, but I never set eyes on them.'

'We don't mix much with the chairborne brigade, the fellows with safe little jobs indoors in offices,' Hawkins offered.

One of the soldiers had flagged down an Adler saloon going in the opposite direction. Now a small bus full of women and children pulled up behind the Minerva. 'Very well,' the officer said. 'You are not the only one with work to do.'

He strutted across to the Adler, a spare man with a

lean, hardbitten face. The NCO handed back the papers and waved Hilde on.

'You know who that was, of course?' Kane said when the patrol was out of sight.

Fischer shrugged. 'He looked familiar, but . . .'

'The same guy who came on so strong about you importing idiot workmen from Austria – the man who almost tumbled to Daventry at the second road block on our way in to Prague last week.'

'Jesus!' Fischer said. 'I must say I'm glad I didn't catch on five minutes ago. No wonder he looked familiar!'

Five minutes later, Hilde took a secondary road that bypassed Pisek and led to the Otava Dam. Back at the checkpoint, the officer was plucking his lower lip as he stared down the dusty, empty road. The sun was low now, and his shadow was long. Four immigrant postal workers and an injured civil servant from Prague – why should the thought of four Austrians and a Czech stir something at the back of his mind that he couldn't quite bring to the surface?

Chapter 18

'It's all timing,' Kane said. 'The timing has to be one hundred and one percent accurate if we're going to pull it off. Here – I've done a rough sketch of the valley so you'll know what's where if we have to get out fast.'

He was standing with Hawkins, Fischer and the girl on a footpath that twisted through the scrub covering the valley floor. Above them, the viaduct's slender arches soared into

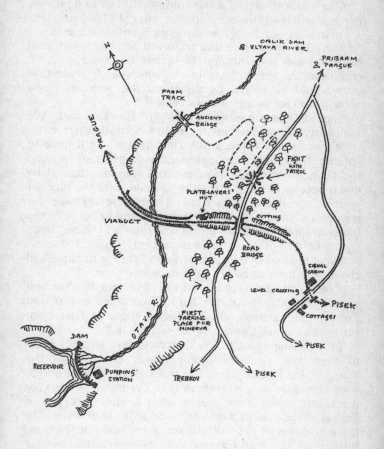

Kane's sketch-map

the afternoon sky; the dam was a mile away, invisible around a curve in the valley.

'One of these piers,' Kane continued, 'has to be blown the moment the train comes out of that cut.' He pointed to a gap in the trees that grew along the lip of the depression. 'If she goes up too late, the train will be across and we'll have lost our opportunity. Blow her too soon, and we could stall the preceding train . . . which would mean that ours would be halted by signals in the previous block section, too far away for us to reach.'

'Shouldn't be too much of a sweat,' Hawkins said. 'We got plenty of material, an' the right kind of detonator.'

'It's not that,' Kane said. 'The thing is, we'll have to split up, three and two. Someone has to be ready to jump the train the moment it stops; and someone has to be down here until the last minute to make sure the plunger goes down at the right time. There'll be no time for anyone to make it from here up to the tracks between the blow-up and the hold-up. The train will have been signalled out of the previous section: when it doesn't arrive at the end of this one, someone's going to come and check. We have to be out of here before then.'

'Right you are,' Hawkins said. 'Me and Fischer will handle the blasting down here. That'll leave you and *Fräulein* Finnemann and Raffles up there to bust open the mail vans and chuck out the sacks. OK?'

'Fine,' Kane agreed. 'We'll have to find another place to stash the car, somewhere nearer this end of the viaduct.' He looked up at the trees again. The Minerva, with Daventry as a watchman and Zygmund still out for the count in the rear, was hidden behind a screen of bushes at the side of a country road half a mile away. On the way down to the valley floor, Kane had noticed that, further on, the road traversed the railway cutting not far from the beginning of the viaduct. 'If we could run her down among the trees from that bridge,' he said, 'that would be jake.'

'I think you can do that,' Hilde Finnemann said.

'Sometimes, when we were children on holiday here from Austria, we would make our picnics down by the water.' She nodded toward the blue width of the river, still showing traces of foam from the sluices below the mile-away dam. 'And sometimes, if it was too hot, up · nong the trees there. I am sure there were motor cars too.'

Fischer asked, 'Which span do you think we should blow?'

'Towards the far side,' Kane said. 'To get as much of the train as possible isolated on the viaduct. I'd say the seventh or eighth pier, counting from this end.'

Hawkins picked up the carpet-bag. He stared up and down the valley. Upstream, the river glinted between alders, osiers, willow, carving an overhang on the outside of a bend, leaving a shingle bank on the inside. Below the viaduct, a farm track twisted through the scrub toward an ancient stone bridge. There were no vehicles on the track, nobody was on the bridge, the only sign of human habitation was a single white vapour trail looping across the blue sky. 'I reckon I could carry the material across right now and start working out the best way to get maximum blast effect,' Hawkins said.

Kane nodded, repressing a smile. He always marvelled at the contrast between the sergeant's correct, rather stiff German and the mind-blowing selection of expletives with which his English was peppered. 'You do that,' he said. 'We'll go back up and move the car. Then we'll backtrack down the line until we find the signal box controlling this section, and check out the time train 243 is due.'

He stopped and stared upwards. A horn blared somewhere among the trees. A moment later, a shunting locomotive hauling a dozen flatbed wagons loaded with tarpaulined munitions crates sidled across the viaduct. 'Use it while you can,' Kane said. 'We'll come back down, Sergeant, and put you in the picture as soon as we know the way the wind's going to blow.'

Hilde stopped the Minerva on the road bridge long enough

189

for Kane to see that there was no signal cabin in sight between the cutting and the next curve in the tracks half a mile away. 'No sweat,' he said. 'It'll take them longer to get here when they hear the bang.' He studied a road map of the area. 'If we go for a couple of miles and then turn sharp right,' he said, 'that road should bring us back to the tracks about a mile away, where there's a level crossing. What price a cabin there, where the signalman can do two jobs for the price of one – operate the gates and control the rail traffic?'

Kane was right. But the wood-roofed hut, with its wide windows, was right beside the roadway, and there were workers' cottages two hundred yards away. There would be no chance of jumping the signalman unobserved or putting pressure on him in any violent way. Kane attacked the problem in his usual positive manner. 'If we can't do it in secret,' he said, 'we'll do it openly. I'm going on in and ask.'

'You're crazy,' Fischer said.

'I know what I'm doing,' replied Kane. 'Hilde, let me out here, turn around, and drive back to the bridge. I'll join you there in a quarter of an hour or twenty minutes.'

The car was still some way short of the crossing. Kane took one of the blank Wehrmacht pay books from Zygmund's case and stuffed it in the breast pocket of his shirt so that the top showed but the part that would normally carry name, rank and an official stamp was hidden. He had borrowed Hawkins's long visored army fatigue cap before they left the viaduct. He was still wearing his officer's boots and breeches. Now, stuffing his Walther in his waistband, he left the Minerva and strode to the cabin. Before he reached it, Hilde turned the car and drove away.

Kane stomped up the three wooden steps and kicked open the door of the cabin. The signalman, a fleshy, moustached Czech of about sixty, was hunched over a newspaper that was spread on a shelf at one side of the shining bank of levers. He held a cup of ersatz coffee in one hand and a hunk of bread in the other. As the door crashed open, he straightened up, scowling. 'Who the devil – ?'

'Field Security,' Kane snarled. He was playing the German bully, relying on a hectoring, au' >cratic manner, the generally Brownshirt effect of his appearance, and the fact that the signalman was old enough to resent Hitler's annexation of his country, to stifle any awkward questions and cut short demands for identification.

'Field what? I never heard any – '

'Be quiet and listen to me,' Kane shouted.

'But the *Feldgendarmerie* . . . only half an hour ago . . .'

'Nothing to do with the *Feldgendarmerie*. I said Field Security. We have had reports that there's trouble expected in this sector. Trouble tonight. My colleague on the far side of the viaduct is dealing with that block section. I am responsible for this. Now, do as you are told or it will be the worse for you.'

'I don't understand.' The Czech was still truculent. 'Nobody told me anything – '

'Of course they didn't, you fool. That's the whole point: to keep the investigation secret. The saboteurs have accomplices among the railway personnel. Once it's known that we're checking up, they'll lie low and we shall lose our chance of unmasking them. Now – tell me what time train 243 is scheduled to pass through here.'

'Train 243? Why should you want to know?'

'Because that is one of the ones they want to wreck. Good God, do I have to write everything down? Train 243 and train 89.'

'I don't have that information,' the signalman said sullenly. 'I just close the gates and accept a train if I'm on a green, and then pass it on. If I'm on a red, then I set the Distant – '

'Of course you do not have the information,' Kane interrupted harshly. 'Nobody would expect a country bumpkin to have an entire wartime timetable at his fingertips. Do you think I don't know how the damned railways run?'

'Then I don't see. . . ?'

'You find out, you oaf. You have a telephone. You call Pisek and you ask. But you say nothing about any investigation, that is most important. Do you understand?'

The signalman shrugged. He moved over to a wall phone, unhooked the receiver and wound a handle. After a while he began speaking. The conversation was short. He replaced the instrument and turned to Kane. 'There is no train 89 – ' he began.

'Excellent,' Kane said without batting an eyelid. 'That shows that at least somebody is using his head. And train 243?'

By now thoroughly mystified – as Kane had intended – the Czech spread his arms in a helpless gesture. 'Not for at least another two hours. Maybe more. 243 is a special coming from – '

'I know where it's coming from.' Kane paused. A bell – one of a row above the levers – was shrilling. The signalman glanced at a light on an indicator board. He pulled one of the heavy levers and moved across to a huge iron wheel mounted vertically near the door. Spinning the wheel, he lowered the barriers with their trailing skirts of wire as a boy on a bicycle ducked his head and raced through. A woman behind him dismounted and wheeled her machine to the side of the road. On the other side of the tracks, two shabby private cars pulled up.

Soon, a three-coach local racketed past, draped with black smoke. The signalman spun the wheel. The traffic moved off. Kane said, 'I shall leave now to rejoin my colleague near the viaduct. Not a single word of this is to be communicated to anyone, do you understand? I shall call you later to find out the exact time of that train's arrival. You had better have the information ready – and I should advise you, unless you wish my report to be totally negative, to be a little more co-operative next time.'

'I am sorry, Herr . . . I didn't know,' the signalman stammered. 'I did not know that Field Security –'

'You know now,' Kane snapped. '*Heil Hitler!*'

Before the man could reply, he jerked open the door, ran down the steps, and strode off along the permanent way toward the viaduct.

Brigadier Honeywell took over the rostrum in the briefing hut from the intelligence officer. 'The fact is,' he told the pilots and navigators grouped in the hut, 'we suspect that the SOE johnnie over there has been nobbled. The last cypher we had was decidedly fishy. It's a book code that alternates except for the last two words – that was his personal sign-off. And, well, this one didn't.' He cleared his throat. 'You see, chaps, if the Jerries did take him, well, by now they'll know we intend to have a bash at their bally dam. So, to save you flying into a hornets' nest, so to speak, we're organising a little change of plan. The party's still on, of course, but we're going to switch targets a bit. Instead of blitzing the Slapy Dam, which is practically on the outskirts of Prague, we're aiming for a new dam on the Otava River, miles out in the country.'

'Jolly good show!' a pilot in the front row exclaimed.

'Wizard! A picnic instead of a firework display,' called another. And a third: 'Any other targets in the area, sir, if the dam's hit for six by the first wave?'

'Oh, yes,' Honeywell said. 'My friend here from the I Corps will brief you on the co-ordinates. There's an important railway junction near a place called Pisek. And a viaduct across the valley some way below the dam.'

Toward the end of the afternoon, a cloud front which had formed earlier over the Tyrol blew up from the south-west. By six o'clock the blue sky was a memory. When heavy drops of rain began to splash down onto the ballast between the rails, Kane kicked open the door of a plate-layers' hut and ushered Hilde inside. Fischer had gone back below the viaduct to tell Hawkins what the leader of the team had discovered from the signalman. Daventry was car-watching among the trees near the road bridge.

The hut was about ten feet square. Through the grimed panes of the solitary window, Kane gazed at the darkening sky. 'Just so long as the damned train isn't delayed,' he said. 'That's all we need – a dark wet night! What are we here? Central European Time, like the rest of Greater bloody Germany? It's not going to stay light long after eight, even if the clouds blow away.'

'It is quite a long time until eight o'clock,' Hilde said. She took off the grey jacket and hung it on a peg behind the door. A pair of dungarees were already draped over the peg.

'Too true,' Kane said absently. He was busy making an inventory of the hut's contents: coils of wire, shears, a red fire-bucket, sledgehammers and crowbars leaning against a wall. On a shelf in one corner, under a pile of steel pitons, he found what he was looking for – earphones, a mouthpiece, a plug and a length of cable: the headset used by linesmen to talk to signal cabins when they were perched on top of a telegraph pole. 'Now we can check the exact time the train is due without going back to the level crossing,' he said.

She was standing quite still in the middle of the hut, her arms straight down by her sides. 'What are you doing?' Kane said, his voice all at once hoarse.

'Waiting for you,' she said simply.

He sensed his pulses accelerating. It was very close in the confined space between the four wooden walls. Suddenly it was also totally quiet, as though the world outside had stopped turning. Gradually he became aware of their respiration, the two of them, breathing faster and faster. 'You feel it too, don't you?' Hilde said. 'I know you do.'

'Goddamn,' Kane choked, 'of course I do.' He had known all afternoon, felt the tension building with every mile they drove, felt it mount unbearably with a sideways glance, the hot pressure of a thigh on the broad front seat of the Minerva. His own tenseness, the coiled-spring energy that always vibrated within him before the action started, was clamouring for release exactly as it had been when he first met her in Prague. Well, not exactly: then it had been, in a way, a therapy, a catharsis; now it was an overmastering urge he would be unable to control even if he wanted to.

Matter-of-factly, she had unbuttoned the cream silk blouse and arranged it neatly over her jacket. The brassière she was wearing this time was white. There was no garter belt, he saw when she unhooked, unwrapped, and then stepped out of the skirt: her stockings, rolled down to the knee, were secured by a coin wrapped within the silk, in the French manner.

Bending, she slid her fingers inside the waistband of her white briefs and pushed them down, over the swell of hips, down her thighs and toward the ankles. At the last moment, she looked up at him from under raised brows and smiled.

In the gloom, her body held an almost translucent quality, like bone china. She opened her lips slightly as Kane moved toward her, moistening the top lip with the tip of her tongue.

He pulled her upright, and entered her still standing up, lifting her and then setting her down on him before they even kissed. She was wet the moment his fingers touched her. Kane closed his mouth over hers, intoxicated through all his senses.

Slowly, they sank to the beaten-earth floor, and as she locked her legs around him, his hands re-learned the lesson of her body. From the sucking clasp of her lips to the hollow of her throat, from the dark stiffness of her nipples to the triangle of damp curls below her stomach, she sent the same messages to his fingertips that they had received in the apartment off the Mostecka in Prague. Her nails dug and her teeth bit the same way; the same beads of perspiration dewed her upper lip and she hissed the same way instead of crying out in orgasm.

And yet it was not really the same at all. Reading his thoughts, she whispered: 'There, back in the apartment, it was, as you called it, fun. Here it is a need. There it was part of my profession; here it is because I want to, want to, yes, want to.'

The blood was singing behind Kane's eyes. 'Do you think I cannot tell the difference?' he murmured.

Later – the hair curling on the nape of her neck was damp too, and she was smoking – Kane sat up. He peered at her in the dim light and smiled. 'Yes, about that apartment . . .' he said.

She raised herself on one elbow. 'What about it?'

'It was just too good,' he said, 'that's what'.

'I do not know what you mean.'

'I think you do. It was too perfect – a set designer's dream, the décor for a business girl's hustling flat in a movie. Someone wanted everyone to believe that you were the perfect whore. But you're not really a whore at all, are you?' He paused. She made no comment. He went on. 'What are you, Hilde? Who are you really – and what were you doing there?'

A sudden gust of wind creaked the timbers of the hut and flung a scatter of raindrops against the window. They could hear the trees threshing on the lip of the cutting above them. After a while she said, 'You ask me three questions. Perhaps there are three different answers. Perhaps – like you yourself, *Herr Hauptmann* Bank Robber – I am indeed not altogether what I seem.'

Kane traced the swell of her belly with a finger-tip. 'The question still stands,' he said.

She grasped the hand and held it against herself. 'You ask what I am. I am quite amoral. You said sex should be "fun". I agree. But for me it is more than that: it is a fascination. The variations in men, the psychological differences, the *alien-ness* of another human being – one moment a cypher in an overcoat that cannot be decoded, the next moment as intimate as it is possible to be – this is what fascinates me.' She smiled, perhaps a little sadly.

'This . . . curiosity . . . is so strong in me that I cannot stay long with one person, I cannot keep a permanent attachment. I tire of a man quickly: it is always more interesting to see how different the next one will be.'

'And this is how you became a prostitute?' Kane used the harsh word deliberately, thinking of the literary works concealed in the drawer of the bedside table in her apartment. 'But is it why?'

'The profession is . . . convenient. As I have explained, the moral side does not interest me – with my particular outlook, I would be seeing a lot of men anyway. Commercially, it allows me to be independent. And after all I can select: I am not like some poor housewife stuck with a drab businessman for ever. Also it is the best cover possible for . . .' She paused. 'For something else.'

'And that is?'

'You asked me what I was doing – in that profession, in that apartment. I accept the question as a compliment. I will explain, therefore, that I have friends – *relations*, as the French say – in the underworld. I act for them, in a way, as a kind of look-out; a reconnaissance unit, if you like. With my connections, I can point out which clients have properties or businesses worth my friends' attention, which are likely to be police spies, which have useful connections in the black market or with the partisans. I can tell them, in case of need, who would be able to help and who cannot be trusted. Because men will confide in a whore things they would not even tell their wives. It is strange, but it is true.' Hilde smiled and shook her head, the pale hair swinging tawny in the gloom. 'I told you: I am quite amoral.'

Outside, the rain was falling steadily now. Kane heard it drumming on the asphalted roof of the hut. He said, 'There was a third question.'

'Who I really am?' The smile widened. 'That will have to wait for another time.' She reached for him and pulled him over her. 'In the meantime, I am not yet tired of *you*!'

Kane, at the top of a telegraph pole into which he had

knocked enough pitons to make the climb, leaned back from the insulators and connected the headset he had found in the hut. He had traced the line from the signal cabin when he regained the viaduct along the permanent way. The Czech signalman answered at ·nce. His voice was surly, but he had the information Kane needed. Train 243 was due at 19 hours 42. It would be preceded by a freight train and then a local going in the direction of Prague, and a diesel railcar travelling toward Pisek.

He shinned back down the pole and rejoined Hilde outside the hut. It was still raining. His shirt was drenched, her hair was already plastered to her skull. She had discarded the skirt and wore her jacket over the dungarees she had found behind the door. 'We have just over half an hour,' Kane said. 'I would like to move the car to the other side of the road bridge. The trees are thicker there, but there's a way in and we can leave it nearer the tracks.'

Hawkins and Fischer, the charges in place, had already climbed up from the valley to shelter in the Minerva. Kane and Hilde slid into the front seat and the girl resumed her place behind the wheel. She started the motor and drove out onto the road.

It was unfortunate that the German patrol, at that moment, was approaching the bridge from the other direction. Less fortunate still was the fact that it was the same patrol which had stopped them near Pisek earlier in the afternoon. Worst of all, Daventry and Fischer had claimed to be in a hurry to reach that town by six o'clock – and here they were, heading away from it, more than an hour later. It was an odd route, too, for Hilde to be taking if she was heading for Austria.

On the positive side, it was perhaps fortunate that they had already removed the Schmeissers from the luggage trunk, reloaded them, and stowed them in the interior of the limousine.

Perhaps. It depended – Kane thought as these pros and cons flashed through his mind – on what the *Hauptmann* in charge of the patrol decided to do. If it was going to be just one more cross-examination, which maybe they could talk their way out of, any visible weapons would kill their chances. If on the other hand they were to be ordered out of the car, searched, possibly arrested, then the guns would be their only hope.

The question was quickly answered. The officer in the scout car took in the situation at a glance. Perhaps, suddenly, he made the connection: four Austrians and a Czech . . . the spurious Todt workers and their 'contractor' . . . that four-day-old report about foreign saboteurs . . . the hold-up killers sought by the Prague police . . . At any rate, he was shouting and waving his arms as soon as he recognised the Minverva.

One of the motorcycle combinations raced past the car and skidded to a halt, blocking the road behind it. The other drew up beside the scout car, barring the way ahead. 'Put your foot down,' Kane hissed to the girl. 'Keep low. Make for the trees.'

The German and his two guards were leaping from the scout car, guns at the ready. Hilde stomped the pedal flat and wrenched the Minerva off the road, smashing through underbrush into an alley beneath the trees. A lot of things happened at once then.

Kane hit the passenger door with his shoulder and rolled out of the car as it jounced over a shallow ditch. He came up with his elbows on the lip of the depression, the Schmeisser in his hands already spitting fire. Daventry knocked out the car's rear window and fired a staccato burst at the men in the first combination. Fischer emptied his Walther in the direction of the other combination and the scout car: At the same time the officer began shooting and a fusillade of 9mm slugs hosed toward the Minerva from the scout car and the sidecar machine gunner beside it. No shots came from the first combination: Daventry's initial burst had taken them by surprise – the rider had been hurled backwards off the saddle; the gunner slumped forward in his cockpit, canting the Parabellum skyward on its rail.

The Minerva jarred to a stop twenty yards inside the wood with a screech of tortured metal: the radiator fan had disintegrated under a hail of lead. Glass shivered and fell from the windows, the windscreen went opaque, the back tyres were in ribbons. As Hawkins and Daventry fell out of the rear door on the side away from the Germans and began firing from underneath the car, a double line of bullet holes pierced the trunk and swept along the side of the tonneau. Hawkins pushed Zygmund to the floor before he dived; Hilde was crouched down under the dashboard, her back against the steering post.

One of the guards from the scout car fell under Kane's first volley. He lay twitching in the centre of the roadway. The officer and the other guard leaped to the far side of the vehicle and began firing over the spare wheel clamped to the bonnet. The two men from the surviving combination were using handguns from the ditch behind them. Kane felt chips of stone from the roadside sting his cheek as a near miss ricocheted off into the trees.

He squeezed the trigger again. The machine pistol roared, bucking and jumping in his hands. The scout car's windscreen shattered. He lowered the muzzle, firing beneath the chassis. There was a strangled cry, and the man standing beside the officer spun to the ground with his shins splintered. From the corner of his eye, Kane saw a shadow reflected in the wet macadam: someone had crawled away and was dashing across the road higher up in an attempt to enfilade them. He jerked around, trying to sight the Schmeisser, but the barrel fouled the stalks of ferns dripping above the ditch. Behind him, shots ripped out from beneath the wrecked Minerva. The German stumbled, fell, rolled over, kicked once or twice and then lay still. His machine pistol skated away and vanished in the verge.

For a moment there was silence: nobody was shooting on either side. Rain bounced off the roadway. A fragment of glass tinkled to the ground. The officer had disappeared from behind the scout car's bonnet. Suddenly Kane saw him: he was hunched down with the driver, sheltered by the car's wheel. Kane heard voices. Mechanical voices? Goddam! The man had unhooked a radio-phone from underneath the facia and was reporting to base, probably, almost certainly, calling up reinforcements . . .

'*Hawkins*!' Kane yelled. 'Stop them! The grenades!'

The big sergeant had already seen for himself. If they could silence the officer before he had pinpointed their position or transmitted co-ordinates. . . ?

He reached through the open door of the Minerva and grasped one of the stick grenades they had taken from the sentries in Prague. He scrambled to his feet and advanced between the bushes, running.

The driver and the surviving machine-gunner opened fire again, while the officer went on talking. Muzzle flashes flickered brightly against the darkness of the trees as lead ripped through the leaves. Hawkins weaved left, right, left again. Ten yards from the road, where the trees were thinner, he drew back his arm.

The firing continued. Kane heard Daventry cry out in pain.

The grenade sailed through the rain lancing down on the road.

Above the scout car, there was a blinding yellow flash. Momentarily, the cracking blast of the explosion rendered Kane deaf. When the ringing in his ears faded, he heard nothing but the steady drip of rain from the trees. Leaves were still fluttering down from the savaged branches across the road.

The German military vehicle was on its side, the steel body-work distorted and pitted with shrapnel. One of the wheels turned slowly. Behind it, flames licked a length of field-grey officers' cloth that covered a tangle of limbs and flesh. The man whose shins had been shattered was no more than a stain in the roadway. 'There should be one more,' Kane said. 'We knocked out four before you launched the grenade. We have the officer, the driver and the guy with broken feet here. It's the second machine gunner. Where is he?'

Twenty feet away among the trees, they found something bloody that flopped from side to side in the undergrowth. Kane hesitated. 'You can't do nothing, squire,' Sergeant Hawkins said. 'He'd be a goner before anyone arrived to pick up the pieces. Th e's fuck-all we can do. It'd be kinder, an' that's the truth.'

Kane nodded. He took the Walther from his waistband and fired three shots.

By the carcase of the Minerva, Daventry sat among wet leaves clasping his left upper arm. Blood seeped through his fingers and stained his suit. 'It's only a flesh wound. Bastard nicked the muscle,' he said through clenched teeth. 'Don't half sting, though!'

'We'll fashion a tourniquet, fix you in a minute,' Kane said. He walked around to the driver's side. Hilde was still crouched beneath the wheel, shuddering. Her hand was over her eyes. From the floor behind the partition, Zygmund said sleepily: 'A fine thing! They have six people in a seven-seater limousine – two in the front, three in the back, and two tip-up seats already – and the guy with a broken spine, he has to sit on the floor!'

'Five people, Ziggy,' Kane said.

Fischer was leaning forward, his head and shoulders through the partition. His eyes and mouth were open, and his chin was red. Pooled blood on the seat below was already congealing. The first volley fired by the German machine-gunner had perforated the coachwork and thrashed across his back, cutting him almost in two and killing him instantly.

'We'll have to leave him with the Krauts. There's nothing else we can do,' Kane said ten minutes later, when they had hastily recuperated the bodies and laid them out as decently as they could beneath the trees. 'At least they'll bury him, which is more than we have time to do.' The wreck of the scout car had been pushed back onto its wheels and manhandled, along with the two combinations, as near as possible to the Minerva. 'They won't be hidden from anyone looking for them,' Kane said, 'but once it's dark they shouldn't be too obvious to a passer-by.'

It was clear that it would be dark very soon. The rain had slackened and finally stopped, but the sky was still covered with ragged clouds hurrying north. Night was going to fall at least half an hour earlier than was usual for mid-August.

To Kane's astonishment, he found that the entire action, including the cleaning up, had taken no more than a quarter of an hour. It was 19 hours 25: they had seventeen minutes before train 243 was due.

'Ziggy, I'm afraid we're going to have to leave you here,' Kane said. 'We'll come back for you when it's all over . . . if we can. In the meantime, we'll leave you a Schmeisser, a pistol and the remaining grenade.'

'If you get held up,' Zygmund said with a brave attempt at a smile, 'I can always take a train.'

'How the hell do we get out of here when we do come back?' Daventry asked. 'The blooming heap's snafu, and the buses around here seem about as frequent as a No.11 in the smoke.'

'Christ knows,' Kane replied. 'You'd better take Fischer's place with Sergeant Hawkins. Don't use that left arm: you can fire the Schmeisser one-handed if you have to. The girl and I will have to handle the train on our own.' He shrugged. 'We'll work out the getaway when – and if – the time comes. Right now, the important thing is to get that bloody letter.'

'Now he tells us!' Zygmund said.

As the four of them hurried along the road toward the railway line, smoke jetted up from each side of the bridge. They heard the hiss of steam and the panting of a locomotive hauling a heavy load. A whistle blew. The freight train was passing on its way to Prague.

Chapter 19

Train 243 was short – three boxcars and a brake van hauled by a saddle-tank shunting loco. 'I can't be sure of making the viaduct in time,' Kane had told Hilde. 'I want you to take one of the machine pistols and hurry along the tracks as fast as you can. Wait at the beginning of the viaduct, and when the train stops take care of the guard or brakeman, if there is one, and then join me by the cab.'

'How will you get there if you say you can't – ?'

'I'm going to jump off the bridge as the train passes underneath.'

'You're crazy!' Hilde breathed. 'You'd never make it. Supposing it's going fast?'

'Don't worry,' he had smiled. 'I've done it often enough before: I was once a stuntman in movies.'

Now he was waiting, a Schmeisser slung over his shoulder, his hands on the parapet – ready to hide the gun if anyone passed on the road, to vault over if the train came.

The local puffed by, whistling, on the up line. A few minutes later he heard it rattling across the viaduct. Two minutes after that, there was a distant hoot, and the railcar clacked past in the opposite direction. Kane saw that the bridge was low: the highest point of the arch was only a couple of feet above the railcar roof. He heard the jangle of lineside wires as the Distant semaphore jerked up to Stop.

He looked at his watch. Another three minutes.

Kane became aware of the thrumming of the rails below before he actually heard the train. The wires moved again. The Home signal showed green.

Billows of smoke, dark against the darkening sky, fountained up as the train approached. The steel tracks sang. The locomotive pistoned beneath the bridge with sparks fountaining from its smokestack. Kane was on the parapet. He balanced, counting the boxcars as they emerged from the arch. One . . . two . . . three . . . Just before the fourth emerged, he jumped.

What he had not bargained for was the clerestory roof – a raised centre-section with narrow transom windows let into the sides – that divided the top of the brake van. Clearly they were dragging out ancient rolling stock for their specials!

Kane hit the raised portion with his left foot, perfectly in equilibrium. But the right, following through, had eighteen inches further to drop. The right leg folded, all of Kane's weight thrown upon it as he pitched forward. He sprawled headlong on the roof, still slippery with soot and rain. Fortunately the train was not going fast – perhaps thirty miles per hour – or he would certainly have been projected over the edge. As it was, he slid, skidded, and finally pulled himself up short grasping the ladder fixed to the end of the van. He pulled himself upright, swayed, and began a crouched, loping, stop-and-start run over the roofs toward the front of the train. Just as long as he pulls the whistle cord, Kane thought – pausing and then gathering himself for the five-foot leap to the next boxcar. *Whistle, you bastard. Pull the fucking cord*! All of the others had whistled before the viaduct, whichever way they came. And the whistle had to blow, because that was the signal for Hawkins to detonate the charge that would blow the bridge. Momentarily, smoke obscured his view.

If Hawkins heard no whistle – Kane jumped again – he might react too slowly to press the plunger before the train had passed. And once beyond the viaduct, even if he could force the train to stop and overpower the crew singlehanded, the time element before the others could catch up would almost certainly bitch the whole plan. He leaped for the front boxcar, missed his footing, and fell on his hands and knees. *Whistle, for the love of God*! Smoke blinded him again.

Raising himself cautiously, Kane could see the inside of the cab of the locomotive. It was dusk in there already:

flame flickered red on the face of the engineer's mate as he shovelled coal into the firebox. The driver himself was leaning out of the window, staring ahead while the tanker rounded the curve that led to the viaduct. He reached a hand up inside the cab and pulled.

A whistle blast echoed off the rock walls of the cutting.

The walls diminished, fell away on either side. The train ran out into the open. The shining rails curved into space.

Kane briefly glimpsed the girl as they trundled past the stone pillars at the entrance to the viaduct. Then a thunderous explosion rocked the sky. For a hundredth of a second, before dark smoke boiled up on either side of the tracks, what remained of the daylight was dimmed by the flash. While fragments of stonework trailing fiery tails still arrowed through the air, the permanent way shivered. Toward the far end of the viaduct the parapet, carrying lengths of iron railing with it fell away. And then, as the mined pillar below disintegrated, a whole portion collapsed into the void.

The sound of the explosion was prolonged by the roar of falling masonry. A tower of yellow plaster dust ballooned out and obliterated the smoke. Brakes hissed, screamed; locked wheels slid on wet rails. The train shuddered to a stop.

Fifty yards ahead of the locomotive, warped rails festooned with sleepers fishboned into the gap where one span of the viaduct had disappeared. Kane was standing on top of the coal in the tanker's stubby tender, pointing his Schmeisser at the cab. 'All right,' he called. 'Out of there and onto the track. Nobody's going to get hurt so long as they behave.'

He jumped down to the footplate. The engineer and the fireman still looked shocked. They clambered to the ballast and stood looking from Kane to the ruin ahead. 'What the devil – ?' the driver began.

'No questions,' Kane snapped. He motioned them towards the rear of the train. Hilde was standing by the brake van. 'There must be a manpower shortage,' she said. 'There's no guard.'

He nodded, staring up at the van. The sliding doors to the freight compartment had jerked open with the sudden stop. Crated machinery took up all the space; there were no mail sacks. Flat steel bars that could be slotted across to lock the doors hung down the wooden sides of the van. 'Where's the mail?' Kane asked.

'The first and second boxcars,' the engineer said.

'Are they locked?'

'Only the second, where the registered stuff is. You're not going to – ?'

'I said no questions. Get up in there.' Kane motioned toward the freight compartment with the Schmeisser. When the two men were inside, looking more scared than ever, he slammed shut the doors on either side and dropped the locking bars in place. 'You take the registered stuff. Shoot away the lock,' he said to the girl. 'I'll handle the rest.'

She looked at him curiously. 'Do you think you'll find anything of value among – ?'

'Talk later,' he interrupted. 'We don't have much time.'

There were about fifty sacks in the leading boxcar. As he heard the girl's machine pistol smashing the locks of the second, he began feverishly hauling them to the door and throwing them out onto the line. The fifth sack bore the stencilled code 15AF/463/BG. Kane breathed a heartfelt sigh of relief. He tossed out another sack, and another.

On the ninth, at last, he saw the legend 15AF/464/BG.

He picked it up, jumped from the boxcar, and ran to the edge of the viaduct. They were well wide of the river. Somewhere below, veiled by smoke and dust or hidden among the scrub, Daventry and Hawkins would be waiting to start sifting through the contents. He blew three blasts on his whistle and dropped the sack over.

All that remained now was to amass enough sacks to convince Hilde that they really were after the contents for their value. He looked at the second boxcar. She already had a dozen or more stacked between the rails and the parapet. 'I'll help you with those,' he offered. 'You were right: there's nothing much in here.'

She favoured him once again with a quizzical regard but said nothing. Kane climbed into the boxcar and began passing out the registered sacks, which were closed at the mouth with wire.

They had shifted perhaps another dozen when he became aware of a distant but continuous mechanical whirring. He ran to the far side of the viaduct and peered over. On the farm track that crossed the river further down the valley he saw two motorcycle combinations, a scout car, and three half-track troop carriers full of German soldiers. They were winding toward a hill that climbed up to the wood and the road where Kane's team had fought the patrol.

'Jesus!' he exclaimed. 'The reinforcements they called up. They must have gotten through before we zapped them after all!'

'It won't be long before they find the bodies?' she said.

'Damn right. There's no train due, either way, for another twenty minutes. But we better get out of here, fast. We'll throw these sacks over and go join Hawkins as quickly as we can.' He was already moving toward the registered mail, but his last words were drowned by a scream of aero engines as a flight of three RAF Mosquitoes swooped low across the valley and headed for the dam.

Pilot Officer Keith Waterstone flicked his control column nonchalantly from side to side as he swerved the fighter-bomber this way and that, surveying the wooded, hilly country fifteen hundred feet below. His wing man and the third pilot in the flight held a steady course. Everyone knew that old Piss-Pierre was a bit of a line-shooter who liked to put on the dog. There was no need for the whole squadron to play silly-buggers just because the boy was on form.

A stiffish breeze had blown away the cloud cover, just

as the met man said it would, and there was a touch of pink in the sky above the undulating horizon in the west. But down below the valley was in shadow: it must be almost dusk down there. Above the treetops, Watersone could see orange flashes and a column of black smoke where the first two flights were laying their eggs on the dam.

Or were they? He banked and stared down through the perspex nose canopy of the Mosquito. There was more smoke down there, obscuring the pewter ribbon of the Otava. And – yes! – the viaduct that old Honeybum had told them about during the briefing. There was a train in the centre of the bridge, and . . . 'I say!' Waterstone exclaimed. 'They must have done in the jolly old dam during the first wave. Because, look, some of the boys have already had a go at the viaduct! See – the span in front of the train's gone for a Burton.'

'You want to see if we can knock down the rest, K.W?' Rusty Moran, his Canadian sergeant-navigator, asked.

'Why not, why not?' Waterstone kicked the Mosquito into a steep bank, signalling the other two planes to follow him and pointing down with a gloved finger. 'And, *look*! Whizzo! There's some kind of Jerry convoy down there too. They're firing up at us, what's more. Bloody cheek! We'll give them a squirt or two with the cannon after we've pranged the bridge.' The three twin-engined fighter-bombers soared up above the lip of the valley, turned in formation, and zoomed down toward the viaduct in a shallow dive.

'Angel Red, Angel Red!' the voice of the wing controller rasped in the pilot's earphones. 'Light flak and no bandits over the dam. We've put the pumping station U.S. and bounced a couple against the base of the barrage, but the dam's still not breached. Red, Green and Blue – aim for the lip with everything you've got.'

'Dammit, we'll have to leave the viaduct after all,' said Waterstone. But Rusty Moran already had one of the arches in his sights and had pulled the toggles that released their bombs.

Hawkins and Daventry had sorted through less than half of the letters in the missing sack when the first wave of Mosquitoes made their run. The sergeant – by no means a pessimist – had already given up. 'It's fuckin' hopeless,' he grumbled. There were hundreds of letters in the sack and the light was fading fast. 'Look for one that's different from all the others, he says. *All* the bleeders are different in this light. Or else they're all the sodding same. It depends, dunnit?'

They were sitting on the bank of the river, in a clearing surrounded by alders. When it became obvious that the planes were attacking the dam, Hawkins began stuffing the envelopes back into the sack. 'We'll have to find time somewhere else,' he said. 'If they breach her and she blows, half this bloody valley's going to be under water, an' we can't afford to get caught in that lot.'

'At least we know we've got it,' Daventry said, nursing his arm.

Sacks, plain and registered, began dropping from the viaduct when the raid started. Daventry and the sergeant recuperated as many as they could and carried them to higher ground. When Keith Waterstone led his flight back down to attack the bridge, they were half-way up the slope on the far side of the valley.

Rusty Moran was a professional. His aim was good. The first of the Mosquitoes' 250-lb bombs burst a few yards from the base of one of the piers supporting the central arch. The second was a direct hit half-way up the pillar.

The stone column shivered and leaned inward, finally cascading to the ground in a shower of dust and granite blocks. The arch and the permanent way above it, which carried most of the weight of the train, subsided, cracked, and disintegrated. As it fell, the other pillar, weakened by the bomb burst so near its base, crashed down with it. For a frozen moment the train, held up only by the steel rails draped over the abyss, hung in space. Then it tipped sideways. The locomotive plummeted down, dragging the four coaches after it. The rails snapped. And half the next pillar too, having lost the anchorage that held it rigid, toppled into the valley.

The noise was appalling. A grey-brown cloud billowed out, rolled up the valley walls, and rose hundreds of feet into the air. Waterstone's two companions dropped their bombs into the maelstrom. The sounds of their cannon attack on the convoy were lost in the uproar.

'Blimey!' said Hawkins. It was the strongest word in his vocabulary, and he seldom used it. 'That's torn it, then. That's what that's done and no mistake: that's fuckin' torn it.'

'You can say that again,' Daventry agreed. 'Look there.' He pointed upwards.

Hawkins craned his neck. Another squadron of Mosquitoes passed overhead on their way to the dam. Then he saw what the safe-breaker meant. Between the gap torn by their dynamite and the larger hole blasted by the bombs, a single pillar of stone still stood. Two ragged quadrants – all that remained of an arch on either side – sprouted from the top. And surmounting these was a short length of track bordered by parapet and rail.

Silhouetted against the evening sky, two figures grasped the rail and stared down into the desolation below.

Kane and Hilde Finnemann were marooned, more than one hundred feet from the ground, on a teetering column that swayed already in the rising wind . . . and could be brought crashing down at any moment if the dam was breached and floodwaters raged through the valley.

Chapter 20

'Well', Kane said, 'I guess that's it. I hope Hawkins and Daventry have the sense to get the hell out while they can. And I hope they remember to collect poor Ziggy first. So far as we're concerned, honey . . .' He shrugged.

'What do you mean?' Hilde asked.

He gave a crooked smile, gesturing left and right at the ragged, ten-yard length of track on which they were isolated. Cinders, granite chips and fragments of ballast were still detaching themselves from each end, where the rails drooped down toward the dust and smoke eddying below. 'I don't imagine that Colbert – That is to say, I can't see anyone steaming up this valley in a chopper and take us off,' he said. 'And if the boys in blue hole that bloody dam, they wouldn't have time anyway: this pillar's about as steady as a drunk on Christmas Eve.'

'We don't need any helicopter,' the girl said. 'All we have to do, after all, is climb down.'

Kane stared at her. 'You must be joking,' he said.

Hilde shook her head. 'No, no. I have looked. Certainly it is too smooth until the ledge where the arches begin, but after that it is no more difficult than a cliff face. And as for the smooth part, we have this.' She picked up a coil of rope. 'I brought it from the plate-layers' hut,' she explained, 'in case we had to tie up the crew or anything.'

Kane looked over the edge. Now that the viaduct on either side had gone, the pillar seemed fragile beyond belief, dizzily high and unstable as hell. 'No more difficult than a cliff face,' he said. 'I see. As simple as that.'

She was knotting one end of the cord around the railing. 'Really,' she said. 'You must not let the thought – or the height – put you off. Mechanically, it is not difficult. If you were only a few feet from the ground, on a beach for example, you would do it without thinking. Looking for birds' eggs, or a wildflower you wanted.'

'Oh, sure,' he said. 'Money for old rope!'

'Have you done any mountaineering?'

'A little rock climbing. But I'm not a professional like you.'

She smiled. 'There has to be a first time.'

And a last, Kane thought. He took a deep breath. What the hell. It was the end anyway, the last time for everything – unless they took this one crazy chance. It was all very well for her to say it was easy: to him that chance seemed a million-to-one outsider. But what, after all, did they have to lose? He prided himself on picking up a challenge: this might be his final opportunity! 'OK,' he said firmly, 'let's not waste any more time. You're the boss on this one: who goes over the side first?'

'You do,' she said. 'I am less likely to fall, but if you are above me and you fall, you will take me down with you.'

He nodded. 'Good thinking.' As he swung his leg over the rail, there was a subdued rumble from his right. Ballast and chunks of stone pattered down into the void. The floor beneath the permanent way trembled. A series of fissures snaked out from the parapet, and a whole section of the lip crumbled and fell away.

When the noise had subsided, Hilde said, 'It is not so much the difficulty of the climb – that, after all, is partly within our control. It is a question of whether we can do it in time – before the whole of this column collapses.'

He was on the far side of the rail, his back to the drop as he took the strain of the rope. 'I'll be as quick as I can,' he said. 'Just so long as I don't fuck up and take the quickest way of all!'

'You won't,' Hilde said.

Kane clenched his teeth and braced his feet against the stonework. Hand over hand, he lowered himself down the rope. About this part of the descent, for an ex-stuntman there was no difficulty. As the girl said, it was only the thought of the drop yawning behind that complicated the manoeuvre. In fact the rope reached some way below the narrow ledge where the arches had curved away from the top of the pier. Taking a turn around his wrist, he made use of its entire length. But finally he arrived at the crunch moment, the moment of truth: he had to let go of the rope and continue on his own.

Kane stared at the granite blocks in front of his face. He felt for, and found, a crevice into which he could insert one toe. He tested it to see if it would bear his weight, and it held. He found another crack. And a third, above him and to the left, for the fingers of one hand.

He let go of the rope.

This was the point of no return. He was alone, spreadeagled like a fly against the crumbling fabric of the pillar almost one hundred feet above the ground. He swallowed, preparing himself for the nightmare descent. The masonry had been eroded by wind and weather. And while this meant that the gaps between the dressed granite blocks were more frequent, it meant also that rain turned the crumbs of old mortar and flakes of decomposed rock into a greasy paste in which fingers and toes could skid more easily than grasp.

Kane knew that he must keep his eyes fixed rigidly on the stone immediately in front of his face. All of his concentration must remain in the fingers and toes searching for crevices beneath him. If he allowed his gaze even once to stray down or outwards, he could be lost. He must will himself into a one-dimensional world where there was no past and no future, no time and no space but the few square feet of rotted stonework before his eyes. 'Fischer,' he murmured, 'I'm beginning to understand how you felt!'

For a few seconds he remained still, his cheek pressed to the cold, damp granite, willing himself to move. Then he lowered his free hand, groped for a crack at the level of his waist, tested it, rested his weight on it as he let go of the first crevice and searched for a fissure further down still, dislodged one foot from its resting-place and probed unseeingly for another that would again take his weight below, repeated the move with his other foot . . . and so on, stone by stone and inch by inch, as the wind plucked at his clothes and the light gradually faded. Only two factors served to ameliorate the situation; to take the task out of the realm of the impossible into the barely conceivable – first, the fact that the pillar tapered towards the top meant that it sloped very slightly away from him as he went down, so that he could lean himself against it without feeling the whole of his body weight trying to tear him away from the face; secondly, the blocks of which it was built became progressively larger toward the foot of the column, so that the interstices between them where the mortar had crumbled away should grow proportionately more important.

Even so, each foot of the descent was a hellish test of will-power, coaxing muscles and overtaxed sinews to hang on for just that second longer while the questing toe sought a temporary resting-place that would take the strain, the fingers searched for a cleft that would not flake away the instant any weight was put on it.

Kane began to suffer from hallucinations. He was still no more than a foot away from the rope. Hilde had passed him on the other side of the pillar and gone off with the others. He had reversed his direction without realising it and was climbing up instead of down.

But gradually he began to make progress. The blocks increased in size, the cracks between them grew wider and easier to find. He passed a section where whole chunks of masonry had fallen away and he could wedge himself in the gap like a mountaineer in a chimney.

The second wave of fighter-bombers attacked the dam. He heard the explosions over the moaning of the wind. The column shuddered each time the planes roared overhead.

Hilde was already on the way down. From time to time rock chips or crumbs of mortar pattered onto his shoulders, and once, in a lull between two waves of raiders, he heard the scrape of feet above him. Was she wearing boots or shoes? He couldn't remember. There had been the grey suit, the cream silk shirt . . . the weight of a breast in the warmth beneath the shirt . . . a wet heat in the gloom of the hut. *Never mind. Concentrate on the stonework. A crevice for the left hand . . . the left hand!* . . .

For several eternities he inched his way down. Above the wooded horizon in the east, a single star glittered in a violet sky from which all clouds had disappeared. Kane was focusing his attention so ferociously on the fissured blocks in front of his face that when his lowered foot struck against something hard, he cried aloud in surprise and alarm. Daring at last to look down, he saw that he was standing on top of a great slant of rubble formed by the ruins of the adjacent arch.

He had made it! Why the hell should he have had any doubts? The girl had told him he could make it. So why should he find that he was supported on rubber legs? The tortured muscles of his wrists and calves were fluttering. He held out his arms as she turned and jumped the last few feet and embraced her, feeling the blood from his lacerated fingertips warm against his palm.

'My God,' Kane said, 'when I think what I would have been paid for that if I'd been doubling for Fairbanks or Flynn!'

She squeezed his hand. 'There is somebody calling to us from below,' she said.

Hawkins and Daventry were on the slope of the hillside beneath the remnants of the viaduct. 'I'd leg it over here, mate, if I was you,' the big sergeant called. 'I think the bleeders buggered up the dam with the last lot.'

'By God, I think he's right,' Kane exclaimed. The drone of the last plane had faded and died; the distant flak batteries were silent. But far away beneath the evening sky a sullen roar, faint at first but rapidly gaining in volume, was audible.

'Quick,' he urged. 'Let's get as far up the slope as we can.' Leaping from block to block of the fallen masonry they made the valley floor and began scrambling up between the bushes towards the two men. The noise was getting louder every second – a menacing, rushing thunder of sound that reminded Kane of a hurricane he had once experienced in the Pacific. A puff of warm wind gusted against them. On all sides, flocks of startled birds rose into the dusk. 'Jesus!' he said. '*By Christ, would you look at that!*'

Two of the raiders' 250-lb bombs had fractured the lip of the dam about fifty feet apart. A third – dropped by a plane in the previous wave – had already exploded against the sloping wall of the barrage at a point equidistant from those bursts. Now, suddenly, cracks in the concrete zigzagged between the three weakened areas. Subjected to the remorseless pressure of hundreds of millions of gallons of water, the wedge of masonry between them erupted outwards, allowing the contents of the reservoir to surge through the breach. The gigantic outrush of water hurtled to the valley floor, throwing a cloud of dust and spume and debris hundreds of feet into the air. And as the flood seethed through the gap, widening the breach as it went, a twenty-foot tidal wave swept down the valley, destroying everything in its path.

Kane and his companions saw a solid wall of water advancing towards the viaduct, an unbroken, terrifying wave whose frothing crest was jagged with planks and crates and uprooted trees.

The wave raced past ten feet below them, thundering between the remaining piers of the viaduct, carrying away the shattered boxcars and the wreck of the locomotive, tumbling blocks of fallen masonry as if they had been pebbles. Behind it raged the floodwaters, foaming in the dusk already with flotsam torn from the hillsides.

The tidal wave was still in sight when a low, rumbling roar shook the ground at their feet. The base of the solitary pillar on which Kane and Hilde had been marooned exploded outwards with the force of the current; the column swayed, leaned sideways, and collapsed into the flood.

Chapter 21

'They say disasters come in threes.' Hilde raised her voice to make herself heard over the roar of the torrent scouring the valley from one hillside to the other. 'We already suffered the meeting with that patrol, the loss of your friend Fischer, and then the raid. Maybe we should be all right from now on?'

'I don't know that I'd call the raid a disaster,' Kane objected. 'If the planes hadn't come, there'd have been plenty of folks around pretty damned quick to find out what the hell, after the viaduct was blown. The way it is now, they'll put the whole thing down to the bombs. Loss of the train, the viaduct, destruction of the mail, everything. My guess is, they'll be so busy at the dam – and the other dams that the flood might wreck – that it'll be some time before they get around to this neck of the woods. Like it gives us a hell of a lot more time. With luck we should be able to make some kind of getaway.'

Luck, for once, was indeed with them. They hurried along the slope, beneath the first arch of the viaduct that was still standing, toward the track that wound up to the wood where Zygmund was waiting for them. There was no sign of the German patrol that had been called in to reinforce the detail annihilated by Kane's team: any survivors not gunned down by the raiders had been carried away by the flood. There was however a vehicle. It was slewed across the trail a few yards above the dirty grey foam that swirled at the edge of the water. Bodies were strewn nearby – Kane reckoned, from the mangled state of the remains, that they had been caught by a burst of cannon fire – but nothing moved. The vehicle itself was undamaged. It was an Sd-Kfz/251, a half-track *Sonder Kraftfahrzeug* troop-carrier capable of transporting nine men in three rows of seats. Each of the caterpillars ran on two driving and six guide wheels; there was a canvas hood;

and the cut-outs beside the seats were shielded by canvas flaps. Kane leaped up onto the track guard and peered at the controls. 'Santa Claus came down our chimney at last,' he enthused. 'We don't even need to use the trail to get to Ziggy in this: she'll go straight up the hillside like a bloody tank! Come on: let's hump in the sacks we saved and be on our way.'

'On our way where?' Daventry asked. The wound in his upper arm was hurting him.

'Home,' Kane said. 'Or as near as we can get.' He looked at the girl. 'Er . . . that is, we must find a place to go over the stuff in the sacks, divvy up the loot, and – well, maybe we should split then. They'll be looking for five guys and a girl. Four when they find Fischer.' He slapped a hand against the half-track. 'This heap has a range of more than a hundred and fifty miles. We'll take the helmets off these poor sods and travel by night. We'd better collect as many shooters as we can too: we left the last couple of Schmeissers on top of that pillar.'

There were seven or eight helmets to choose from. Even for Kane, the task of removing some of them was too much. He took the five they would need and helped Hawkins bring the sacks to the troop-carrier. Only nine had survived the explosion, the raid and the flood – the one with the vital letter and one other from the first boxcar, and seven containing registered mail. They found three undamaged machine pistols among the dead.

At the back of the carrier, there was an armoured trunk surmounted by trenching tools, a spade, and two spare wheels. Inside, to Kane's joy, were two five-gallon jerricans of gasoline and half a dozen army greatcoats. In the coats and steel helmets, at night, they could pass for a regular Wehrmacht unit on urgent business: no Czech police would attempt to stop them, and only a *Feldgendarmerie* road block would be likely to halt them while the hours of darkness lasted. The police, after all, would be looking for civilians.

Four of the sacks squeezed into the trunk; the

remaining five had to be stowed on the third row of seats and in the footwell in front of them. They were visible from the road, but that – along with the chance of running into an MP patrol – was a risk they had to take. 'With the jerricans, we should be able to make between 280 and 300 miles without a refuel,' Kane said. 'We'll keep to the minor roads, head south . . . and play it by ear when she runs dry.'

He pressed the starter. The big Büssing-NAG motor rumbled into life, and the Sd-Kfz/251 lumbered up the hill towards the wood.

At four-thirty in the morning, Kane called a halt. They had covered rather less than 130 miles in seven hours driving, but the route – avoiding all sizeable towns – had been circuitous and they were climbing almost all the time. Now they were 4,000 feet up in the Sengsengebirge, near a village called Micheldorf, half a mile off the road along a game warden's trail in the middle of a pine forest.

The troop-carrier was hidden behind a logpile in a small clearing. The journey had been without incident except for one astounding piece of good fortune: emerging from a side road forty miles south of Pisek, they had been waved angrily on by an MP . . . and found themselves on the tail end of a long military convoy heading for Linz. Maintaining his position there, Kane, who was driving, found himself waved as urgently past the Austrian frontier post without so much as a glance from the *Feldgendarmerie*, SS and immigration officials grouped around the raised barrier.

He had swung away from the convoy on the outskirts of the city and continued up into the mountains during the small hours.

They slept until seven thirty, grateful for the army topcoats in the chill mountain air. As soon as it was light, they got to work on the sacks. 'Do you still have the Reichsmarks you took from the safe in Prague?' Kane asked Daventry in a low voice while Hawkins and the girl were dealing with the wire that bound the mouths of the registered sacks.

'Sure I do.' The safe-breaker patted the bulge of his body belt with his good arm. 'Why? You want to buy us breakfast?'

'Pass them over to me when you can do it unobserved,' Kane said. 'They're no use to us; we'll give them to the broad as her cut, pretend to find them in some packet or something.'

Kane began sorting through the hundreds of envelopes in the Operation Cornflakes sack while Hawkins and Hilde ripped open the contents of the registered mail. The team leader had been well briefed, but he had to examine the entire contents of the sack three times before he located the vital letter . . . and then it was only because the feel of the paper was different from the fake German envelopes fabricated in Italy that he caught on. The letter was addressed to an *Unteroffizier* in charge of the stores at a military canteen in the Friedrichstrasse, Berlin. As soon as he opened it, Kane knew it was the right one. It contained two sheets of rice paper covered with single-spaced typescript.

The first page comprised nothing but five-figure cypher groups: clearly the rundown on Cornflakes. The second was in clear: a list of names, addresses and telephone numbers, all of them in England, against which professions or activities had been indicated.

Kane whistled to himself. This was dynamite! Obviously the Nazi agent in London, suspecting that he was blown, was sending his bosses a checklist of his fifth-column contacts, while he could.

The discovery changed everything. Once the vital envelope was in his hands, the original brief – to destroy the contents, and with them the exposure of the Cornflakes ruse – was no more than a formality (Kane chewed up the rice paper and swallowed it then and there). But now that he had found the attached list, a new dimension was added: it had become equally vital that he return safely to base and hand this over to his chiefs, so that the German ring could be rolled up. In other words, Kane's team was no longer dispensable. They must get back to Italy at all costs.

Apart from the minor hazards of escape from an occupied country and passing through the front lines on a battlefield, there were three specific difficulties to overcome: lack of suitable ID papers, the presence of the girl, and the fact that two of the team were injured, one seriously. Daventry's arm had stiffened up and was throbbing very painfully: Kane was afraid it might be infected. As for Zygmund, he was semi-conscious most of the time now, running a high temperature, and growing progressively weaker. If he didn't receive expert attention within the next twenty-four hours, Kane feared that he might not survive.

But how the hell could they make Perugia in that time with half the Austrian Alps, the Dolomites, the Po valley and the Tuscan Apennines to cross, almost all of it enemy territory? And a vehicle that was going to run out of fuel in less than half that distance?

I'll deal with the problem when we're bloody doing it, Kane told himself characteristically. In the meantime – a question he *could* resolve now – there was Hilde. It was important that they kept up the local crook façade. However seductive he found her, he was on a mission . . . and you never knew, when it came to spies. In any case, it would be common criminals the police were looking for. Luckily.

'Where were you hoping to go, honey?' he asked her. 'If you'd delivered the taxi to your friend the way it was planned?'

'I have contacts in Graz,' she said. 'It's my home territory. I can fence the stuff there. Don't worry. I won't delay you. It's difficult enough without a female passenger, I know.'

'Shit,' Kane said, 'it was through us you lost the car, missed out on your buddy in Budejovice – and lost your skirt!' She was still wearing the dungarees from the plate-layers' hut. 'The least we can do is put you on a train. We – er – we have our own contacts in Klagenfurt. Can you make Graz from there?'

'Oh, yes,' she said, 'via Glandorf and Bruck.'

'OK,' he promised. 'We'll drop you there. Right now – well, I guess you'll have to replace the Minerva. Take this, and replace the clothes you wrecked as well.' From the inside of a ripped packet (which had in fact contained a shipment of watches consigned to a jeweller in Leipzig), he removed the banknotes that Daventry had passed to him and handed them over.

She stared at the sheaf of bills. 'Oh, but . . . No, I couldn't,' she protested. 'Not all that. We said fifty-fifty.'

He nodded. 'Sure. But some things can't be matched in cash. I can't explain, but there are certain papers we need . . . stuff that's of more use to us than money.'

'And you think they are here?' She moved towards the piles of envelopes littering the grass. 'Let's find them, then.'

He patted his breast pocket. 'I already did. Now, what say we check out the rest of the stuff and then bury the evidence right here?'

Hawkins was already using the trenching tools to dig a deep hole beneath the trees. The haul from the remainder of the registered mail was nothing sensational: money orders, bank drafts, more watches, a few small items of jewellery, cash payments to black marketeers, illegal transfer of articles in gold. Kane made a show of dividing up the booty and handed Hilde her share in Zygmund's carpet-bag. He would give her the half that was supposed to be theirs when she left them, and ask her to fence it on their behalf. It would help to console her after the betrayal – for he would make a date, several days ahead, for them to meet in Graz, when she could give him the money realised on the team's half . . . and maybe resume their interrupted relationship. And of course he would not be there.

When the mountain of paper had been safely interred, Kane went off into the woods with a Schmeisser. An hour later he was back with food: he had machine-gunned two pheasants and a rabbit. Hawkins, who could organise fire without smoke, cooked the game and they ate. A steel helmet brim-full of icy spring water was all they could offer Zygmund. The wounded Pole's temperature was still rising.

Clouds covered the sky all day. Nobody came up or down the forest track. Even the birds were silent in the alleys beneath the close-packed pines. Kane kept them there, sleeping in turn, until two hours after dark. The crow-fly distance to Klagenfurt was just under ninety miles. But the road mileage, twisting between the Salzkammergut and the Rottenmanner Tauern, circling the great mass of the Schladminger, was likely to be at least twice as much. The troop-carrier's top speed was only 35mph, and it was dubious if they could even approach that over most of the mountain route. The probable length of the journey had nevertheless to be balanced against the risk of trouble if they started out too early or travelled in daylight. Kane planned to make the outskirts of the city at dawn. And after the girl had gone? Leave that until tomorrow, he told himself.

Driving hard, taking ninety-minute spells at the wheel, they pressed on non-stop through the night and made the schedule. Nobody tried to stop them. Judenburg, the only sizeable town they hit, was blacked out and deserted; the mountain villages were dead.

Kane parked the half-track in a disused quarry a mile outside the city limits. The snow-capped peaks of the Carinthian Alps were rosy pink against a clear sky in the north as Hilde shrugged out of the army greatcoat and removed the helmet. She took out pins and shook the straw-coloured hair loose. With the soiled overalls, an unsuitable jacket and her carpet-bag, she could have been one of the itinerant female labourers working in the potato fields. Kane had promised to escort her as far as the streetcar terminus.

There was a café across the cobbled street from the turn-around at the end of the tracks. Early customers – working men in dungarees, a woman tram conductor – clustered around the bar drinking ersatz coffee, hot chocolate, steins of Pils. 'Let me buy you a coffee,' Kane said. 'Warm you up. It's kind of chilly at this hour.'

She frowned. 'Is it all right? Do you think it's safe?'

'Whyever not?' he replied, smiling. 'You see any cops?'

There was a radio with a fretwork speaker above the

steamy urn at one side of the counter. An announcer was reading out the news headlines. Our glorious armies were still pushing the Bolsheviks back in Lithuania. Field Marshal Model's *Heeresgruppe* B was making a strategic withdrawal toward the Seine. There was an insurrection in Paris: terrorists had fomented a general strike and barricaded some streets. There were rumours – entirely without truth, the *Führer* himself had denied them – that Rumania, faced with the Russian threat from the Ukraine, was suing for a separate peace. A gang of killers who had robbed a postal centre in Prague and then butchered an army patrol near Pisek were thought to be heading for Austria on foot. There was a woman with the gangsters, one of whom had been killed and another was thought to be wounded. The news reader made no mention of the raid on the dam.

Hilde looked at Kane over the rim of her cup. 'So much for the famous East-Central Experts,' she said teasingly.

'Come again?'

'The bank robbers, remember? They would have said if they were suspected. Besides, those boys have never been interested in money orders.'

'I never claimed that was who we were,' Kane said. 'You jumped to that conclusion. If you wanted to think that . . . OK, I let you. But you never answered my third question: like who are *you*?'

'I'll ask one of my own first. Who is Colbert?'

Kane tapped his breast pocket. 'A friend in need,' he said.

The conductress and her driver left the café and walked across to the streetcar. 'I must go,' Hilde said. 'There may not be another for half an hour.'

The car was full of workmen. She stood on the step and held out her hand. 'And my question?' Kane repeated.

'Like you,' she said, 'I told the truth – but not all of it perhaps..I do act as a kind of look-out for friends, but they are not actually underworld people. I suspect that we are maybe on the same side of the fence – or, rather, the right side of two different fences. Did you ever hear of the MVD?'

A bell clanged. The streetcar began to move. Kane let go of her hand. He smiled into her eyes. 'I have the address,' he said. 'See you around.'

She nodded. '*Un de ces jours*,' she said.

One of these days.

Kane was heading for one of the remoter parts of the Austro-Italian border with no particular plan in mind when he saw the aircraft. It was a tiny high-wing monoplane with a single tailfin and a fixed undercart, one of the Fi-156 Fiesler Storch artillery spotters used by the Wehrmacht.

The plane was being thrown about the sky like an autumn leaf in a gale. From time to time it sank below the crests of a line of foothills to the south, then it would soar up again, dipping and wheeling, to skim the treetops and shoot up high. Finally the pilot executed an immaculate loop, sideslipped to lose height, and glided down behind the swell of downland through which the troop-carrier was climbing. The Storch did not reappear.

'Aerobatics!' Kane said. 'Must be an airfield, maybe some kind of training school, nearby.' As he spoke, they breasted a rise. In front of them now the land fell away into an upland valley. And in the centre of the grassy depression were two canvas-covered hangars, a small hutted camp, a single tarmac runway. In front of the hangars, three more Storch monoplanes stood like outsize mosquitoes among Heinkel trainers, a three-engined Fokker, and a Dornier transport. There were Luftwaffe vehicles in front of the huts, and Luftwaffe personnel by the aircraft, but no fighters, bombers or other warplanes on the apron. The perimeter was bordered by a simple wire fence, and the only sentries on view stood at the gate leading to the hutted camp.

The road ran within a hundred yards of the end of the runway – they were separated only by a wide, rough verge and a row of lime trees. Between the trees, beside a windsock on a mast, the Storch that had just landed was visible. It was standing with its motor idling, clearly awaiting a signal to take off again.

Kane had been intending to look for a place where they could lie up again until dark. But with more high ground ahead, he was worried about the fuel situation: he had underestimated the Büssing-NAG's consumption and the amount of low gear work the heavy vehicle could do in the mountains. They had used the two jerricans, and the tank was rapidly running dry.

Now, typically, he rejected all his former plans. An opportunity presented itself. He would seize it, and the hell with the consequences. 'Hawkins!' he rapped. 'Greatcoat. Helmet. Get two of the Schmeissers ready.'

He trod on the accelerator and swung the wheel hard over. The carrier left the road and churned across the verge, the caterpillar tracks biting into the soft earth and sending clods flying on either side. Kane aimed the stubby bonnet straight at the wire perimeter fence. The heavy iron bumper-bar smashed into the wire, tearing out supporting posts and flattening it to the ground. The half-track skated over and slewed to a halt fifteen yards from the plane. Kane and Hawkins leaped out, brandishing their Schmeissers.

The pilot of the Feisler was just turning the machine around into the wind. Seeing a Wehrmacht vehicle by the windsock, and what appeared to be an officer with no jacket and a *Fedwebel* in a greatcoat and steel helmet running toward him, he throttled back and frowned out of the perspex greenhouse.

Hawkins stood in front of the plane, aiming his machine pistol at the propeller; Kane was below the door, gesturing with his weapon for the pilot to get out. The pilot, a young man wearing a fleece-lined leather coat and flying helmet with the flaps undone, looked puzzled. He opened the door and half rose from his seat . . . and then, perhaps with a flyer's mistrust of the army, perhaps because of the flattened fence, maybe because he saw the

227

wounded men inside the half-track, his suspicions turned to certainty. His right hand dived for the gun holstered beneath his flying coat.

Kane shot him twice with the Walther from his waistband – once through the right forearm, once in the shoulder. The pilot toppled forward and fell from the plane. Kane seized his gun and ran for the carrier, with Hawkins close behind. Daventry was already on his feet and heading for the plane. He climbed inside and squeezed himself behind the rearmost of the tandem seats.

Leaving everything else behind, Kane and the sergeant dragged Zygmund from the half-track and ran with him towards the plane.

Three hundred yards away outside the hangars, Luftwaffe men were shouting. Two steel-helmeted guards piled into a scout car and raced toward the runway. Sentries at the gate ran to a machine gun in a sandbagged emplacement.

Zygmund cried out in anguish as he was bundled up into the tiny cabin. Daventry reached forward and eased him into the second seat. Hawkins swung his huge frame aboard and crouched over him; Kane slid behind the controls, flipped off the brakes and opened the throttle. The tiny plane surged forward.

The scout car was a hundred yards away, veering onto the runway. Kane was already hitting 50mph. He dare not head directly for the car: the machine gun in the rear, aimed by the man behind the driver, was already spitting fire, and a single bullet touching the airscrew could signal the end for them all. But he wasn't going fast enough to lift off before he reached the car. He swerved the plane off the runway, kicking the rudder hard left, and bumped across the rough grass, outflanking the car. Hawkins crouched in the open doorway, spraying lead from his Schmeisser.

The scout car squealed to a halt, skidded around, and resumed the chase. Only now it was a stern chase – and although its speed had been cut down off the runway, the plane started gaining as soon as it was back on the tarmac. The machine gun at the gate had been swung round and was firing as the Fieseler roared past. Slugs punctured the fabric at the rear of the fuselage; two of the greenhouse side panels starred; there were holes in the starboard wing. Hawkins kept shooting.

One of the machine gunners slumped over the sandbags. Men running for one of the planes on the apron threw themselves flat. A Luftwaffe officer aiming a machine pistol crumpled to the ground.

Then they were beyond the hangars, gaining speed still more . . . and lifting. No winged aircraft in the world, except for an autogyro, could take off and land in such a short distance as the Fi-156. The runway was sixty feet beneath them before they had covered half its length.

Hawkins slammed the door and tried to keep himself off Zygmund's lap. 'That was a fuckin' bit of all right, squire,' he shouted in Kane's ear. 'Home in half a soddin' hour now, eh?'

Kane grinned. His eyes were shining. Against the odds, by acting decisively, seizing an opportunity, they had made it again. That had always been his creed: hit fast, hit hard, and hit unexpectedly. 'You guys are going to be cramped as hell,' he said cheerfully. 'According to this chart' – he gestured toward a clipboard – 'it's 400 kilometres to Perugia, half of it over the Adriatic. And the plane's maximum range, with full tanks, is 385. So we should be in the air around two and a half hours . . .'

'Jesus wept!' Daventry exclaimed.

'. . . if it wasn't for the fact that we don't have enough juice to make the whole distance. I'll see if I can find a nice quiet beach near Rimini, and ditch you there.'

'What's all that crap in real miles?' Hawkins demanded.

'About 230 to Perugia. The crate will just about stagger up to the ton if there's a tail wind. In still air, she'll go as slow as thirty.'

'Thank you very much,' Daventry said. 'We'll be blooming good target-practice for the Kraut gunners anyway.'

Kane shook his head. The wind was shrieking through

the bullet holes in the canopy. 'We go hedge-hopping,' he yelled. 'That way, we're below the Jerry radar screen, and nobody knows we're there until we've bloody gone.'

'Except the Polish flak gunners behind the Gothic Line, and the Raf fighter boys, and the Yanks in their flying fuckin' arsenals, an' they'd all just love to claim another kite with black crosses hit for six, wouldn't they?' Hawkins said sourly.

'Yeah . . . well . . . Maybe it's as well we're all set to spend a day at the seaside,' Kane said.

'A day at the seaside already? I'd trade it all for a nice salt beef sandwich on rye bread,' Zygmund's weak voice broke unexpectedly into the conversation.

Before the Germans at the field could get another plane off the ground, the Fieseler left the training field tilting below, swept over the foothills, and flew towards a cloudbank blowing up from the south.

'You really mean,' Hawkins said to Kane later that day, 'that the skirt was working for Uncle Joe? She wasn't a brass at all? Or a bent hooker on the lam? She was doing our kind of work on the sly?'

'Not exactly,' Kane said 'She hinted that she worked for the MVD. That's a branch of the NKVD, the Soviet security service. I would think she used her . . . her position, shall we say, in Prague to finger left-wing sympathisers, likely fifth-columnists, people in a position to be blackmailed – characters who could be of use to the Russkies when they overrun Czechoslovakia, as I guess they will soon.'

'And the loot, the Spondulicks, all that booty we handed over?'

'We wouldn't be entitled to spend it ourselves. I figure it'll be well spent – however it's spent – if it helps to end the war more quickly.'

'Well, bugger me!' the sergeant said.

They were back at the hotel in Perugia. Kane's calculations had proved correct. The Fieseler had glided the last few miles with empty tanks and made a perfect three-pointer on the sand at Ascona. They had been driven under armed escort to the intelligence headquarters by a suspicious Royal Engineer major whose mine-sweeping squad had rescued them from the beach. Daventry was having his arm dressed. Zygmund was in hospital. He would recover, the doctors told Kane, though he would probably limp for the rest of his life. 'Have a salt beef sandwich ready when he comes out from under the anaesthetic,' Kane recommended an outraged ward sister. 'On rye bread.'

All that remained then was the official debriefing.

It took a long time. Colbert, Georgopoulous, Brigadier Honeywell, and an Intelligence colonel from GHQ, MELF, all had a lot of questions to ask. Then Kane astonished everybody with a last-minute, rabbit-out-of-the-hat flourish –the revelation that he had secured a list of Nazi agents and fifth columnists in Britain. Patience, Honeywell's blonde WAAF assistant, took copious notes . . . and proved that, however eclectic the literary curriculum, the Ladies' College had certainly failed to instil in her a talent for speedwriting. By the time it was all over, the clock above the Governor's Palace in the Piazza Italia was striking midnight.

The brigadier and the three colonels pushed back their chairs and rose to their feet. Patience gathered together her papers. As she stooped to pick up a sheet that had fallen to the floor, Kane noticed that, instead of the regulation-issue grey lisle, her stockings were now sheer silk with a dark seam. He found it hard to believe that it was no more than a week since he had interviewed the Wehrmacht NCO, Bergmann, in this very room, in this hotel, in this same Italian town.

Colbert and Georgopoulous left the room together. As they passed Kane, who was standing waiting by the door, Colbert nodded and drawled, 'Jolly good show. Spot on.' The American held up a thumb. 'Swell,' he said. 'See you around, Kane.' And then, to Colbert, 'I have a driver standing by. I was figuring on making it to Rome. They tell me there's a dancer at Mario's, in the Via Veneto, who's sensational. You care to tag along?'

'Actually, no,' Colbert said. 'Thanks just the same. There's a fresco in a small church in Arezzo. Lawrence says it's the greatest painting in the whole world. Or was it Huxley? Anyway, I fancied tooling along to see it tomorrow morning. I'm not on duty until mid-day. But it does mean an early start, I'm afraid.'

Kane's celebration was to be restricted to a drink in his quarters with Hawkins. The sergeant had already managed to lay his hands on a small keg of English bitter. Kane refused to ask how and where. He was about to leave when Georgopoulous's words raised an echo in his mind. See you around. Yes, indeed.

He turned back into the room. Brigadier Honeywell was saying, ''fraid there are – um – one or two things still to do, me dear. If you wouldn't mind toddlin' back to my quarters for – ah – half an hour or so? Time off in lieu, of course. Goes without sayin'.'

'Righty-o, sir,' the blonde said. 'It'd be a pleasure.'

Honeywell fussed toward the door, and then, seeing Kane's expectant expression, asked, 'Yes, Kane? Was there something?'

'Yes, sir,' Kane said. 'A small favour I'd like to ask, if I may. Something personal.'

'A favour?' the brigadier repeated. 'My dear boy! But of course, of course. Anything you want. Just name it. What is it, hey? Two days extra leave? Three?'

'No, sir. I should like to know the date of the next delivery scheduled in the Cornflakes operation.'

'God bless my soul,' Honeywell said. 'Whatever for?'

'I'd appreciate permission to make use of it myself, sir,' Kane said. 'For . . . as I say, for personal reasons. I want to send a letter of apology to an address in Graz.'

'In Graz? In Austria? Sending letters to an enemy country?' Honeywell looked scandalised. 'But, my dear chap, we can't have that! Don't you know there's a war on, Kane?'

STAR BOOKS BESTSELLERS

FICTION

THE PROTOCOL	*Sarah Allan Borisch*	£2.25*
SEASON OF CHANGE	*Lois Battle*	£2.25*
LET'S KEEP IN TOUCH	*Elaine Bissel*	£2.50*
DANCEHALL	*Bernard F. Conners*	£1.95*
DREAMS OF GLORY	*Thomas Fleming*	£2.50*
DEAR STRANGER	*Catherine Kidwell*	£1.95*
PHANTOMS	*Dean R. Koontz*	£2.25*
THE PAINTED LADY	*Françoise Sagan*	£2.25*
LAMIA	*Tristan Travis*	£2.75*

FILM TIE-INS

EDUCATING RITA	*Peter Chepstow*	£1.60
TERMS OF ENDEARMENT	*Larry McMurtry*	£1.95*
PARTY PARTY	*Jane Coleman*	£1.35
THE WICKED LADY	*Magdalen King-Hall*	£1.60
SCRUBBERS	*Alexis Lykiard*	£1.60
BULL SHOT	*Martin Noble*	£1.80
BLOODBATH AT THE HOUSE OF DEATH	*Martin Noble*	£1.80

STAR Books are obtainable from many booksellers and newsagents. If you have any difficulty tick the titles you want and fill in the form below.

Name _____

Address _____

_____

Send to: Star Books Cash Sales, P.O. Box 11, Falmouth, Cornwall, TR10 9EN.

Please send a cheque or postal order to the value of the cover price plus:
UK: 55p for the first book, 22p for the second book and 14p for each additional book ordered to the maximum charge of £1.75.

BFPO and EIRE: 55p for the first book, 22p for the second book, 14p per copy for the next 7 books, thereafter 8p per book.

OVERSEAS: £1.00 for the first book and 25p per copy for each additional book.

While every effort is made to keep prices low, it is sometimes necessary to increase prices at short notice. Star Books reserve the right to show new retail prices on covers which may differ from those advertised in the text or elsewhere.

*NOT FOR SALE IN CANADA

STAR BOOKS BESTSELLERS

CHILLERS

CHAINSAW TERROR	*Nick Blake*	£1.80
SLUGS	*Shaun Hutson*	£1.95
SPAWN	*Shaun Hutson*	£1.80
EREBUS	*Shaun Hutson*	£1.95
CARNOSAUR	*Harry Adam Knight*	£1.95
SLiMER	*Harry Adam Knight*	£1.95
BLOWFLY	*David Lowman*	£1.95
THE PARIAH	*Graham Masterton*	£1.95*
THE MANITOU	*Graham Masterton*	£1.50*
THE PLAGUE	*Graham Masterton*	£1.80*
THE SENTINEL	*Jeffrey Konvitz*	£1.65*
SATAN'S LOVE CHILD	*Brian McNaughton*	£1.95*
SATAN'S SEDUCTRESS	*Brian McNaughton*	£1.25*

STAR Books are obtainable from many booksellers and newsagents. If you have any difficulty tick the titles you want and fill in the form below.

Name_____

Address_____

_____

Send to: Star Books Cash Sales, P.O. Box 11, Falmouth, Cornwall, TR10 9EN.

Please send a cheque or postal order to the value of the cover price plus: UK: 55p for the first book, 22p for the second book and 14p for each additional book ordered to the maximum charge of £1.75.

BFPO and EIRE: 55p for the first book, 22p for the second book, 14p per copy for the next 7 books, thereafter 8p per book.

OVERSEAS: £1.00 for the first book and 25p per copy for each additional book.

While every effort is made to keep prices low, it is sometimes necessary to increase prices at short notice. Star Books reserve the right to show new retail prices on covers which may differ from those advertised in the text or elsewhere.

*NOT FOR SALE IN CANADA

STAR BOOKS BESTSELLERS

THRILLERS

FLIGHT 902 IS DOWN	*Hal Fishman & Barry Schiff*	£1.95*
DEBT OF HONOUR	*Adam Kennedy*	£1.95*
THE DOMINO VENDETTA	*Adam Kennedy*	£1.80*
THE FIRST DEADLY SIN	*Lawrence Sanders*	£2.60*
DOG SOLDIERS	*Robert Stone*	£1.95*
IKON	*Graham Masterton*	£2.50*
HUNTED	*Jeremy Scott*	£1.50
DIRTY HARRY	*Philip Rock*	£1.25*
MAGNUM FORCE	*Mel Valley*	£1.50*

WAR

BLAZE OF GLORY	*Michael Carreck*	£1.80
CONVOY OF STEEL	*Wolf Kruger*	£1.80
BLOOD AND HONOUR	*Wolf Kruger*	£1.80
PANZER GRENADIERS	*Heinrich Conrad Muller*	£1.95*
THE RAID	*Julian Romanes*	£1.80*
GUNSHIPS: NEEDLEPOINT	*Jack Hamilton Teed*	£1.95
THE SKY IS BURNING	*D. Mark Carter*	£1.60
TASK FORCE BATTALION	*Tom Lambert*	£1.60

STAR Books are obtainable from many booksellers and newsagents. If you have any difficulty tick the titles you want and fill in the form below.

Name_____

Address_____

Send to: Star Books Cash Sales, P.O. Box 11, Falmouth, Cornwall, TR10 9EN.

Please send a cheque or postal order to the value of the cover price plus:
UK: 55p for the first book, 22p for the second book and 14p for each additional book ordered to the maximum charge of £1.75.

BFPO and EIRE: 55p for the first book, 22p for the second book, 14p per copy for the next 7 books, thereafter 8p per book.

OVERSEAS: £1.00 for the first book and 25p per copy for each additional book.

While every effort is made to keep prices low, it is sometimes necessary to increase prices at short notice. Star Books reserve the right to show new retail prices on covers which may differ from those advertised in the text or elsewhere.
NOT FOR SALE IN CANADA

STAR BOOKS BESTSELLERS

NON-FICTION

OIL SKEIKHS	*Linda Blandford*	£1.95
THE COMPLETE JACK THE RIPPER	*D. Rumbelow*	£1.60
CRIME SCIENTIST	*John Thompson*	£1.60
THE ELEPHANT MAN	*Sir Frederick Treves*	95p
TODAY'S THE DAY	*Jeremy Beadle*	£2.95
COLA COWBOYS	*Franklyn D. Wood*	£1.95
THE BOOK OF FOOTBALL LISTS	*Robert Hutton Moss*	£1.95

BIOGRAPHIES

RICHARD BURTON	*Fergus Cashin*	£1.95
CLINT EASTWOOD: MOVIN' ON	*Peter Douglas*	£1.00*
CHARLES BRONSON	*David Downing*	£1.95
IT'S A FUNNY GAME	*Brian Johnston*	£1.95
IT'S BEEN A LOT OF FUN	*Brian Johnston*	£1.80
CHATTERBOXES	*Brian Johnston*	£1.95
ORDEAL	*Linda Lovelace with Mike Grady*	£1.50*
BETTE DAVIS:		
MOTHER GODDAM	*Whitney Stine with Bette Davis*	£2.25*
PRINCESS GRACE	*Gwen Robyns*	£1.75

STAR Books are obtainable from many booksellers and newsagents. If you have any difficulty tick the titles you want and fill in the form below.

Name _____

Address _____

_____

Send to: Star Books Cash Sales, P.O. Box 11, Falmouth, Cornwall, TR10 9EN.

Please send a cheque or postal order to the value of the cover price plus:
UK: 55p for the first book, 22p for the second book and 14p for each additional book ordered to the maximum charge of £1.75.

BFPO and EIRE: 55p for the first book, 22p for the second book, 14p per copy for the next 7 books, thereafter 8p per book.

OVERSEAS: £1.00 for the first book and 25p per copy for each additional book.

While every effort is made to keep prices low, it is sometimes necessary to increase prices at short notice. Star Books reserve the right to show new retail prices on covers which may differ from those advertised in the text or elsewhere.
*NOT FOR SALE IN CANADA

STAR BOOKS ADULT READS

FICTION

THE ADVENTURES OF A SCHOOLBOY	*Anonymous*	£2.25
THE AUTOBIOGRAPHY OF A FLEA	*Anonymous*	£2.25
ALTAR OF VENUS	*Anonymous*	£2.25
MEMOIRS OF DOLLY MORTON	*Anonymous*	£1.95
LAURA MIDDLETON	*Anonymous*	£1.95
THREE TIMES A WOMAN	*Anonymous*	£2.25
MY SEX, MY SOUL	*Anonymous*	£2.25
JOY	*Joy Laurey*	£1.95
NYMPH IN PARIS	*Galia S*	£1.95
BEACH OF PASSION	*Donald Bowie*	£1.95*
DRY HUSTLE	*Sarah Kernochan*	£1.25*
FOLIES D'AMOUR	*Anne-Marie Villefranche*	£2.25

STAR Books are obtainable from many booksellers and newsagents. If you have any difficulty tick the titles you want and fill in the form below.

*Name*_____

*Address*_____

_____

Send to: Star Books Cash Sales, P.O. Box 11, Falmouth, Cornwall, TR10 9EN.

Please send a cheque or postal order to the value of the cover price plus:
UK: 55p for the first book, 22p for the second book and 14p for each additional book ordered to the maximum charge of £1.75.

BFPO and EIRE: 55p for the first book, 22p for the second book, 14p per copy for the next 7 books, thereafter 8p per book.

OVERSEAS: £1.00 for the first book and 25p per copy for each additional book.

While every effort is made to keep prices low, it is sometimes necessary to increase prices at short notice. Star Books reserve the right to show new retail prices on covers which may differ from those advertised in the text or elsewhere.

NOT FOR SALE IN CANADA

STAR BOOKS ADULT READS

FICTION

BEATRICE	*Anonymous*	£2.25*	☐
EVELINE	*Anonymous*	£1.95*	☐
MORE EVELINE	*Anonymous*	£1.95*	☐
FRANK AND I	*Anonymous*	£1.95	☐
A MAN WITH A MAID	*Anonymous*	£2.25*	☐
A MAN WITH A MAID II	*Anonymous*	£1.95*	☐
A MAN WITH A MAID III	*Anonymous*	£1.95*	☐
OH WICKED COUNTRY!	*Anonymous*	£1.95	☐
ROMANCE OF LUST VOL I	*Anonymous*	£2.25*	☐
ROMANCE OF LUST VOL II	*Anonymous*	£2.25*	☐
SUBURBAN SOULS VOL I	*Anonymous*	£1.95*	☐
SUBURBAN SOULS VOL II	*Anonymous*	£1.95*	☐
DELTA OF VENUS	*Anaïs Nin*	£1.60*	☐
LITTLE BIRDS	*Anaïs Nin*	£1.60	☐
PLAISIR D'AMOUR	*Anne-Marie Villefranche*	£2.25	☐
JOIE D'AMOUR	*Anne-Marie Villefranche*	£1.95	☐

STAR Books are obtainable from many booksellers and newsagents. If you have any difficulty tick the titles you want and fill in the form below.

Name_____

Address_____

_____

Send to: Star Books Cash Sales, P.O. Box 11, Falmouth, Cornwall, TR10 9EN.

Please send a cheque or postal order to the value of the cover price plus:
UK: 55p for the first book, 22p for the second book and 14p for each additional book ordered to the maximum charge of £1.75.

BFPO and EIRE: 55p for the first book, 22p for the second book, 14p per copy for the next 7 books, thereafter 8p per book.

OVERSEAS: £1.00 for the first book and 25p per copy for each additional book.

While every effort is made to keep prices low, it is sometimes necessary to increase prices at short notice. Star Books reserve the right to show new retail prices on covers which may differ from those advertised in the text or elsewhere.
*NOT FOR SALE IN CANADA

STAR BOOKS BESTSELLERS

GOR SERIES

STAR Books are obtainable from many booksellers and newsagents. If you have any difficulty tick the titles you want and fill in the form below.

Name_____

Address_____

Send to: Star Books Cash Sales, P.O. Box 11, Falmouth, Cornwall, TR10 9EN.

Please send a cheque or postal order to the value of the cover price plus:
UK: 55p for the first book, 22p for the second book and 14p for each additional book ordered to the maximum charge of £1.75.

BFPO and EIRE: 55p for the first book, 22p for the second book, 14p per copy for the next 7 books, thereafter 8p per book.

OVERSEAS: £1.00 for the first book and 25p per copy for each additional book.

While every effort is made to keep prices low, it is sometimes necessary to increase prices at short notice. Star Books reserve the right to show new retail prices on covers which may differ from those advertised in the text or elsewhere.
NOT FOR SALE IN CANADA